I0788423

BULLETINS AT THE END OF THE WORLD

A short story collection set in the Godsverse

By:
Russell Nohelty

Edited by:
Lily Luchesi

Proofread by:
Toni Cox

Cover Design by:
Lily Luchesi

TABLE OF CONTENTS

Bulletins At The End of the World 1

Table of Contents 3

Introduction 1

Break Down At the End of the World 1

A Thief Emerges… 7

Interlude at the End of the World 36

The Great Unknown 38

Akta's First Hunt 42

Not Another Haunted House Story 57

Homecoming 76

Clombarge 82

The Case of Flossie and James 84

The Last Death of Oscar Hernandez 93

Intruder at the End of the World 102

Not Tonight 105

Little Wifi Girl 116

Akta's Ice Headache 120

Gamesmanship 131

Bulletins at the End of the World 143

The Horrors of Vending 146

There Are No Jobs on a Dead Planet 158

The Blacksmith 166

Out of the Frying Pan 168

Visitors at the End of the World 201

Author's Note 1

Bonuses 3

Katrina Hates the World 5

Limbo 30

The Last Bravery of Dulcie Eynes 40

New Armor 46

About the Author 52

INTRODUCTION

THIS IS NOT a normal short story anthology. I don't think I've ever done things the normal way, so why should this collection be any different? No, I needed this anthology to have a story. I had to come up with a narrative that might need an explanation for you to fully understand and enjoy this collection.

Well, maybe that's not true. You might be able to pick this book up and enjoy it just fine without listening to me ramble, but I'm going to explain it anyway because it's my book, and I can. If you want to give it a go, then flip through my rambling here. If you want the set-up, then keep reading.

The idea for this collection came to me in a flash. Most of my ideas come this way, both good and bad ones. It wasn't even going to be a short story collection at first. I didn't know what it would be, just that I liked it. So, I dutifully filed it away in my folder of ideas, sure I would never hear about it again.

But this little bugger was persistent.

It kept popping up again and again. I moved it into my development folder and back to my idea folder a half dozen times in those first weeks because I really didn't have the energy to work on yet another project.

However, it wouldn't stop nagging me. Then, like all ideas eventually do when they demand to be made, it gave me a way to use it that I couldn't resist, combining it with something I've been working on for a long time—a short story collection of my past works.

Smashing multiple good ideas together to get something great is a staple of my career, so in a way, it makes perfect sense for that to be the reason this collection exists in the way it does.

Fans of my writing have been diligent about buying and tracking down my old work, but it's hard not to miss something when my stories are in dozens of different places, so I decided to put out a collection of my published work, along with some stories that were never placed anywhere but I thought deserved attention.

This is not a novel concept or even an interesting one. It's something just about every writer has ever done, but I never thought I would have enough short story work to warrant this kind of collection.

Yet, here we are.

The work inside this book has been collected from the beginning of my career, in 2010, through 2023, containing everything I have the right to republish from those years. I believe there is only one story I missed from that time, which is *Anastasia's Escape* from *Unpopular Tales* volume 1. You can track that book down if you want the complete, complete works. It's a depressing story, though, so be warned.

That said, simply doing a collection of my old work didn't seem…interesting enough to me, I guess, which is where the narrative comes into play.

The idea is this…

The world ended six months ago. Stephanie Mills "survived" the Apocalypse, whatever that means, and now travels across the country, looking for safe harbor. Along her way, she finds a radio station, a stack of papers from an author she has never heard of named Russell Nohelty and decides to read the author's work over the air.

That's it. That's the premise.

When Stephanie is in the picture, you are following the "story of the book". When you are reading one of my short stories, then you are listening to one of Stephanie's radio broadcasts.

It's an absolutely bonkers premise, and I love it so much. It's extra in the exact kind of way that my work often is, and I hope you can get behind it. If you don't like that premise, you can simply flip through Stephanie's story and read each story in this collection as a standalone, but I hope you will play the game with me and enjoy the experience.

Several stories have never been published in print anywhere, and that, along with Stephanie's story, will hopefully be enough for even hardcore fans who have my work to pick up this book, too.

Through these pages, you'll read fairy tales, science fiction, fantasy, horror, and even tales of the Godsverse, which is the last thing you should know.

This is a Godsverse story, set in the time between the Apocalypse described in *Darkness* and the beginning of Katrina's story in *Death*. This does not overlap in any other way, except that it happens in the same universe where I have now inserted myself as a character.

I have always wanted to make stories that were more pastiches set in the world but smaller stories, and this is my first intention to do so. While the short stories exist in other universes and aren't part of the Godsverse, Stephanie's story is.

Does it make any sense? Not completely. But somehow, to me, it makes all the sense in the world. If you have loved the Godsverse up until now, I have to think it makes some sense to you as well because we resonate on the same frequency of weird.

You might have to make some mental leaps to get there, but I hope you'll give it a go like you always have with my work.

All I ever wanted in my life was to make weird things with, and for, weird people. I have written movies, directed TV shows, produced audio dramas, and written books. Through all that, I am eternally grateful for you allowing me to follow my weird proclivities all over tarnation and back.

I hope you enjoy this collection, whether you are new to my world or have traipsed across the universe with me many times before. It's truly only because of you that any of this work exists in the first place.

BREAK DOWN AT THE END OF THE WORLD

"MAMA NEVER GONNA keep me down!" I sang at the top of my lungs as I sped across the Oklahoma landscape. I hadn't seen much for the last hundred or so miles, and that was just fine with me. I had seen too much death and destruction over the last six months for the rest of my life. So, the quiet of the country was a welcome change.

I lived in Los Angeles for most of my life and never thought I would like the quiet, but leave it to an Apocalypse to change everything you valued about the universe.

"I'm gonna fly higher, higher, higher!"

Music was everything to me. I often thought I would be a DJ, but that was before the world ended, and all the good boys and girls were sucked up to Heaven, leaving us to deal with monsters that wanted to rip our arms from our bodies and flay our minds in half.

Now, I don't think about the future. I don't think about much except surviving. Music was even more important to me now because it gave me a respite from the horrors of the world that were all too prevalent these days. It let me forget for a moment, just a moment.

"Would you—" The next song started, but as I began to sing, there was a pop from the engine, and it started to smoke. "Shit."

I pressed the gas over and over, but the car wouldn't do anything except decelerate to a slow roll.

"No, you stupid car!" I shouted as black smoke plumed from the ugly yellow Yugo I hot-wired three hundred miles back. It wasn't my preferred vehicle, but beggars couldn't be choosers, and the longer the Apocalypse dragged on, the fewer cars became available that had gas in the tank.

In the early days of the Apocalypse, it wasn't uncommon to find a Mercedes or BMW with a full tank, but as gangs of roving marauders formed, they gobbled up all the good cars. They collected all the good everything until there was nothing left for the rest of us.

It didn't take long for power to centralize until it was held by a few, just like before the Apocalypse, except that now the thugs were at least blatant about it. They didn't hide behind suits and smiles but the barrel of a gun.

That wasn't a game I wanted to play, so I decided to try my luck on the open road. I left Los Angeles a month ago, moving slowly at first, making sure to travel only during the day when the monsters that rose from the depths of Hell were less active.

That was a sentence I never thought I would say. Don't get me wrong; I expected an Apocalypse in my life. I just thought it would be a climate one or some sort of crypto bullshit. I did not think monsters would literally rise from the bowels of Hell six months ago. I didn't think they would rampage across the land like locusts until they took control of the whole world in a matter of weeks.

"Please, baby," I shouted, begging the car smoke to abate so I could keep going. "Don't do this to me."

But it was no use. The car jerked forward soon enough, popped, and then began to slow down no matter how hard I pressed the gas.

"You mother f—" I slammed on the steering wheel as the car rolled to a stop, dead. "This is not happening."

I grabbed the backpack from the back seat and threw my CD case into it. I had never used a CD before six months ago, but when Sirius, Spotify, Pandora, and just about every other streaming service went down without capitalism to fuel them, there weren't many ways to get music except the old-school methods my parents used.

It wasn't easy to pull together a decent collection, but I was able to scavenge and barter for the best rock from the

70s, 80s, 90s, and today. I pulled my CD player out of the auxiliary jack and stuffed it in the front of my backpack.

"Fine, asshole. Be that way. I don't need you." I reached into the glove box and pulled out the only thing I kept with me; a Colt 45 with two full clips.

After slamming closed the car door, I decided to stay off the street and walk through the untended cornfields that could hide my tracks. I didn't expect many to come down the road, but if they did, I wanted to make sure they couldn't find me easily.

The coarse stalks of the corn cut at my arms as I walked through them. I cursed my delicate Los Angeles skin as I twisted to avoid the stalks as best I could. As I walked, I hummed "Millions of Peaches" by the Presidents of the United States, the only song about going to the country and picking peaches I had ever heard. I thought about it a lot, being on farmland. I reached into my pack and pulled out my CDs. I had traded that CD for Audioslave's first album, but I had *OK Computer* from Radiohead, which scratched a similar itch, and I could mix that with Beck's *Odelay* for a potent one-two punch.

I hadn't even started the first track when the corn began to thin, revealing a steepled house with a huge radio antenna sticking out the top like it had been built into the foundation. I instinctively reached for my gun, fearing somebody would jump me, but that was not a good attitude in the new normal.

I fought against it every day. All the best things that happened to me came from trusting people. All the worst things, too, but I knew one thing to be true. If I pulled my gun, they would pull theirs, and that was not a good first impression.

AJ would not have approved. He would have called me naïve, but it was his death that solidified that lesson. If he didn't pull his gun before going into that Ralph's, the people he accidentally walked in on wouldn't have been so jumpy, and they wouldn't have shot him in the back of the head.

That's when I knew I had to get out of town. He desperately wanted to make it work in the city, but I thought salvation would be found in the country, away from the prying eyes and itchy trigger fingers found among masses of people.

"Hello!" I shouted as I walked to the door. "I'm not here to hurt you."

It wasn't so bad on the road. Most days, you barely knew it was the Apocalypse. Monsters went where the people were, and most people concentrated near a big city. That herd instinct was hard to fight in people.

I stepped up the porch and grabbed the screen door that banged against the wood in the wind. I knocked loudly on the door. "I broke down on the road. I don't need anything from you, though, except for a safe place to sit for a spell."

As I spoke, the door creaked open, which was never a good sign. Even in the country, people locked their doors these days. You never knew what was out to get you.

I stepped into the house carefully. The air smelled of musk, and the whole floor was covered with a thin layer of film. I wandered around the living room until I reached the kitchen. When I opened the fridge, I found it full of food, and the cupboards were fully stocked.

Somebody should have been home, but there were no tracks in the house across the dust, which meant nobody had come through in at least a couple of weeks. They could have used another entrance, though, or so I thought before I cased the whole first floor and found every surface just as dusty.

I made my way back to the main room and up the stairs to the second floor. I found an office, a bedroom, and a guest room, along with a study filled with more books than I could read in a lifetime.

I followed the stairs down to the main floor and went down to the basement, the only place in the house I hadn't explored yet. There was a buzzing sound the closer I got to the bottom, and when I reached the door that blocked me from continuing, there was a handwritten sign that said "87.9 FM. The lowest number on the dial."

A radio station? In somebody's basement? Is that even legal? Before the end times, everyone and their brother had a podcast, which operated out of basements and attics around the world, but I had never heard of a radio station broadcasting out of one. Maybe it was licensed for commercial use or—*no, Stephanie.* Don't go into your old life. You don't have to think about commercial real estate ever again. That was one of the positives about the Apocalypse.

I knocked on the door but only heard a buzz from behind it, so I pushed the door open and walked into a small room with several microphones and a mixing board, along with enough chairs for three people and hundreds of dials along the metal walls.

Lights were flickering on the board, and dials were flickering wildly on the walls. On top of that, the red light was on, which always indicated that they were broadcasting in movies and TV shows.

"Anyone here?"

I stepped to the desk and smiled. I had always wanted to be a DJ, but wasn't it dangerous to play with something that could broadcast far and wide? No, Stephanie. It's not like they can track a radio signal that comes into their car or anything.

Besides, when are you going to get another chance?

I shrugged and sat down in front of one of the microphones. Next to me was a little mixer that jumped from green to yellow and then red as I moved around.

"Hello?" I smirked. "Is this thing on?"

I looked over at a stack of papers and pulled one close. It was a short story by somebody named Russell Nohelty. They all were, in fact, a whole collection of little stories. *Was he going to broadcast them to the world? Was he ambushed before he could?*

"This is random, but so is everything else." I cleared my throat and spoke. "Who wants to hear a story?"

What could happen if I read just one and then got back to finding a way out of here? Wouldn't be any harm in it. It's not like anyone was listening anyway.

"Alright then." I nodded. "You're listening to Sammy Chops on 87.9…the low down." I chuckled as I used my best radio voice. "This one's called…"

A THIEF EMERGES...

"ER'KATA," SINTIA WHISPERED into the ear of the fruit merchant as she walked up from the alley on the side of the stand, pulling her wooden cart behind her. Chrin was always so aggressive with his customers, and a sweet word from her mouth calmed him and made him slightly more suggestible to a deal.

Her mother taught her to love magic, though she didn't like that name because she could do more than control love. She was a magic user, like her mother before her and her grandmother before her. That was how they survived in the north for so many generations.

Unfortunately, the "gift", as her family called it, was weaker with every generation until Sintia could barely do more than push an emotion slightly, nudging it to barely being in her favor. She could tamp down a fit of rage into seething anger, while her grandmother could calm a stampeding bull until it was putty in her hands, and her mother could turn annoyance into trust.

Her mother promised she would deepen her gift with time, but Sintia was not so sure.

Still, even the small amount of love magic she learned was helpful enough to get her through an average day, as long as she used no more than two spells from waking to falling back asleep. Many people called her lucky, but it wasn't that. It was magic, plain and simple.

"Good morning, Sintia!" Chrin, the fruit vendor, shouted. They called him ogre because he was as ugly as the beasts of legend and twice as hairy. His temper didn't make it any easier for him to find a wife, nor did it endear him to the people of Nhilvarna. Still, he had the best plums in town and handled his wares with the kind of care normally reserved for young children. "Bright today, eh?"

It was a joke he made every time Sintia visited his booth because of the light gray sunglasses that framed her face. All people from Ishafar wore them to cover the dichromatic eyes that allowed them to see as perfectly from their pale blue in the night as their brown one in the midday sun.

"It's always bright in your brilliant glow, Chrin."

Chrin was also the only fruit stand on a street corner next to an alley, making it easier to manipulate him with her limited magic without being spotted. His stand was also in the full sun, and she always felt her powers were better in the full sun of midday.

"Ain't that the sweetest thing?" He took a big breath of the air. "You know, I was in a bit of a slump the last couple of hours, but seeing you always perks me right up."

Yes, that was the point of the spell, Sintia thought. "Well, that's kind of you to say."

Most people in Nhilvarna treated Sintia as a second-class citizen. No, worse than that. They thought her no better than vermin, even though she had the same blood pumping through her veins as they did. It was a hard life in Nhilvarna, and the baron she lived in service of made sure everyone knew he thought her existence was a sin.

"What can I get you, Sin?" he asked.

The sound of her nickname sent shivers down her spine. Some, like Chrin, didn't know what they were saying and meant no malice with it, but that didn't stop it from digging deep into her heart. Most were more malicious, wanting to curry favor with the baron by hating all whom he hated. Still, she had errands to do, which meant swallowing the pain that followed her every day.

"Can I get sixteen plums, fourteen apples, and thirteen pears?" Sintia asked, pointing to each as she made her ask.

"Here ya go," Chrin said, handling her fruit more delicately than his rough, callused hands should have allowed. "That will be five copper."

Sintia cocked her eyes at him. "Come on, Chrin. You can do better than that. How about three?"

He chuckled. "You'll put me out of business. If anyone else asked, I would pop them in the jaw, but—" He leaned forward. "If you don't tell anyone, I'll let it go for four."

She leaned forward and kissed his rough cheek before depositing four copper into his hand. "You're the best."

Every copper she saved at the shops was another cent she could use to buy her freedom and that of her family. She stuffed the extra copper in a hidden pocket under her armpit and then walked off to finish the rest of her errands.

When she was done with the butcher, the church bell rang from the center of town, indicating it was after 1 pm. If she didn't get the meat and other ingredients back to the baron's house soon, they would not have the time to prepare dinner before his guests arrived.

As much food as she collected that day would have fed a normal family for a month, but the baron and his guests would go through it in an evening and then throw away the waste, except for what Sintia and her family could save for themselves.

"Where have you been?" her mother shouted as Sintia walked into the kitchen. "Were you dawdling around town again?"

"No, Mama," Sintia replied. "The butcher took longer than I thought. I'm sorry."

"You can swallow your sorrys, missy." She held out her hand. "Well, let's see it."

Sintia handed her the groceries and inspected them carefully.

"You have a good eye, at least. These will do."

Sintia reached into her hidden pocket and pulled out a copper piece. "I also saved a copper today, Mama."

Sintia's parents had been indentured servants her whole life. It was supposed to be a seven-year contract, but the baron never told them that interest was compounded monthly or that he would charge them for room and board. By the time Sintia was 16, they had accumulated a debt of almost two hundred silver. They could not void their contract until it was paid in full.

Her mother rolled her eyes. "You're going to get yourself killed if you keep sneaking around like this, taking from the baron and pilfering his friends."

Sintia's parents scraped every copper and pinched every penny but had only been able to save what amounted to fifty silver by the time Sintia was old enough to do chores. Since then, she had been able to beg, borrow, and steal for another hundred.

"Or we'll be free." Sintia smiled. "You can look after things tonight, right?"

"Is Ihrisa coming to help?" her father asked, hobbling into the room with some difficulty and putting more wood into the hearth. He was a kind man with a stern face and thick beard.

"She should be here before I leave, but you know how she is."

"By the Almighty, she will come in time." Mama nodded. "Your father and I will cover for you, but you best be quick. You know how fast the baron can eat when he's in a mood."

"I'll be back by the main course," Sintia said with a smile, kissing her mother on the cheek. "I promise."

Sintia left her parents and walked upstairs to get ready for the night. The baron would be entertaining the richest family in town tonight, which meant if she could get in while they were distracted, she could steal enough to make up the fifty silver she was short of, and by the end of the week, they would be free.

* * *

Sintia watched the Duke of Bhacasta, the feudal lord of Nhilvarna and ten other cities built on his land, brother to the king of Cvintavha, and the purest noble blood outside of the royal palace in the capital, arrive at the baron's manor with all the pomp and circumstance of a king. Her dichromatic eyes gave her near-perfect night vision, which allowed her to track the duke from a quarter mile away.

Every year, the barons and lords of the realm had to kiss the duke's ring twice, once on the midsommer festival and again after the harvest. The duke came to collect his rent, but the nobles used the opportunity to prove how well-off they were by treating it like a celebration. In doing so, they invited all the duke's men to dine with them, which left his manor lightly guarded. At the midsommer festival, Sintia snuck out of the manor before dinner to spy on the manor and make a plan for his next visit.

Usually, the property was guarded by a dozen men, but when the duke traveled, he pulled people off his detail in every city to provide extra protection, which meant that the usually fortified domicile was now only guarded by two people, and if last time was any indication, they didn't take their job too seriously without their boss around.

Sintia was nervous, as she expected her friend, Ihrisa, to help her parents with serving, and she was late. Her parents were old and could only do so much to help satiate the ravenous appetites of the duke's men, who required kind words and loose pours all night.

Perhaps I could wait another six months, Sintia thought, except that she had a buyer for a pair of greaves that she spotted in the duke's armory and another for a broach that his wife wore to the midsommer festival two years ago, along with a pair of silver candlesticks that together would fetch enough to cover her debt and give her family enough to start a new life somewhere new; somewhere people didn't hate them for how they looked. If she waited, the buyers would get cold feet or move their attention to other opportunities.

No, she had to go, now or never, and never wasn't an option. She only hoped her family could keep them busy enough that the baroness didn't come looking for her.

When the last of the procession ambled inside, she grabbed onto the vine trellis next to her bedroom and slid down it onto the ground. *Tomorrow I will chastise Ihrisa for leaving me in a lurch,* she thought. *She was probably busy thinking about boys.*

Sintia used the coaches lined up out front of the baron's house as cover to move through the path to the gate and then slid through it. Ihrisa would have to answer for herself, but that had to get out of her head if she ever hoped to succeed.

Making her way across the city dressed in a black cloak and headdress that covered all but her eyes would have drawn attention during the day, but Sintia kept to the shadows and avoided the eyes of the few merchants left closing up their shops by slinking through the darkness.

The duke's manor was close enough to the baron's that she could make it in less than ten minutes if she pounded her legs hard enough to burn. She needed to be back within the hour to make it in time for the main course, giving her just half an hour inside the house if she wanted to return in time.

With little effort, Sintia made it to a crack in the duke's wall she'd eyed on her last visit. It was scheduled for repair within the month, which would have seriously impaired her ability to enter the manor any other time; just one more reason why taking such a risk was worth it now, even as her gut tightened thinking of Ihrisa's abandonment of her.

She tossed a bag over her shoulder and pulled herself up through the crack. Her hands were only just small enough to fit through the fissures, and she pulled herself onto the wall, rushing around it in the darkness until she found a small outhouse that allowed her to crawl down on the other side.

She hid behind a pile of wooden crates, clocking both guards as they made their staggered, listless patrol through the grounds. When they both had their backs turned, she rushed forward toward the open doors the duke never closed to prevent the acrid heat that hung over the city from suffocating him.

The duke only stayed in this manor for two weeks every year, and it was usually closed up tighter than a drum, but when he came, the windows all opened, along with the doors, to make it comfortable for the duke's visit. Lucky for her.

She slipped through the door on the guard's next patrol and into the armory. When she was in school, she took a trip to the duke's manor, where she saw the gaudy, jeweled gloves that the duke only brought out for his parade through the city that came with the end of every visit. She would have usually never thought about taking something so precious, but, only by luck, on her visit, she heard them talk about a spare set they kept just in case of emergencies.

Those were her target. She pulled out a set of thieves' tools and set out to break the lock under the glass case where the gloves were on display.

She spent hundreds of hours practicing her skills on every lock in the baron's manor, often staying up until the wee hours training her ears to hear the click of the tumblers. It paid off, and soon enough, the lock clicked open. She opened the cabinet and slid the dragon greaves into thick cloth bags to prevent them from clanging together before stuffing them into her sack.

When she was done, she returned the lock and rushed out of the room. The candlesticks were in the kitchen, with the rest of the fine serving plates. She hopped across the shadows and into the back of the house. She didn't need any information on where to find the candlesticks. The baron had asked them to design their kitchen just like the duke's, thinking it would impress him. Little did he realize that a duke would never be caught in a kitchen and wouldn't recognize the resemblance if he did.

The kitchen cabinets weren't even locked down, so little did the duke think about them, and Sintia bent down to find five pairs of candlesticks in a cupboard under the sink. She carefully reached into the back and pulled two out in the back, where they would not be noticed. She hid them into her sack, wrapped in a precious set of spare clothes.

The hardest of all the items was the duchess's brooch, as it was locked in a jewelry box upstairs. Luckily, the trellis next to the kitchen led up directly into the bedroom antechamber, and she climbed up it with little effort. However, when she reached the top, she noticed a third guard walking up and down the hallway.

This was not part of the plan, and her heart choked in her throat as she watched the guard walk closer. There was only one spell she knew which could help her now. It was the one her mother told her would put fear into the hearts of even the most stone-willed man.

She did not often have use for it, especially after she left school, but she felt it bubble up in her throat. "Er'salma."

Her whisper floated on the wind and into the guard's ear. She saw his stony face drop, and a shiver went up his spine. He tried to take a step forward but instead spun around and walked in the other direction and then down the stairs.

Sintia smiled to herself as she made her way down the hallway and entered the duke's bedroom. The baron had expensive taste, but it was nothing compared to the gold and silver embossed across every inch of the duke's room.

Sintia thought the decorations quite gauche but didn't have time for criticism. The gaudiness of the duke's taste hopefully meant they would not notice one missing brooch. She walked over to the three-tiered jewelry box and pulled out the smallest pieces in her kit, making short work of the precious lock.

She slid the lock off just as she heard voices outside. "Are you crazy? There's nothing up here."

Her heart jumped into her throat as she heard people walk up the stairs. Sintia kept her attention on the box and searched until she found the broach buried under a hundred different pieces of jewelry the duchess never wore. It was so tempting to take more than she needed, but she was not a thief. She was just trying to survive.

She clipped the lock on the jewelry box just as the footsteps mounted the stairs. "How can you be a guard for the duke if you are scared of the dark?"

"I'm sorry. I don't know what came over me."

There was a turn on the doorknob, and Sintia rushed to the window. She didn't like the idea of jumping down into the brambles below, but as the door opened, she had no other choice.

The thorns nicked at her arms and legs as she fell into the rose bush below, but she stayed there, stifling a whimper until the shadows left the duchess's room and the sounds of footsteps walked away.

When she stood, the thorns ripped at her arms and legs, slicing at her clothes and leaving her bleeding from a dozen cuts. Luckily, she never planned to use those clothes again, and she would be sure to burn them later in the night. The cuts were a different matter. The baron liked his servants perfect, and if he touched her in the wrong way, Sintia would wince and reveal her deception.

That was a problem for another day, though, she thought. What was done was done, and she hobbled off into the darkness, pushing herself over the wall, and scampered off into the night, back toward her home and freedom.

* * *

Sintia managed to make it back to the gate with minor effort if a bit of pain. Two guards chatted by the carriages, and she waited until their backs were turned to sneak in behind them and scuttled up the trellis before they turned back around.

Sintia slid silently against the boards of the room, careful not to make a sound to alert the people downstairs that she was up. Her parents had concocted a lie that she was sick from her chores and needed time to rest. The baron didn't like that, but Sintia was usually a good worker, so he would have to put up with it. Ihrisa was originally supposed to fill in for her, but she hoped Mom and Dad did okay by themselves.

She knelt in front of the loose floorboard and pried it up as quietly as possible. Sintia placed the bag inside the crevice, and her heart sank when her hand failed to find the 150 silver she had collected over the past decade. She scrambled to her feet and found a lantern, which she lit and poked into the hole.

Nothing. It was all gone, except for a note in the baron's handwriting.

We will talk about this once dinner is over, thief. Do not make a scene, or I will have you arrested. – Baron Mhartine Dubhois

Sintia's stomach twisted in knots as she realized the baron knew what her family had been doing for the past many years and was wise as to where she had been that night. Sintia wanted to scream into the night, but she had to make sure her family was okay first.

She tore off her clothes and tended to her wounds, ripping pieces off the thorn-tattered clothes to stop the bleeding from the worst lashes from the bramble and then slipping into a serving uniform before walking out the door. There was no need to lock it now that her family's secret was out.

The blustering of the baron echoed through the manor as she stepped down the stairs. "I have no great love for the church, but their knowledge is second to none."

The duke's voice quaked the house when the baron fell silent. Her mother's eyes found hers when she reached the middle of the stairs, and the fear plastered on her face told Sintia that her mother knew that the baron knew everything.

"That is the problem," the duke blustered. "In that knowledge is incalculable power, which must be stopped."

"How will you do that?" the baroness's voice cooed.

"It will be hard," the duke growled. "Their power comes from my brother's protection of their cause, but they flaunt his edicts at every turn. I work to bring them down but have not had the ability yet."

They spoke of the Jhangasi Church of Grina, an overtly religious sect worshiping the goddess of wisdom. Cvintavha and the surrounding regions had historically worshiped Ghata, but the Jhangasi weaseled their way into the king's ear by offering to absolve him from all his extramarital infidelity, telling them that every time he deflowered a woman was a prayer to Shala, who equally represented sexual desire as wisdom and cunning.

The queen deplored the king's religious conversion, which happened with near immediate speed, but her consternations did not matter to the king. As long as his proclivities were seen as religious observance, he took full advantage of it, often flaunting his conquests at court. The blessing of the royals caused the Church of Shala to catch on with nobles and gave them a foothold in cities all over the countryside.

"I do not trust them," the baroness said, a hard woman with a stiff lip for all encounters. She was as ruthless as her husband and reveled in demeaning those that displeased her. Sintia fell into that camp, young and nubile, which offended her world-weary bones. "I will worship the goddess Ghata until the day I die, no matter what the king demands."

"As you should!" shouted the duke. "Shala is the goddess of fools. To think they converted our beautiful temple into a church for that heathen."

"It's hideous," the baroness tutted. "An abomination."

"Hear, hear," yelled the duke. "If we let this madness go on much longer, they will warp all our sensibilities and make us a laughing stock in the eyes of Cvintavha."

"I am surprised Fhalama has not crossed the Eternal Desert and declared war on us for our insolence." The duchess piped up, agreeing with the duke. She was considerably younger than the baroness but cut from the same cloth.

"Where have you been?" Sintia's mother whispered to her daughter when she finally reached the bottom of the stairs.

She stuffed a carafe of wine into her chest. "You know exactly where I have been."

"The baron—" Her eyes widened as she shook her head.

"I know," Sintia replied. "I found the note. Let us just get through this, and we will figure it out."

Sintia took the carafe into the room, where the knights of the duke's court yelled and hooted at her entrance. They squeezed her thighs and reached under her dress as Sintia tried to fill their glasses. She wanted to slug them, but all Sintia could do was smile at their insolence, lest she have her hands cut off for trying to defend herself. She was already in enough trouble.

"There you are, my dear!" the baron bellowed. "I'm glad you feel better now, Sin. Huzzah!"

Every word was filled with enmity from his forked tongue, but he said them with a smile.

"Thank you, sir. I am feeling a bit better now."

"Oh, that's nice," the baroness said through puckered lips. Her eyes showed even more disdain for Sintia than usual, which told her that the baron's wife likely knew about the truth that fueled the baron's rage. "I would hate for you to bring the sickness that fell you for a whole afternoon here."

"I would never dream of it," Sintia replied, bitter at the baroness's twist on her namesake. "Nor would I wish to leave you short-handed. I feel much better now. Please accept my humblest apologies."

"Yes, yes!" screamed the duke. "Enough of this jabber! Servants should be seen and not heard. Fill our glasses and bring out food, wench!"

"Yes, sir." Sintia gave a humble nod and finished filling the glasses before dipping into the kitchen to help with the platters of food her father had slaved over all day.

"Thank Grina," Sintia's father said, grabbing her around the neck and kissing her forehead. He had taken Grina for his god before the Jhangasi curried favor with the king. All from Demajios did, if only in lip service. "We feared the worst."

"I'm fine," Sintia replied, wincing. "Though I am tender to the touch."

Her father pulled away. "You must—the baron knows everything. He pulled us aside before the duke arrived and told us to keep a stiff chin tonight, or he would see our heads on a pike, but I fear our heads will be on the chopping block either way."

Sintia's father was a kindly man, but he had seen his share of pain in his life. He met his wife in Cvintavha and thought love would be enough to set them free. Time and betrayal had hardened him, so the fact that Sintia could see the fear on his face made her stomach knot even tighter.

"I will figure it out," Sintia replied with whispered determination. "Let us just get through this night, and once it is over, we will figure out a way to make it okay."

The baron screamed for his food, and Sintia's mother jumped in her skin. "I tried to calm him down, but even with my powers, it did not work." She grabbed a tray. "Let us just pray to the Almighty that the baron is kinder than usual."

They brought the food and acted the perfect servants for the rest of the night. The baron, to his credit, kept an amicable front, never belying that anything was wrong in his home. When the hour grew late, the duke took the tax that was the pretext for his visit and departed with great bluster, leaving the dining room a wreck for Sintia's family to clean.

The duke hugged the baron tightly and gave him glad tidings before the door closed. The baron and baroness watched out the window until they were out the gate, and it closed behind them.

The baroness kissed her husband on the cheek and yawned. "I will take my leave to bed. Don't be too long."

"I won't, my dear," he replied. "I just want to make sure our servants do not cut corners on the cleaning, and then I will be right up."

"Yes," she said, glaring at Sintia and her family. "I thought I saw a smudge on one of the platters tonight, and I nearly died of fright. Luckily, the duchess did not see, or it would have been quite the scene."

"I'm sorry," Sintia said quietly. "I know it was hard for my parents while I was waylaid with sickness. I will be sure to make my health a top priority from now on."

"See that you do, Sin," she replied.

"Of course, my lady." Sintia filled her voice with deference. "I will be sure to keep that in mind."

"You have it good here," the baroness said as she walked to the stairs. "You should see what my friends do with their servants. I hope you appreciate it."

Sintia nodded. "Of course, ma'am."

It was a horrible truth, but a truth nonetheless. As nobles went, the baron was nicer than most. Sintia and her family were rarely beaten, and he never took advantage of the poor girl, even though it was his right whenever he pleased, but that did not make them good people. It was the least they could do to treat Sintia and her family like humans, even if it was not expected of them.

The baron, though, loved to play head games, and as the baroness disappeared into the dark, he turned to Sintia with a great grin on his face. "Now, let us talk, Sin."

* * *

Baron Dubhois crossed the room and pulled out a small serving plate Sintia had swiped from his collection several years ago. It was her boldest move in all her years as a thief. She regretted it immediately after the fence bought it off her but couldn't stomach the thought of turning the silver back in to get the plate back. She had never forgotten about it in the ensuing years, using it as a lesson in being more discreet. Now, it had come back to bite her.

"Do you know what a sin is?" the baron asked Sintia.

"A vile thing," Sintia replied. It was all she could think of after all the times she had been called it.

"Not untrue," the baron said. "But it is more. It is an immortal act in violation of the gods and giants above them, in contradiction to the divine law. Do you believe you were born a sin against creation, Sintia?"

"I don't think so," she replied. "I try to be good."

"And yet, every word out of your mouth is a lie, which is a great sin. Two years ago, I asked you about this plate," the baron said, turning to her. "Do you remember that?"

"I—yes, sire," I replied.

"And do you remember what you told me?" he asked, stepping toward Sintia. His gait wasn't threatening, but a growling gravelly nature to his tone made her skin crawl.

"It wasn't her fault—" Sintia's father said, but the baron uncharacteristically smacked him across the face before he could finish and knocked him to the ground.

"Do not interrupt me," the baron said before turning calmly to Sintia. "Do you?"

Sintia nodded. "I told you that I didn't know. You—you gave me ten lashes for losing it."

"A mercy, it turns out," he said. "Four weeks ago, I saw this plate at a lord's house halfway across the city. I asked him where he got it and offered to buy it from him. I tracked down the seller, who told me they bought it from a young girl with two different colored eyes some years ago." His brow furrowed. "There are very few girls with dichromatic eyes in this town, let alone ones that would have access to my private collection. So, tell me. How long have you been stealing from me?"

"I didn't, sir—I mean, I don't."

He raised his hand. "Don't lie to me, girl. I am not as stupid as you would believe me to be."

Sintia squeezed her eyes closed, bracing for a hit with his open palm. "I did—I did that once, but I haven't taken anything since."

He dropped his hands. "Then how did you collect the hundred and fifty silver I found in your room?"

"That was us, sir," Sintia's mother said, cowering from the baron's hand. "She had nothing to do with it."

"No, Mom!" Sintia shouted. "Don't li—"

"Be quiet!" her mother screamed to her.

"Do not raise your voice in my presence," the baron growled at Sintia's mother before he turned to her. "Speak, then."

"I have been haggling with the vendors and taking the remainder of their reduced prices for myself." Sintia's mother choked on her words for a moment, clearing her throat to dislodge them. "I have done so for years, and that is how I acquired so much money."

"And you hoped to pass it off as your own and give it back to me to buy your freedom?" He chuckled. "I have to admit; I admire the cleverness of such a plan. That said, what you have told me is impossible. I keep records of how much I have given you over the years. At best, you could have taken a hundred silver from me in that time. Where did the rest come from?"

Sintia's mother swallowed hard. "That is all I have done. You have my truth."

"I don't believe you," the baron said, turning his head toward the top of the hallway. "Did you find it?"

"Yes, husband." The baroness came down the stairs and into the kitchen. "It was exactly where you said it would be. All from the duke's estate."

The baron took the bag and looked into it. "Very impressive, child. Tell me, do you have the same gift for magic as your mother?"

"I do—" Sintia's mother started, but now she found the back of his hand, giving out a little yelp as she stumbled backward.

"We are not stupid," he said. "I have heard you murmuring, plotting, and talking in the darkness. This is my house. Nothing happens that I do not know about. I chose to keep your secret until it benefited me, which it now does."

The baroness turned to her. "Well, do you, Sin?"

Sintia sighed and nodded. "A bit, ma'am. Nothing like my mother."

The baron narrowed his eyes. "That is a powerful ability for a thief to have. I'll bet it has gotten you out of many jams."

Sintia couldn't help but smirk with pride. "A few, sir."

He stepped forward. "And then perhaps it can help me, as well."

Sintia looked up at him. "I don't understand."

The baron handed the bag to his wife. "I will keep this and the money you stole from me as collateral, but if you want to earn your freedom, then perhaps we can work together after all."

"How, sir?" Sintia asked.

"You may have heard us talking about the Jhangasi—the scum of the kingdom." He spat. "Do you know of them?"

Sintia nodded. "I hear their bells every day."

"Yes, they are loud and make my skin crawl," he said. "Every one of their churches keeps a library of forbidden magic—the kind of thing that could get you killed by the king. I need you to break into their library and steal a book for me."

"I—I am not that good a thief."

"I think you are." He smiled. "But if not, get better quickly because if you do not steal this book for me by midday tomorrow, I will call the guards and have you arrested. You will be tried as a traitor to the duke and hung next to your mother and father." He turned from Sintia. "However, if you do this for me, your freedom is yours, and I will give you the money you stole to start a new life far from my sight."

Sintia's eyes perked up. The baron had never spoken of her freedom before, and it was hard to contain her excitement. "What is this book?"

"No!" Sintia's mother shouted. "You can't!"

"I have no choice!" Sintia had never screamed at her mother, but she did so now out of fear and anger before turning to the baron. "If I do this, you guarantee our safety?"

He smiled. "You have my word as a noble and on my family's name."

Sintia had no choice but to bow her head. "Then I agree."

The baron nodded. "Perfect. Get some sleep. Say your goodbyes to your family, and get your affairs in order. I cannot overstate the danger of this mission. If you fail, you will be thrown into prison until you are old and gray."

"Come dear," the baroness said. "Let us leave them to clean up and say their final goodbyes."

Yes, they still expected Sintia and her family to clean, even though this might be their last night for the rest of their lives. The baron took his wife's hand and walked up the stairs. They did not even worry that they would run. If they did, Sintia and her family would not get far, and when they were dragged back to him, they would be in the exact position they were now. Nobody cared for them. Nobody liked them, and thus they had no choice but to do as he said, no matter how bad the terms.

"What have you done, my child?" her mother said, wrapping her tightly.

"I've given us a chance for freedom," Sintia replied through her tears.

Her father rubbed her back. "Silly girl. It is us who are supposed to save you."

Sintia swallowed. "Not this time, Papa. Just keep the faith that the Almighty will save us."

"I fear he is not enough to save us this time," her mother replied.

Sintia cleared her throat and then wiped the hot tears streaming down her face. "Come, let us clean. We don't want the baron any angrier with us."

"He can burn," her father growled, spite in his throat.

"He will, Papa," Sintia replied. "In time, I swear they both will."

* * *

The next morning, Sintia rose early after a fitful sleep, and her mother dressed her wounds. It was a tense, wordless affair. They both knew the stakes of what would happen should Sintia fail and that this might be the last day they breathed free air.

"I love you," she said, wrapping Sintia tightly when she was dressed in the white robes the baron insisted she wore. They were loose-fitting, which she hated since it meant she had to be extra careful not to snag them on anything.

Her hair had always been short, but today it completed her look as an altar boy for the Jhangasi. When she was ready, she walked out of the room and down the stairs to find the baron at a table with a bowl of hot oatmeal and an empty place next to him.

"Please, sit, Sintia," he said, extending his hand to the place setting next to him.

Sintia had never eaten with the baron before, and she hesitated for a moment until the baroness came with a second bowl of oatmeal and gave her a curt smile.

"Thank you," Sintia said, taking him up on his offer.

"You'll need all your strength today," he growled, slapping her on the back like they were old friends.

Sintia ate the bowl hungrily, and a ham hock and thick coffee followed the oatmeal. When the baroness finished delivering food, she sat down next to the girl, who smiled at her. "I didn't know you were such a great cook."

"I had other interests before becoming the lady of this house," she said. "I'm glad you like it, Sin."

"I really do," Sintia replied, trying to swallow the anger at the blasphemy of her name.

"Your family worships the Almighty, right?" Baron asked. "She is the single goddess of your people, I mean."

I nodded. "My parents say the words, but we have not practiced since I was a little girl."

"And they do not go to their accused church, do they?"

She shook her head. "No, you forbid it."

"Hrm, well, you have done plenty that I forbid, like stealing, so I was not sure." The baron leaned in toward her. "How much do you know about the Jhangasi, then?"

"I know the king made Jhangasi the official religion of the land and forced Ghata's worshippers into the fringes. I have heard you say they are a blight on all of Cvintavha."

The baron chuckled. "You aren't wrong, but they are so much more. You see, the Jhangasi covet knowledge above all other things. They believe that if they understood how the world worked, they could—well, I'm not sure what they plan, but I know that they aim to have more knowledge than the gods, which is heresy of the highest order. The duke's brother has been seduced by their ways, and we must break them from that curse."

"And this is what you need help with?"

He nodded. "There is a book inside the confines of their sanctuary that I have heard tell it contains every spell ever cast with lore magic. Could you imagine what a group like the Jhangasi could do with something that powerful?"

Sintia thought for a moment but couldn't think of anything. "…No?"

"That is for the best." He bit his lip. "I can assure you, though, they would do dangerous things."

"So, you need me to get this book and bring it to you?"

He nodded. "Exactly."

"And what do you plan to do with it?"

"That is not your concern," the baroness said smugly.

"It's okay, darling." He smiled. "I aim to bring it to the duke, and together we will show this treachery to the king and break this spell they have on him."

"And if it's not enough?" Sintia asked, ripping off another piece of meat and stuffing it into her mouth.

He leaned back. "Then Ghata help us all, for if he is not broken off this curse soon, then all of Cvintavha will fall."

Sintia pushed her plate away. "Well, I don't care about all that, but if it's going to free my family, I'll do whatever you need."

He smacked his hand on the table. "Do this for me, and you will find your freedom and my grace."

"And your money," Sintia said, matter of fact.

"And that." He handed her a drawing of a circle with three smaller circles inside it, all inside a box with a small gap in the lower left corner. "This is the symbol on the book you are looking for. It will be made of gold and on the front of a book bound in black leather."

Sintia stood up with conviction. "And why am I dressed as an altar boy?"

The bells rang in the distance. "Service starts in ten minutes. Join the altar boys walking into the church and turn into the first left you find. Take the spiral stairwell all the way down, and follow the hallway to the end. The library will be behind the double doors."

"And if I am seen?" Sintia asked.

"Then I expect you to use your power, just as your mother has on me all these years."

The baron and baroness had never been half as nice to Sintia in all her time with them combined. The baroness never so much as lifted a finger in the kitchen, and now she made Sintia breakfast? What was happening?

Maybe the baroness was cooking to prepare for a life without them, should she recover the book for them. It didn't matter much, though. The reasoning did not change her assignment. She needed to stay focused on the prize.

Sintia turned onto the main street and lost herself in the procession headed toward the church. The parishioners were dressed nicely in black, and speckled with them were altar boys in white robes identical to the ones she wore. It was not uncommon to see a man that looked like her in the pack of parishioners, as this was the religion of their home, so nobody gave her a second look.

Two older men dressed in green and purple robes stood at either side of the entrance to the Gothic church, adorned with statues of screaming giants on every landing and intricate roses carved up each side of it. Brand new stained glass told the story of a woman bursting with wisdom that offered love and compassion to all.

She had watched them break the old stained glass when the Jhangasi moved in ten years ago, removing every remnant of Ghata from the building, save for the roses that adorned the church from its days as a temple to her. The baron forced her to crawl through the trash to collect as much of the broken molding and stained glass as her poor, bloody hands could carry.

"Good morning," one of the old men said as she passed them on the steps of the chapel. She kept her head down and nodded curtly. "I don't think I've ever seen you before."

"I'm new," she said in a gruff voice. "From far away."

Sintia's face convulsed at the horrible lie she told, but the priest barely noticed it and instead turned to greet the next parishioners after wishing her well.

Sintia moved toward the left when she passed the threshold to the church, where she found the spiral stairwell and disappeared down it. The whole of the community seemed caught up in the service, which made it easy to vanish without being seen, and Sintia kept her feet light on the wrought iron metal to avoid being heard by anyone. Being invisible was something she had practiced since birth.

When Sintia reached the bottom of the stairs, she found a hallway just as the baron described, lined with burning torches of a brilliant red she had never seen before. Torches usually burned orange and yellow, and she wondered if magic had something to do with it…or if the burden of knowledge turned the torches red.

As she continued down the hallway, Sintia passed paintings of a beautiful woman with long red hair, bringing books to the people, and making peace between warring factions on either side of her. The Jhangasi certainly made Shala seem like the type of goddess deserving of worship. Sintia could see why she ascended to godhood if she was as wonderful as the lore depicted and wondered for a moment why her parents never spoke of her. But a moment later, she let the thought flitter out of her head and turned her attention back to the hallway.

Sintia passed thick wooden doors carved with vines until she reached a pair of double doors at the end, depicting Shala reading a book on either side. She took a deep breath. Books were a precious gift from the giants, hand painted by scholars and passed between them like holy relics. The idea of touching one brought a shiver through Sintia's back. If this book was as powerful as the baron mentioned, was it even safe to touch?

Before she could decide whether the pursuit of knowledge was worth the terrible price she might pay, she heard a creak from a door behind her, and her breath left her as she heard somebody enter the hallway.

"Excuse me, young man," a creaky voice said. "But what are you doing here?"

* * *

"Er'kata," Sintia whispered under her breath before turning and blowing the spell over the ancient priest shuffling toward her. She had never been strong in magic, but she channeled every bit of her will into the spell and hoped it would be enough. Her breath hit the priest like a sack of bricks, and he stood straight when he smelt the magic on her breath. "Oh, I'm so sorry. I'm new, and one of the fathers upstairs asked for a book from inside the library. I could really use your help."

The priest furrowed his brows, trying to make sense of the lie Sintia weaved. It seemed like he would scream for help for a moment, but then his mouth went slack. "Odd. They must have forgotten the Hilarjax. Was it Father Ulthet? He would forget his head if it weren't attached."

"Yes," Sintia said with a nod. "I think that was it. Although I'm not sure. I'm very new. Frankly, I think they might be playing tricks on me."

The old man shuffled forward and pushed the door. "I would not put it past the altar boys. They are scamps like that. Come, let us see if we can find what you need before they begin the service."

The doors to the library opened with a creak, and Sintia's nostrils were filled with the musk of a thousand books stacked on top of each other on the floor, tables, and rising high into the sky on shelves filled with leather and parchment.

"I have never seen anything like this," Sintia muttered to herself, a fear rising in herself that she had never felt before. If books were as powerful as the baron said, then the amount of power in that library was incomparable to anything she could imagine.

"This is one of the bigger libraries in all the parishes around Cvintavha." He turned. "What parish did you say you were from?"

"I'm—" Sintia thought for a minute, spinning a lie in her mind. "My parents are refugees. We were told that the church is accepting of people like us."

"Of course, my child. Grina protects all who seek knowledge, no matter how wretched." He hobbled to a big table filled with books and dust. "Now, I see that the Hilarjax was taken, so I fear that you are right that the altar boys were having a laugh with you. Nevermind that, the mass is starting. Let us—"

"Wait," Sintia said, scampering forward. "Since we are here, may I ask a question of you that I have heard about only in stories?"

The priest sighed. "Do it quickly."

Sintia didn't have any good segue, so she simply dipped her hand into her pocket, pulled out the piece of paper, and whispered her spell a second time. She had not rested enough to use the er'kata spell so quickly, but she fought the pain to cast it again.

The priest's eyes went wide for a moment when he saw the sign but then settled once again. "This is a very powerful book."

"Would you show it to me?" she asked. "Please. I would be ever so grateful."

Sintia made sure every bit of her breath hit the priest's face, her magic fighting against his natural reaction to call her out for what she was, a liar. His face twitched, fighting against the spell, but eventually, he succumbed to it and nodded.

"For a moment."

He walked slowly across the room and shuffled through several books, pulling them off a pile, until he grabbed a book nearly as big as Sintia's chest and turned to her. The baron was right. It had a massive golden emblem on it that looked exactly like the crude drawing he gave, and Sintia walked toward it.

"You treat books of such power as if they were nothing?"

The priest smiled. "All books have power, young man; sometimes, it is best to hide that which has the most power in plain sight."

"May I hold it?" Sintia asked. Fear filled her mouth as she asked the question. She knew the book had power and wondered if she was worthy of carrying such a thing. Still, she had no choice but to keep going.

The priest tried to fight his baser instinct but finally relented and handed her the book.

Sintia grabbed the book gingerly, expecting to be ripped apart at once, but when she wrapped her arms around it, not even so much as a jolt of energy shot through her, and she let out a sigh of relief.

"I'm so sorry about this," she said after a long moment.

"About what?" the priest asked.

There was no way to extricate herself from this situation without using a third spell, which was more than she ever had the strength to do in her life. Her will had been sapped, but she gritted her teeth and forced the words out of her mouth.

"Er'salma," she whispered, feeling the magic leech from her bones as it floated across the room. She had never used so many spells so close to each other, and her eyes felt heavy at the weight of it.

A cold chill crawled up the priest's body, and he turned from Sintia immediately and rushed away from her into a small alcove in the back of the room. His feet shuffled away until she could barely hear them, and she turned to run, out of the library, out of the hallway, and out of the church as the cantor droned on with a sad dirge from the pulpit.

She had to leave Nhilvarna and never show her face again lest the priest be able to point her out to the guards. The thought of freedom overwhelmed her fear, though, and she smiled. With the book held tightly in her breast, she would have liberty for herself and her parents.

Nobody bothered her on the way back to the manor, even though she held a large book in her hands. She was often seen with odd items for the baron, so even those that milled around town didn't take notice of anything strange about her. She appreciated that because she was so weak, she wobbled with the heavy book in her hands, drained from the magic that flowed through her.

Her heart fluttered as she passed through the gates to the baron's manor, and she let out a deep breath as she slammed the door behind her. She leaned against the door to steady herself. "I'm back!"

She expected her parents to find her first, but it was the baron who walked out to see her. "Very good, child. Is that it?"

Sintia nodded and held it out to him. "Yes, this is what you asked for, isn't it?"

The baron smiled for a minute, looking at it, and then walked to a cabinet behind him in the foyer. He placed the book inside and locked it behind him. "You have done well, child."

"And so then it is done? We have won our freedom?"

The baron's cold face drew a small smile. And then he shook his head and snapped his fingers. From the bedroom upstairs, four guards emerged. Two held her parents, who struggled against them through their gags.

One of them, Sintia knew as the captain of the guard, and his plumage was more vibrant than the others. "Is this her?"

"What is happening here?" Sintia asked. "What are you doing to my parents? Let them go!"

The baron reached into the banquet room and pulled out the sack Sintia had kept her spoils from the night before. She realized what was happening all too late as the baron threw them on the floor.

"Yes, sir." The baron nodded. "This sinner and her parents used our dinner last night to sneak into the duke's house and steal these from him. I'm sure you recognize them."

Sintia dropped to the ground, weeping, as the captain stepped forward. She didn't have the strength even to speak. "I do, and you are sure these three are responsible?"

The baron tutted, offended. "How else would I come into possession of them? Are you calling me a thief?"

The captain shook his head. "Of course not, sir. Do not worry. We will take care of these three criminals, and you will be well compensated for your loyalty to the crown."

"The gold will be welcome, but justice is its own reward."

The captain grabbed Sintia tightly and bound her with shackles. She kicked and screamed, reaching out to her parents for comfort, but finding nothing but the cold, hard air to grasp at.

"No! Please!" Sintia shouted. "You have no idea who this man is. He's a liar!"

"Quiet, girl!" the baron said. "It's unbecoming of you to besmirch my name after everything I have done for you."

The captain pulled Sintia out of the house and through the gate. She grabbed onto the stone, trying to break away, but she was left drained from her experiences in the church. All she could do was scream out weakly in agony and curse her betrayal, vowing one day to get vengeance, even if it was the last thing she did.

INTERLUDE AT THE END OF THE WORLD

WHEN I FINISHED the story, my hands buzzed with energy, and I had a smile on my face as bright as any I had over the last few months.

"Ha!" I shouted. "That was a pretty good one. Um…alright, kiderinos. I'm going to get some water, and then I'll do another if you're really well behaved."

I pushed myself to stand and rubbed the sides of my mouth. What did I mean I was going to do another one? I couldn't just sit down here and read stories all day, could I? I needed some water and a good think.

I walked up the stairs and pulled a water bottle out of the fridge I had seen there before. I chugged it immediately, and then another. *Why shouldn't I stay here?* It was defensible with a little work, and nobody else had come around for a long time. There was food and, after turning on the water to confirm it came from a well, clean water, too. It was as good a place as any to make a stand if you wanted to make a stand.

But you aren't one to make a stand, Steph. No, you're a runner. You are quick on your feet and spooked easily. Still, who knew how much longer it was to another unguarded place? I only found this one because it was off the main road, and you couldn't see it through the thicket of corn and trees surrounding it.

If I was going to stay, I needed to get the car off the road. I went back to where it was holding up and pushed off the parking brake. I threw the car in neutral and eased it off the road, covering it with corn stalks so nobody could see it. Luckily, the Yugo was a piece of junk and light, which made it easy enough for one person to move, but by the time I was done, I was parched.

I scarfed down two more glasses of water and downed three protein bars. Then, I locked the front door and boarded it up as best I could. I ripped some planks off the floorboards and found a hammer in a shed out back.

I moved everything that could be used as a weapon into the basement after I finished converting the house into a little fortress, and then I sat at the desk again next to a microphone, ready to make another broadcast.

"Did you hear all that? If you come for me, I'm going to beat yer ass. Got that?" I smiled. "But if you're good, then I can read you a couple more stories. What do you think about that? Yeah, I like it too." I pulled another story from the pack. "Here we go."

THE GREAT UNKNOWN

Originally appeared in "Itty Bitty Writing Space"

"DO YOU KNOW why I hate Santa Claus?" I asked with a deep gasp. Technically, I couldn't breathe, but that didn't stop me from gasping when the occasion arose.

"I have no idea," Doctor Trevor replied from across the room. Humans didn't take kindly to my presence, even though I never did anything malicious to them. He was bald and rail thin. His hand shook uncontrollably as he scribbled illegible notes.

I had been seeing him for over a month to help with my crippling jealousy of other supernatural beings. He had yet to get comfortable with the fact that I was Death, that it was my job to take people to their final salvation, or that I spoke so casually about it with him.

I lay on the red couch next to a bay window that looked out on the park across the street. The couch was clearly made for a much smaller man than I, though I'm not sure I had ever been a man or human at all. I dangled my bony feet off the end of it as the light shone on my pale face.

"People idolize that jolly fat man for delivering presents once a year," I said to him. "Yet, here I am, the last, final comfort in their loved ones' lives, and most of them fear me. He works one day a year, but I don't get one second off, not even one. I even work on Christmas."

"And yet, you are here," he said.

"Am I?" I replied. "I am in so many places at once these days that I'm not even sure which is the real me."

"That must be hard for you."

"It's never been harder," I replied, tilting my head toward him. "Every day, there are more and more of you people, which means there are more and more people dying, and I am tasked with ushering you all into the afterlife.”

“May I ask you a question?” he asked, mumbling under his breath.

“I should hope so. I’ve been coming here for weeks, and you haven’t asked me anything of import yet.”

“Did you…shepherd my mother?” he asked.

I smiled. People didn’t think Death could smile, but the idea of death was so laughably ridiculous I often couldn’t believe I did anything but grin at the thought of it.

“I did. She was a lovely woman.”

“And my father?” he asked without another moment’s hesitation.

“I have shepherded every member of your family for a hundred generations, dating back to when you could barely be considered human at all.”

The doctor lowered his pen to the pad in front of him. “Does it hurt?”

I pushed myself up and turned toward him. “I’m not sure. They never say it hurts. Usually, they are scared or confused, but they are never in pain. On my best days, my job is to relieve people from pain.”

“Where do you take them?” he asked, tears welling in his eyes.

“Beyond,” I replied.

“That’s not a very good answer,” he said, scoffing through gritted teeth.

“I know,” I replied. “I wish I had something better to offer, but I only play a small part in the grand design. I am only the conduit that transitions you into the next phase of your journey. When you reach the end, I return.”

“What is the meaning of all this?” he asked me. “It feels so pointless.”

“That is the question people ask me most of all and the one I am most unqualified to answer.”

“Try,” he said, venom bubbling in his throat.

"From what I have seen, the meaning of life is to love and be loved, to laugh and cry, and come to peace with your existence so that you can welcome death as an old friend."

"You're saying all of life is just to become comfortable with meeting you? That sounds like an overinflated ego to me."

"Perhaps, but you asked my opinion. I am as prone to myopic thinking as anyone."

"Do they welcome you? The ones you shepherd."

"Some do. Others curse me. It varies. The happiest are the ones who have found some peace in this life."

He placed his paper down and stared at me with watery eyes. He choked back what remained of his emotions and took a deep breath.

"Why did this have to happen to me?" he said. "Why did I get cancer? I'm only thirty-six."

"Now we come to the crux of it," I replied. "Bad luck, I'm afraid. No, that is not exactly correct. Random chance would be more appropriate."

His whole body convulsed in sadness. "I had so much to do, so much left to do."

"We all do."

"Not all of us," he replied. "Some get to live long, full lives. They accomplish everything they set out to do. It's not fair."

"And some die at birth without accomplishing anything. You're right, though," I said, standing. "It isn't fair. None of this is fair. It is just as it is, and that's all we can do."

He looked up at me. "And it won't hurt?"

I shook my head as I moved toward him. "Not even a little bit."

He dropped his head and cradled it with his hands. "Then do it already."

I held out my hand. "It has already been done. You have been dead for the past month. I have kept you here until you grew accustomed to it and accepted me willingly." A white light grew above me until it filled the office. "Come, let us away."

Doctor Trevor grabbed my hand and stood up. Together, we were enveloped by the light. It is not fair that Santa Claus gets all the glory when I bring people the greatest gift of all—a warm hand to travel with into the great unknown.

AKTA'S FIRST HUNT

Prequel story to "Hell"

"I DON'T SEE why you won't let me carry you," Akta shouted down from the sky at her mentor, Sir Cleybourne, as he stomped through the woods in full chain metal armor. "I'm very strong."

"I'm fine on the ground, and no, you're not," Cleybourne hollered back, hacking at the trees in front of him, his white hair and beard glinting with his sword in the sunlight. "You're supposed to be learning how to be a proper fighter, and proper fighters don't fly."

Akta flitted her dragonfly-like wings and swooped down from twenty feet in the air to hover in front of Sir Cleybourne, flying backward inches from the ground but never once touching it. "How do you know what fighters would do if they had wings?"

Cleybourne half-heartedly swung his broadsword at her, ducking it just as she had a million times before. She wasn't wrong, though. Cleybourne had trained many fighters before her, but never a pixie, never one who could fly easier than he could walk.

"I know the ground steadies you and allows you balance."

Akta swirled into the air. "Who needs balance when you can fly?"

Cleybourne stopped in his tracks. "It also gives you the power to thrust at your enemies. Take, for instance, that boulder there." He pointed to a rock stuck in a crevice in front of them.

Akta flew over to it. "Yeah. I see it. What about it?"

"Say you wanted to move that boulder. How would you do it?"

Akta scratched her head for a second. "Well, I wouldn't. I would just go around it."

Cleybourne shook his head firmly. "That's not an option. You must go through it."

Akta flew onto the boulder and stood atop it, her bare feet sliding across the smooth rock. Cleybourne hated that she didn't wear shoes, but Akta didn't know why she needed shoes if she never touched the ground.

"Yeah, it is an option, though. I can even stand on top of it if I want," Akta said. "Just look. I'm doing it right now."

Cleybourne sighed. He didn't know why he was stuck training the pixie. There were many mightier knights who could benefit from his attention. But the King insisted that it be him.

He watched the twelve-year-old pixie swing through the sky with the greatest of ease and wished he were back training Prince Odgeir, the crown prince of the

Kingdom. At least the boy listened to reason. At least he had respect, even if he was a talentless fighter. "Could you come over here?" Sir Cleybourne called to her.

Akta zipped through the air toward him. "Sure thing. What are we supposed to be doing again, anyway? I meant to ask."

Sir Cleybourne sighed. "Once again, we are here to hunt, kill, and bring back a boar for the royal supper."

"I guess I know that part. The part I don't understand is why *we* are doing it. I mean, you're kind of a legend, and I'm kind of amazing. Why can't they get a butcher or somebody to do it?"

Sir Cleybourne pulled Akta by the belt strap. "A butcher cuts the meat, but a hunter kills it. However, that is irrelevant. We will do it because it was tasked to us. The King decided this was a mission even you couldn't screw up, though I know you will do your best."

"I don't think that's fair, Cley. It's not like I've been on missions before." She crossed her arms and gave him a petulant look.

"No, but you have been around the castle and caused enough catastrophe for ten lifetimes. You just about gave your poor chambermaid a heart attack."

Akta yanked free of Cleybourne's grasp and flew in front of him. "That's definitely not fair. She walked in on me, practicing disappearing. How come she didn't knock, huh?"

"A knight is always prepared."

"Maybe I don't wanna be a knight. There are many ways to be a good hunter without being a knight."

Cleybourne grumbled. He'd trained a hundred knights in his day, and none were as thick-headed and disobedient as Akta. "If you want to work for the king, you will learn his rules. You cannot go around behaving like you do, sullying his good name."

"But it's so *boring*. Look at this." Akta shot into the sky. In a moment, she was a hundred feet in the air. "Look at this. Why would you want to train me like all the other knights when I can do this?"

"Because that is the way it is, young one. The sooner you learn that, the sooner you will get back your precious pixie dust."

"Oh, I could get that back whenever I wanted. I know you keep it in the stables under the horse feed. I'm not an idiot. I'm just being polite."

"That's never been your strong suit."

Akta peered off into the horizon. She squinted her eyes tightly and saw the black outline of a four-legged animal with sharp tusks. "Hey, do boars have tusks?"

"Yes…" Cleybourne tilted his head, wondering what she was getting at. "Adult ones, at least."

"Then I found one!" Akta zipped away.

"Wait!"

But it was too late. Akta had already left Sir Cleybourne behind.

The pixie did many things well, but listening wasn't one of them. She was singularly focused when she set her mind on something which had its advantages and disadvantages.

Now, at the moment, all Akta saw were the advantages. If she returned to the castle with a boar she'd caught herself, maybe she could skip all this training nonsense and finally be given a mission to fight real monsters. After all, that's what she'd wanted since she was a little kid. Sir Cleybourne and all the greatest knights in the land made their bones fighting monsters and sending them back beyond the Veil, where they couldn't hurt the good people of the kingdom anymore.

They weren't fighting stupid boars and bringing them back for supper, Akta thought bitterly. Well, Sir Cleybourne was, but only because he was old. Not many monster hunters made it to old age, and when they did, the King put them to use, training a new generation of fighters. The King thought Akta could be the best monster hunter in the land, and no matter what Sir Cleybourne thought of her, he was a humble servant of the realm, so he had to obey.

Akta pulled out her daggers when she was within sight of the boar. It was a big, fat thing, waddling through the mud and rooting for truffles. From the sky, Akta had the element of surprise. She slowly lowered herself down to the mud and readied herself to make the fatal stab. She raised the dagger over her head and dove it down into the boar's front leg with all her might.

The boar screamed out in pain, but it didn't die. In fact, Akta's dagger barely made a dent in the hide of the boar. It shook off the knife, which landed harmlessly at Akta's side.

Then, the boar's eyes turned a bright red as it dug its feet into the ground and charged. Akta rose into the sky out of the way.

"Whoa! Easy now!"

But the boar wouldn't calm down. Akta had tried to kill it, and it demanded vengeance. The boar turned and charged again. Akta easily flew out of the way and landed gracefully atop a tree near the mud pit.

The boar caught sight of Akta and slammed itself at full speed into the tree. It backed up and rammed again. The vibrations sent Akta into the air and out of the boar's sight. A few seconds passed, and the boar calmed down, content that its message was clear: *Do not mess with me.*

It hobbled off into the woods, and Akta followed close behind. "Let's see where you go when you're not rooting around."

*

Akta floated behind the boar for ten minutes before it finally came to rest in front of a large rock cave. The boar snorted and honked until another fully-grown boar came out of the cave. Then, and only then, the boar lay down, wounded and bleeding.

The new boar waddled over to it, licked the wounded boar's blood, and stretched out beside the boar. This was Akta's chance to attack when they were distracted. She swooped in again, startling the boars, who raised onto their haunches and kicked at Akta. She swung around, trying to dig her daggers into the wounded boar's thick hide, but to no use. She had no power in her thrusts, just like Sir Cleybourne had said.

"Get over here!" Akta shouted.

The boars charged together, and Akta swerved for her life. She ended up in front of the cave, where she heard a light, high-pitched honking. She looked inside the cave to see a small boar curled up in a corner.

Akta picked it up as the two adult boars' eyes glowed bright red. This was their child, clearly, and they didn't like strangers playing with it.

"Yeah!" Akta shouted. "You don't like that."

The boars charged, and Akta floated into the air, the tiny pig in her arm, cooing soundly. "Alright. The King wants a boar. I'll give him a boar."

Akta raised her dagger into the air. It shook in her arm. "Just do it already. You're a monster hunter, for Velaska's sake!"

But her arm wouldn't strike. The baby was so cute when it looked up at her with its big saucer eyes. "You're coming with me. Cley will know what to do with you. The crown prince loves suckling pig."

Akta zoomed off, faster than the boars could give chase, with the little pig under her arm for safety. It nuzzled into the crook of her elbow, comfortable as ever.

* * *

It was no time at all before Akta returned to where she'd left Sir Cleybourne. "Cley! Sir Cley!" Akta screamed.

There was no response. Something was wrong. The brush where Sir Cleybourne had stood was trampled, and broken branches lay scattered across the ground. Great three-toed footprints embedded deep in the mud.

Trolls.

Akta saw a glimmer on the ground and walked toward it. Cleybourne's sword was underneath one of the branches. Not far from there, Akta spied a trail of massive footprints leading deeper into the woods. She put Sir Cleybourne's sword in her belt, picked up the little porkling, and followed the tracks. The ooze of the mud on her feet gave her an uncomfortable new sensation.

The tiny pig honked curiously.

"*Shhh…*" Akta whispered to her. "Not another word or I'm cooking you up and making pork belly mutton. That's what I'll call you—Pork Belly."

Akta followed the trail of footprints at a glacial pace. She was used to flying through the air with the greatest of ease. Walking on the ground put a tremendous strain on her joints. She didn't like it.

She fluttered above the ground momentarily to avoid the squishy feeling under her feet, and when she reached a clearing, she rose higher in the air hoping for a glimpse of Cleybourne. Meanwhile, the pig that was once so relaxed in her arms began to squiggle and squirm.

"Stop it, Pork Belly, or I'll drop you."

That didn't do much to allay the pig's nerves, and it scratched its hooves along Akta's breastplate, honking as it scrambled up her body.

"Ow!"

That's when she heard it. The unmistakable sound of Sir Cleybourne's maddening shouts berating the troll. "I don't know what you think you're doing here. Let me go!"

Akta listened for another moment until she tracked Sir Cleybourne's voice back to the source, a craggy rock face deep in the distance. She shot through the sky toward the screams, which grew louder and louder as she closed in.

The pig in her arms squeaked and dug its hooves into her shoulder. "Careful, Pork Belly. Careful."

She'd grown to like the stupid little pig. It would be a shame when Sir Cleybourne forced her to cut its throat, but that was a worry for another time. Right now, Akta focused on the task at hand—saving her mentor before a big, gangly troll ate him.

* * *

Akta landed in the forest near the rock wall where she'd heard Sir Cleybourne. Not far away, in a small clearing, an ugly green troll, with sharp teeth poking out of his underbite jaw, stirred a black cauldron sitting atop a burning fire. Behind him was a great cave, twenty times larger than the one that housed Pork Belly and her parents.

"You don't have to do this, you know," Sir Cleybourne said, tied to a large boulder, not unlike the one he'd asked her to move a few hours before. Akta heard his voice in her head, *"Say you wanted to move that boulder. How would you do it?"* She wondered if he saw the irony. Probably not.

The troll shoved his massive hand into a cloth bag and pulled out two heads of lettuce. He gave them a sniff, shrugged, and tossed them in the cauldron, which already bubbled with carrots and celery and other things.

"Seriously!" Sir Cleybourne shouted. "We can come to some sort of arrangement, I'm certain. I hear there is some lovely boar in this area. I could rustle you up some. I assure you it would taste much better than human, especially an old man like me. I'm quite gamey, you see."

As Akta watched the troll, she realized Pork Belly wasn't wriggling in her arms anymore. She no sooner had that thought than she saw Pork Belly scamper into the open field toward the troll.

"You see!" Sir Cleybourne said, seeing the pig. "Much nicer meat in that pig than in me, don't you know?"

Shut up, you stupid old knight, Akta thought.

The troll rose until he stood twenty feet high and lumbered toward Pork Belly. Now she would have to save both Sir Cleybourne and the pig simultaneously. *Great.*

"Come!" the troll shouted when he saw Pork Belly. The pig turned on her haunches and ran the other way. She was fast, but her stubby little legs couldn't outrun the troll.

Luckily, Akta was faster than both of them. As the troll reached out his claws to grab the pig, she swooped in and snatched Pork Belly away at the last second.

The troll scratched his head for a moment, wondering where his meal had gone. Meanwhile, Akta flew to the top of the cave and placed Pork Belly on a small cliff next to a large boulder. "Stay!"

Sir Cleybourne caught eyes with Akta as she flew down toward him. "What are you doing here?"

"Saving your hide, thank you very much," Akta whispered.

"You aren't ready to take on a mountain troll. I can barely do it."

Akta grabbed the thick rope that bound Sir Cleybourne to the rock, pulled the sword from her belt, and cut ferociously into the twine. "Well, you didn't do it, actually."

Cleybourne watched her working at his bindings and mumbled, "I've lost a step in my old age but were I still in my youth, that troll wouldn't stand a chance."

"Clearly, you're not in your youth anymore, sir."

The troll turned, hearing the commotion, and saw Akta chopping at the rope. "What are you doing?"

Akta dropped the sword and hung in the air, trying to look nonchalant. "Oh, nothing. I'm just trying to see if you tied these ropes tight enough. You know how slippery humans can be."

"Pixie?" The troll cocked his head.

Akta nodded and spoke slowly. "That's right. I'm a pixie."

"Not many left. Only know one other."

"Another? I heard I was the only one. Maybe you can introduce me, and we can have a tea party."

The troll lumbered toward her. "First eat. Then me take you tea party."

Akta hovered between the troll and Sir Cleybourne. "About that. I have an interesting idea. What if you…didn't eat him? How would that be?"

The troll swatted at Akta, who avoided his palms at every turn. "Hungry!"

"I know you are, but look over there. You got a nice stew going. Lettuce. Some carrots. A little celery. That's enough to fill you up."

The troll took another swat. "Need meat!"

Akta dropped to the ground and planted her feet deep into the mud beneath her. "I'm afraid I can't let you do that."

The troll raised his arms in the air and pounded them into the ground where she stood. Akta dodged the attack and pulled out her knives. She flew around the troll and sliced his shin above the ankle.

"OW!" The troll bounced on one foot, holding his injured shin.

Akta whizzed around to where he could see her. "Look, if you just leave him alone, I'll leave you alone."

The troll charged Akta. A troll is a powerful creature but miles slower than a pixie. When she flew into the air to dodge the attack, the troll blundered right into the oak tree behind her. Akta rushed over to Cleybourne and dug her knife into the rope.

The old knight squirmed against the boulder. "Hurry up, would you?"

"I'm trying. These ropes are thick."

The troll rose from the ground and wrapped his arms around the tree, uprooting it and flinging it toward Akta, who covered Sir Cleybourne as the tree crashed in front of them.

"What, you're going to protect me? And what can a pixie do against a tree crushing me, really?" Sir Cleybourne said. "Think with your mind, not with your gut."

Akta grumbled, "This is not the time for lessons!"

"It's the perfect time!"

The troll roared and charged. Akta looked around, searching for a plan to keep the troll away from Cleybourne. Before her, the cauldron steamed and bubbled over. The idea was still forming in her mind as she hurried toward it and kicked the pot with her feet. It burned something fierce, and she let out a pained scream. "Yeargh!" She dug her feet into the cool mud, but it gave no relief.

The boiling water splashed through the air toward the troll, who covered his face in a panic. The scalding water washed over him, but it didn't take him down. Instead, he picked up the tree and swung it violently at Akta. The branches clawed at her as she ducked low to avoid them.

"We can still talk about this!"

"No talk! Eat!"

The troll stormed forward again, and Akta backed closer to the cave. With another swipe, the tree crashed into the cave, dislodging small rocks from above.

Pork Belly squealed piteously, and Akta noticed the boulder next to the little pig giving way a bit. She flew up to the top of the cave, barely avoiding another swing of the mighty oak. Her feet still burned, but she wedged them against the boulder.

Sir Cleybourne was right. There was a reason to have your feet on the ground, if only for moments like this. She pressed with all her might, but the boulder didn't budge. The great troll aimed another blow, and the whole cave shook with the force of impact. The boulder trembled, working its way closer to the edge, even though she did nothing to help it. This gave her an idea.

"Come out!" the troll shouted.

Akta flew over the cave and hovered in front of the boulder. "I'm here. Quit causing such a racket!"

The troll screamed with rage and wound up for another strike at Akta, who deftly moved out of the way. The tree slammed into the cave, dislodging the rock more. Akta hovered carefully, staying close to the boulder but also out of reach. "That's not very strong. You can do better than that, can't you?"

The troll took a step closer, snarling, and swung the tree, again and again, hitting the rock face and the walls of the cave. The boulder was beginning to tilt. Akta zipped around, dodging each blow. One more hit would tip it over the edge.

"You couldn't hit the broad side of a building, could you?" Akta said, laughing.

The troll pulled back with the tree and slammed it full force into the wall right below the boulder. By the time he saw the rock tumbling toward him, it was too late. The boulder flattened him to the ground.

Akta scooped up Pork Belly and flew back to Sir Cleybourne. "See. I told you I could handle it. And look, I have dinner too."

Sir Cleybourne gave her a withering look. "Not much of a dinner."

Akta cut through the thick rope that held Sir Cleybourne. "That's all you have to say to me? I saved your life."

"I had it handled."

The rope frayed. "You were about to be troll food."

The rope broke and freed Sir Cleybourne, who rubbed his wrists gratefully. "Yes, well…it was unorthodox, but you got the job done, didn't you then?"

"And I learned that sometimes boots are important." She lifted her scalded feet for his approval.

"Yes, quite." Sir Cleybourne picked up Pork Belly. "You know, this really isn't much of a meal."

Akta sighed. "I know. And I have to be honest; I don't think I can kill the poor thing."

Sir Cleybourne picked up the sword in his free hand, twirled it in his fingers most expertly, and sheathed it. "Yes, well, I think we can find a place for her in the castle, don't you? After all, she did help slay this beast."

"That would be nice."

From the woods, two wild boars broke through the brush. Sir Cleybourne grinned from ear to ear as he placed Pork Belly down and drew his sword. "Ah, the sweet smell of battle."

Akta kneeled down to the ground and pushed Pork Belly back to her parents. "I myself have had enough fighting for one day. Besides, I don't think I have it in me to make this one an orphan. I know what that's like."

Pork Belly hobbled over to her parents. The boars sniffed their baby, and for a moment, they seemed placated. But then they turned their attention back to Akta and Sir Cleybourne, and their anger returned. The male boar huffed and lowered his head aggressively.

"I think it might be time to vacate the area, then," Sir Cleybourne said slowly, beginning to turn and make a break for it.

Akta scooped up Sir Cleybourne and flew away as the boars charged at full gallop. "On it."

"I don't like to be carried!"

"Yeah? How much do you like being gored by pigs?"

Sir Cleybourne looked down at the charging boars. "I could have easily handled them…in my youth."

"This ain't your youth."

The boars chased after Akta and Sir Cleybourne until they had either tired themselves out or felt satisfied that they'd made their message clear: "And stay out!" They headed back to rejoin their daughter.

Sir Cleybourne let out a sigh. "This is quite embarrassing."

"What? Being carried by your student? Get over it. I'm sure this won't be the last time."

"Possibly," Sir Cleybourne said. "You do know I will have to mark your first mission down as a failure."

Akta looked back at the boars disappearing into the woods, and she smiled at them. "Yeah, well, that's how it goes sometimes."

NOT ANOTHER HAUNTED HOUSE STORY

Originally appeared in "League of Monsters"

HOW DID I *end up with Gillman?* The thought kept going through Henry's brain as they took a skimmer boat across the lake to Highland Island in Northwestern Oregon, just outside Portland.

If it were Ned, who was pretty nice except for the constant shedding and bouts of fleas when he turned into a werewolf, or Moira, who was uptight but could talk about French wine with the best of them, or even Dracula, though his penchant for blood freaked even him out, it would have been fine, but to be stuck with silent the gill creature for two days had been absolutely horrible.

When Doctor Gordon joined them on missions, at least he could have a conversation, but having to communicate through nothing but a series of flash cards that Stephanie gave her test subject made for the absolute dullest stretch of days in recent memory.

Luckily, the island had grown large on the horizon since they left the pier, and they would soon be on dry land.

"How much longer?" Henry shouted toward the captain of the skiff over the sound of the engine.

"Just a few minutes Fra—I mean Henry." She smiled sheepishly at them. "Sorry about that."

"It's okay." It really wasn't, but Henry was used to it. "Just remember, I'm Frankenstein's *monster*, which means I didn't have a name when he made me."

"I know," the captain said. "No matter how many times I see it in the papers, though, I keep just saying Frank. I'm a bad person."

"You're not a bad person." He shook his head. Secretly, though, he kind of thought she was at least a *slightly* bad person. How hard was it to remember a name when the person was standing right in front of you? "Seriously, it's fine. Happens all the time."

That didn't make it any better. He had saved the world countless times over the years, yet he still couldn't shake his origins. Everyone else seemed to get a second chance at life, even murderers, everyone except for him. He was stuck on the day he was born, and there was nothing he could do to change that.

"You're too kind," the captain said. He hadn't bothered to get her name. It might have been rude, but he would never have remembered it, and in a couple of minutes, he would never have to see her again.

Except on the trip back. Maybe he should have gotten her name. *Was it too late?*

It was a pain he would have to deal with later because as he went to get her name, a great quake rocked the boat. Gillman shouted in a high-pitched squeal. He pulled a flashcard out of his pocket in the shape of a lake.

"Hold tight!"

"Yes, we're on the lake, Gill." He felt bad calling him by the name people assumed for him even when he asked for more from people, but he had yet to come up with a name, and Doctor Gordon refused to give one to him, which made things even more awkward.

Gill pointed to the water again, but Henry could do nothing but throw up his hands. "I don't know what you're saying!"

Henry didn't have time to ask any follow-up questions because a second quake of the boat sent him tumbling over the side of the boat into the water. Henry didn't like water. Maybe it was that he couldn't swim or that his corpse-like skin absorbed water after a very short time and made him bloated, but either way, he found himself kicking against the pull of the surf, trying to drag him underwater.

This is a neat way to die, Henry thought. He had saved the world from fifty-foot-tall monsters and unfathomable creatures from the depths of the Earth, yet would be taken down by a ripple on a lake. *Wonderful.*

The water was murky, and the visibility wasn't helped by Henry's arms flailing like crazy or his mouth creating bubbles as it gasped for air, but in the dark water, he swore he saw something in the distance, circling toward the far side of the island. However, before he could get a better look, he felt two claws on his jacket and was yanked out of the water.

He broke the surface of the water and took a deep breath of air. He was drenched in water from head to toe but didn't seem to have taken any into his body, slowing his movements. That was the good in the bad. Henry was trying to look at the bright side of things, but it wasn't easy.

Henry looked up to see Gill staring down at him, nodding in approval. Henry slipped onto a bench and nodded back.

"Thank you."

Gill clapped in front of him and pulled out a card from his pocket that showed two people hugging.

"That one I understand, friend," Henry said. "I appreciate you, even if I do not always show it."

"Are you okay?" the captain asked from the bow of the ship.

"I'm fine." It was then that Henry noticed the ship was filling with water. "It doesn't seem like the ship can stay afloat much longer, though."

"Not at all." She shook her head. "I think I can beach us in shallow water if we don't get any more interruptions. Did you see what hit us? Did I miss a rock or something?"

Henry stood and shook his head. "Nothing so banal as that. I can't be sure, but I swear I saw a creature lurking by the island. However, Gill here saved me before I could get a closer look."

Gill tapped Henry on the shoulder and tapped his own chest. Then, he pointed into the water. It didn't take a genius to understand those gestures. "You want to go in the water. Yes, I think that's a capital idea. If anything comes to attack us, you can bash them on the nose or something of the like."

Gill nodded and then effortlessly dove into the water. Henry waited for the ripples to die down before he turned to the captain. "And how can I help us get to shore?"

The captain dug under the cockpit and pulled out a large, red bucket. "You look strong. Get to bailing."

Henry didn't need to be told twice. He grabbed the pail and started to scoop water out of the schloop furiously. He knew the only thing preventing him from finding a watery grave was the wood between him and the sea, and he worked like that was the case.

His father gave him strength among his many curses, but that was often enough to save his life and those of the people he tried to help. He always wondered why, in a world powered by knowledge, strength was valued above all else, but that he had in spades. He was not as smart as he would like, despite his best efforts, or as charming, but he was strong, for what that was worth.

At this moment, it meant a whole lot. His strength and speed were enough to keep the ship seaworthy until the captain could navigate it to solid land or within enough feet of it that Henry could walk to shore without worrying about being swallowed by the sea.

"Well," the captain said, "I'm definitely billing you for that boat."

"That's fine," I replied. "Dracula will cover it."

She looked over at me. "That's the coolest sentence anyone has ever said."

"For you, maybe." I took a deep sigh. "For me, it's Wednesday."

She turned around to the island. "What are you doing here anyway? Don't get much call for charters since the old Greaves's manor was closed to the public."

Henry growled. "That's exactly why I'm here. Boss thinks there's something hinky going on with this place, and I aim to figure out what it is."

The captain stared out at the ocean and her ruined boat. "You mean besides the giant monster that destroyed my ship."

"We don't know it was a monster." Henry turned back to the water. "Where is Gill anyway?"

"He makes it a habit of rushing off like that?"

Henry shrugged, taking note of a trail that wound up a nearby hill. "I haven't been around him by myself before. Usually, his handler's with me." He pointed to it. "That the road to the mansion?"

"It is. Come on. I'll walk you."

"You don't gotta do that," Henry replied. "I can handle myself."

"It's fine. I used to come up here a lot as a kid. If there's something hinky going on here, maybe I can help you figure it out."

"People who hang around me usually end up dead unless they're monsters. You a monster, captain?"

"Alice," she replied with a smile. Thank the gods Henry didn't have to get it from her now. It was the one good thing that happened today. "And not that I know of. Seems like that's the kind of thing a girl would know."

"You would think," he replied. "But you would be surprised what people don't know about themselves. It's your funeral, though. You want to get yourself killed; it's a free country."

"That's mighty hospitable of you to let me chart my own death." She started toward the path. "Seems like chivalry isn't dead."

"Well, I am technically dead, so there's that."

"You got me there." Alice finally reached the trail and then turned to Henry. "I think I heard about Gillman's doctor. Stephanie Jordan, right?"

"Gordon, not Jordan." She had a habit of mangling the names of Henry's friends and acquaintances. It was beginning to get annoying. "But you have a pretty good memory."

"It's a curse more than anything."

"I understand all about curses," Henry replied. "How do you figure, though?"

She took a deep breath. "Just seems people are happier if they don't remember the past, ya know? I got a lot of things I'd like to forget."

Henry nodded fervently. "Sister, you said a mouthful, but at least we get a nice walk, and that's a good thing, right?"

Henry had over 150 years of regrets, and they weighed on him heavily most times, but when talking with Alice, everything came easily. He barely thought of the hellish circumstances of his birth or the conditions of his enslavement by the mesmerist Prospero at all on their hike up to the manor, which was something of a minor miracle in his eyes as those thoughts nearly always swirled in his mind like the eddies on a mighty river.

"Yes, it is," Alice replied with a flashy smile. Henry didn't know that people had so many teeth or could be so white.

When they finally reached the top of the hill, the manor stood looming over the whole island. Henry could see 360 degrees to every side of the lake, and the first thought through his head was that it would make a perfect vantage point to see anyone coming to attack you. Probably most people didn't think that, though. They were probably just happy to enjoy the nice view.

"The Greaves family a superstitious bunch?" Henry asked as he walked up to the steps.

It would have been a nice home if he had found it fifteen years ago, but now it needed some serious upkeep. The paint was chipped in large patches all around the exterior, revealing the rotten wood underneath a faded yellow veneer, and the stiff wind that blew through the island looked as if it could knock the whole structure over with how much it shook the foundation of the house.

"This place should be condemned," Henry said, trying to decide if his heavy foot would break through the soft wood that made up the porch in front of the house.

"Didn't used to be this way. Five years ago, after the war, Victor disappeared in the night, and it's been abandoned ever since. Before that, it was a nice little house, and they didn't even mind if people came to hear the legend of the house."

"Let me guess," Henry said gruffly. "Another haunted house story?"

"Something like that. Legend goes that Victor's father had a bit of a fascination with the occult, and he built this house at the intersection of two Ley lines that gave him the ability to speak with the dead."

Ley lines. Henry would have thought they were bunk if they weren't part of the reason his father was able to bring him to life. Doctor Frankenstein's castle rested at the intersection of five Ley lines, allowing him to access immense power from beyond the grave. Without them, Henry would never have been born. He wasn't sure that was a good thing, but he was convinced Ley lines existed. He would bet his life on it.

"Of course he did." Henry scratched his head. "I'll bet the old man had a wife he lost too soon."

"A daughter, actually," Alice said. "He devoted all his time to trying to bring her back."

"That's a familiar story. Well, let's get this over with." Alice started to walk forward. "I really can't emphasize enough how much you shouldn't join me."

Her eyes narrowed. "And I can't emphasize enough how much I don't care. I've lived on this lake my whole life and desperately want to see the inside of this house that has dominated local legend."

Henry stepped on the wood and was pleased that his leg didn't fall through it. "Can't blame you there."

Henry walked carefully to the front door. He didn't know why he knocked, but it seemed the polite thing to do. While he did, Alice walked to the window and peeked inside. Even if nobody was home, it still felt rude to peer into the house, as if you were looking under the skirt of an unwilling dame.

"Nobody's in there, and it doesn't look like there's been anyone in the house for a while." She walked to the door and jiggled the handle. "Locked."

"Hrm, maybe we should find another way inside." Henry didn't like to intrude, even though that was part of his job. If there was a ghost living inside, they had every right to privacy, same like him.

He didn't even know why he was here at the end of the day, aside from drawing the short straw back on the ship and then being greeted with the news that Doctor Gordon had been unable to join them due to a bout of food poisoning.

He usually left the investigating to Ned. He was the journalist, after all, while Henry preferred assignments where he got to smash and break things. This didn't seem like that kind of job. If the Eye of Zchash was inside this house, then it was not going to be his brute strength that found it.

This sorcerer crap wasn't for him, either. That was Dracula's bag. Henry liked things he could see and hear. He was a punch first, ask questions later kind of guy, and magic wasn't something you could put your fist through.

He was brought back from his crisis by the smashing of a window and shards of glass falling to the ground. Henry looked over to see Alice sliding inside the broken window. "I found a way in."

"That's very rude," Henry said. "This is private property."

"You tut and tut, feeling superior for following the rules," Alice said, opening the door from the inside. "But I bet you come in now that the door is open."

He smirked. "Of course, I will. After all, it would be rude to ignore an open-door invitation, even if it is from a criminal. I am not, of all things, rude."

"Then please, come in." Henry was having a decent time, despite being in a terrible situation. Mostly he dealt with monsters and burly men who smelt like they hadn't showered in weeks, so bantering with a lovely woman was a welcome relief.

The inside looked as if somebody was ready to move but never did. The couches and tables were covered with blankets, and layers of dust caked on them as if nobody had been there in years. He looked down at the floor, where his feet made soft indentions in the hardwood as if he was walking in snow instead of the mess of a life.

"You said he left suddenly?" Henry asked.

"In the middle of the night, like a vamp—ghost."

"I'm not a vampire, Alice. I don't get offended when you talk about them. I'll bet if there is a ghost here, though, they would be pretty miffed right now."

"I'm scared," she replied sarcastically.

"Hello!" Henry shouted. "We're not here to hurt you. We just need to ask a couple of questions."

"Who are you talking to?" Alice asked.

"Ghosts, of course. If this is built on Ley lines, then it could be a conduit for ghosts, and I would hate for them to think I am some uncivilized brute. I have enough trouble with first impressions as it is."

"I never knew you were so erudite," Alice said.

"That is a very good word," Henry replied. "Well done."

"I went to finishing school back before the war. Got out in June '41, but then—well, you know what happened then."

"Yes, I do. The world went to Hell and derailed everyone's plans. Did you lose somebody special there?"

"Lots of people." Alice looked over at Henry. "But who didn't? Now come on. I want to see what else is in this house."

"You can check this floor, and I will take the upstairs."

Alice nodded and then walked off while Henry took to the stairs. They creaked like an unhappy duck as he took them, one at a time and yet sometimes in a chorus as well. They were sturdier than the water-logged ones outside, but only just. They were in desperate need of some attention from a handyman, but they would not get any from Henry. He had a job to do.

On the second floor of the house, there were four doors, and Henry decided to take them in turn, from left to right. The first door seemed to be a child's room, with a small bed and dresser and a ceiling painted with stars and planets. If the child was to be an astronomer, then it was a long time ago, as the telescope out the window had gathered dust just like the rest of it.

After cleaning it thoroughly with his shirt, Henry placed his eye in the eyepiece of the telescope but was disappointed to see that it looked out into the lake and not up to the heavens. After having his fill of the room, he went back into the hallway. The next door was a bathroom, and the one after was a sewing room, complete with several unfinished pieces.

Henry wondered what happened to the family that lived there, as most people do not leave their homes in such a lived-in state. Though the child's room was neat, there was a bedspread still on the bed, and this room had clothes still in the process of being mended.

It was all odd, but he saw nothing to indicate that ghosts still took up residence in the house. There were no pockets of cold or shivers that came from nowhere to indicate a spirit trying to communicate with him.

Another strange thing as ghosts would have loved this little house. It was so quaint and secluded from humanity, which was everything a ghost wanted in a home.

Henry walked out of the room and pushed open the last door. This looked to be the bedroom of the child's parents, with a larger, four-poster bed and several dressers. Henry walked over and opened one. Not surprisingly, they were filled with clothes, as if the owner of the house left in the dead of night, never to look back.

"Did you find anything?" Alice shouted from downstairs.

"Not yet," Henry said, noticing a door on the leftmost wall of the room. When he opened it, expecting a closet, he found a stairwell into what must have been an attic. "This is interesting, though."

"Should I come up?"

"Not yet. Keep scouring."

Henry squeezed himself through the door and shuffled up the stairs to the attic. If the dust downstairs had a mother, it would have come from the attic. The dust balls in the attic were not small things but seemed large as tumbleweeds, and with the draftiness of the floor, they swayed across the room with the movement of the gusts.

The attic was small and cramped, but Henry immediately saw something that caught his attention— aside from the massive dust balls, that is. In the center of the room was a long metal rod stuck from the ceiling to the floor, wrapped with several different colors of cables and fastened with duct tape around the base.

"Alice!" he shouted but got no response. As he breathed in to try to speak again, the dust balls attacked his lungs and made him cough. He heard the floor creak underneath him as he tried to stop the violent outburst, but he could not abate them. He tried and tried but just kept hacking violently, and before he could correct his disposition, the floor creaked again, and this time Henry fell through it.

He crashed into the floor underneath him, covered with the trappings of mold and dust and other debris that came with a dilapidated house. It did not hurt, as it was hard to make anything that would hurt him, but he was quite embarrassed.

It did not help his shame that the force of his fall made the floor around him crack, and again he fell, this time to the main floor. He saw Alice rush to him, but he was not done falling as the ground cracked again, and he fell onto a rocky surface that finally made him groan in pain.

"Are you okay?" Alice asked.

"I'm fine." Henry sat and brushed himself off. "I seem to have fallen into some type of basement." He looked around and saw that it was more a cave than anything. "Or maybe a cave. That is weird. Why would a cave be—I don't like this."

"Well, I was just about to tell you that I found a way down there," Alice said. "Should I join you?"

"As I said before," Henry said, grunting to stand, "I think you should leave this place and never come back, but as you have made clear that is impossible, I think you should do whatever you want."

"Then, I'm coming. Wait for me."

Henry cracked his back after he stood upright and let out a contented moan. In turning around to find the stairs that Alice might come down, he found instead the bottom of the pole he caught wind of in the attic. It still had several cords and cables stuck to it, but from the bottom, a collection of them bound together and lined the cavern floor.

"What is that thing?" Alice said, walking toward him, having found her way down the stairs with much less flair and pain than Henry had managed.

"I have no idea, my dear, but I aim to find out."

Henry followed the strands of wires through the cave until he started to hear the lapping of water in the distance. He had hope in his heart that he would see Gill again but also feared his possible encounter with whatever monster lurked in the deep.

"Stay back," Henry grumbled as he walked forward slowly toward the edge of the water. He followed the cables down toward the shore. The ground was filled with loose rocks that made the terrain tough, but he kept his balance about him.

There was an acrid smell to the air that Henry knew to be blood. He would recognize it anywhere, especially since meeting Dracula. While the old vampire pretended to be civilized, in the presence of blood, he could become quite feral and forget himself. Henry had taken to washing himself twice after any mission just in case he carried any back with him and not interacting with the fellow unless he was free of cuts.

"Listen here, fish," Henry growled. "Or whatever you are. I don't want to hurt you, but if you've hurt Gill—"

Henry came around the corner of the cave and saw a great beast let out a guttural scream at the sight of him. The monster stretched out its long neck toward him and screamed again, pounding its four flippers against the water to cause a great echo in the chasm.

It was as tall as a house and just as wide. Henry had seen worse in his day, but this was one of the most gigantic creatures he had ever encountered. Against the horror of the monster, no sight brought a smile to his face as much as the gash he saw in the monster's hide. The blood did not come from Gill but the beast that tried to attack him.

"What did you do to my friend?" Henry growled, stomping up to it into the water.

That was a mistake, as the monster was quicker than it seemed and snatched Henry with one of its flippers and tossed him toward the sea monster's chomping mouth. Henry righted himself just as its jaws bit down against him and could sock it across the face until it reeled in pain.

Henry fell to the ground and was swept off his feet with the force of the monster's tail. It fell on Henry with its flippers, sinking him under the water. Henry tried to pull the flippers away as he wriggled in pain, but it was no use. The monster was larger than he could move by himself, so all he could do was thrash as the air left his lungs to be replaced by the briny water of the deep.

He started to welcome death when he saw a flash of shadow, and in another second, the monster's head fell from its body. Blood splattered on the water as Gill dove into the water and pulled him from under the monster's weight.

Henry bobbed to the surface and took a wonderful gasp of air. "Thank you, friend."

Gill helped him to the shore, and when he used his hands again, he pulled a flashcard out of his pocket. Henry didn't want to humor him, but Gill just saved Henry's life, so he looked at the picture of water. Then, Gill tapped his eye and pointed to the edge of the cave.

It took him a minute, but then Henry nodded. "You were waiting by the edge of the water for a chance to attack in secret. Very smart old chap. Very smart indeed."

"Yes," Alice said, walking out from the edge. "Very clever indeed. I've been waiting for somebody to kill that monster for as long as I relieved that doddering old fool from his mortal coil."

"What are you talking about?" Henry asked, turning to her as she pulled out a wand from under her coat. As she removed it from her coat, it expanded into a billowing black cloak with a swastika emblazoned in red on it. "Ah, I see. You work for the Final Reich then, I see."

"Oh, very good, Henry." She smirked. "If only you had figured that out long enough ago to make a difference."

Henry looked over at Gill, who tapped the water. Henry nodded and grabbed several loose rocks scattered around the shore, throwing them at the sorceress as a distraction as Gill jumped into the water.

"That simply won't do." The sorceress twisted her wand, and Henry screamed out in pain as his arms were bound tightly together like he was being squeezed by an invisible hand ten times his size. "Call your friend back here."

"Friend?" Henry chuckled. "We barely know each other. If you think I can understand half of what he says, then—"

"Enough!" the sorceress shouted.

"Tell me something. Is your name even Alice?"

She scoffed. "Of course not. Even if it were, I would have cast it off long ago when I came into my power."

"Wow," Henry said, shaking his head. "So, you really were an Alice, huh? And what is your name now? Ventriza or Falbina? You witches all have really stupid names if you ask me."

"I am eternal as the sun!" she screamed, twisting her wand and Henry tighter. "You will not speak to me that way."

"Well, I won't, but he might. If he could talk, that is."

Henry pointed to the water just as Gill leaped from it in a blur. He unleashed his claws, but the sorceress barely batted an eye. She simply waved her wand, and Gill rose high in the air.

"That's better. Now, let's go." The sorceress forced Henry to his feet and held Gill in a trance behind him."

"Where are we going?" Henry asked.

"To the end of these cables. That monster was brought here to protect whatever secrets Victor was building in these caves."

"Then why wasn't it terrorizing people all this time?"

"Because I let it out, okay?" she said with spite in her mouth. "I was not ready for that beast's magical immunity, and in the ensuing fight, I blasted a hole from which it could leave this cave. It was unintentional and unavoidable."

"Excuse me for saying so," Henry got to the other side of the monster and saw the cables continue through a small crack in the wall, "but it seems entirely avoidable. All you would have to do is not work for monsters."

"You are one to talk. You are and work for monsters."

"No, sis," Henry said, ducking into the crevice. "We only look like monsters. You are the ones who act like it. Tell me this, then. All that bull about you losing people in the war. Was that true or just a ruse?"

She cleared her throat as if she didn't expect the question. "We all lost people. I happened to lose them in Germany when the Russians broke through the German line and took no prisoners."

As she spoke, her German accent came through clearer. Henry took note of it before he responded. "And so that is why you work with The Final Reich? For revenge?"

She scoffed. "Nothing so petty as that. I have lived long and lost many. I work with them for the promise of eternal youth. Revenge against my enemies is just a bonus."

"Of course. Too much to ask you to have the courage of your convictions."

Henry needed a plan, but he was nearly useless against magic. That was Dracula's thing. He was the one that saved him from Prospero after all, and if he were here, this wouldn't even be a challenge. Oh, if only one of the bats that lined the cave were him.

If the sorceress wanted a fistfight, then he would have clobbered her, but in a battle of wits, he was at a supreme disadvantage. All he knew was the more time he bought, the most likely he was to find an opening to do something; anything.

The crevice widened and then broke open into a large cavern. The cables continued into the center of the room, which attached to a cylinder that glowed orange with an orb at the top. Henry wasn't a genius, but he knew enough to know that it sure looked like a magical object.

"The Eye of Zchash!" the sorceress screamed. "Do you know what we could do with Victor's knowledge of the Ley lines and a way to focus it?"

"I don't, but I know two things. It can't be good, and it will surely be evil."

"You are so small-minded, Henry. I should talk to your creator about that. Now, go fetch me that orb and take care of any nastiness you might run into along the way."

"Don't want to get your pretty cloak all soiled?" Henry asked, knowing the answer.

"Why, when I have a big lug like you to do it for me?"

Henry growled as he stomped across the room toward the Eye of Zchash. It pulsated an energy that even a non-magical person like him could feel from a dozen feet away. By the time he was on top of it, it singed his arms until he could smell the burning of his undead flesh.

He looked back at the sorceress and found an idea tucked away in his brain. Back in the circus, he was pretty good at the dunk tank and could break the jug on even Horace's rigged game to win a stuffed animal for whatever girl he was trying to impress that night.

It was the same game he just ran, but he wasn't much more than a one-trick pony, even after all these years.

A charge of pure energy went through his body as he grabbed the orb with one hand. He felt the power of it flicker through him as he pulled the orb off the stand. It would have killed a lesser man or a more alive one, but Henry was able to wind up for the throw. Before he did, a beautiful woman made of the pure energy of the orb took shape. He had seen a picture of her on one of the walls, but she was much more beautiful in person.

"She killed my Victor?" the woman said, and Henry nodded, only partially understanding what was happening. This was sorcerer crap, after all. "I have waited every day for him to return to me since I found this place."

"I'm sorry for your loss, but I'm in the middle of a battle."

"Throw the Eye. I will do what I can."

As if time started again, everything sped up to triple speed as he chucked the orb at the sorceress. She was well composed but watching something that powerful rush toward you would break anyone's concentration. As the orb shot forward, the woman did as well, crossing the path toward the sorceress and slamming against her chest before she could react.

In the confusion, she dropped Gill, just for a split second, but it was enough for him to dig his claws into the sorceress's back and send her reeling to the ground. The orb shot past her and crashed into the wall of the cave, shattering it into a million pieces.

"You fool," she choked, blood streaming down her body as she struggled for her wand. "Do you know what you have done?"

I picked up the wand. "Yeah, we saved the world and destroyed a really powerful object that shouldn't fall into the wrong hands."

"You fool," she choked. "Now you can't use it, either."

"That's probably for the best. I saw what the good guys did with ultimate power before, and I'm not sure we should have it either."

Henry snapped the wand in half, and in doing so, a jolt of power crashed through the sorceress. A white light shot through the room, and in her screams of agony, she aged a hundred years in a matter of seconds.

She was as old as Henry, maybe older, but this time she was done. It took all kinds in The Final Reich. It wasn't just monsters looking to enslave the world. Some people just wanted youth, no matter the cost.

"Come on, Gill. I'll buy you a sausage." Henry looked over at Gill. "You feel like a sausage?" Gill nodded, and Henry chuckled. "I understand that as good as anyone."

There were bumps along the way, but in the end, Henry thought it was a very good day, and he would even get a sausage out of it. What more could he want out of life?

HOMECOMING

"WHAT ARE YOU going to do now, Jess?" Tommy asked as he pulled up in front of my house. It wasn't much, but I liked it enough…and it was quiet. People minded their own business, which I appreciated, given that I didn't like thinking about my business when I was off the road.

"I'm gonna sit in front of a TV and watch dumb movies for the next week 'til we get a call again."

Tommy blew out a big breath. It was the type of sigh you only knew if you were a hunter and you had seen one, or a hundred, too many battles in your day. I knew it well.

"That sounds pretty nice."

"How about you?" I asked, opening the door.

He pointed to the back of the truck, where a two-ton horror lay dead, wrapped in a burlap sack. "Gotta deliver proof of death. Then, I don't know. Maybe I'll do some painting."

I chuckled. "You been talking about taking up painting since five years on, and I ain't never seen you paint anything more than the side of a barn."

"There's a first time for everything, Jess." He shook his head. "Just cuz some of us wanna better ourselves, ain't no reason to get all upset about it."

"I'm not upset about it, bud." I stepped out of the car. "In fact, you paint something, and I'll hang it right over my mantle. That's a promise."

"What if it's ugly?"

"Hell, even better!" I said. "Why do I need anything fancy lookin' for? Just don't paint any monsters but like a flower or a real pretty sunset. Yeah, I think I'd like that."

He nodded. "Alright then, well quit yakkin' so I can get back home then."

I slammed the door and waved as he peeled off the gravel road. I turned to my house when the light fell into the distance. The grass was mostly brown and patchy as I walked to the door, and the walkway was cracked from when I laid the foundation wrong, but it was mine, and nobody could take that away from me.

Not without a firefight, anyway.

The doorknob was loose when I turned it open, but it did the job. If somebody wanted to steal anything from my house, they could have at it. I spent most of my life on the road. This was just a place to hang my hat.

Of course, that didn't mean I wanted nobody squatting in my house, either, which was why when I heard the light breath of a child coming from my kitchen, I pulled my six-shooter.

"Come out now," I said, cocking the trigger. "I know you don't mean nothing, but you picked the wrong house—" a small girl with ratty pigtails rose from the edge of the counter and stared at me with big, green eyes "—Rosaline! What the hell are you doing here? Don't you know I coulda shot you and been well within my rights?"

Rosaline was the daughter of my closest neighbor, by proximity, of course, since I didn't make it a habit to learn too much about the people I lived near if I could help it. Still, sometimes her momma would make too much casserole and leave me some. They took pity on me, seeing I lived alone and didn't have many friends coming and going.

"I—I—it got Papa!" she screamed, rushing forward toward me. She didn't get halfway across the room before I saw her white dress had been stained red with blood. She wrapped her arms around me, and her hands were sticky with blood, too.

"What are you talking about?" I said. "Who got your papa?"

She shook her head. "They couldn't see it. I tried to tell them, but they said I was going crazy and everything was safe. Then…then it attacked and…it took Papa!!!"

She started to cry, and I pulled her to me until she was done. It wasn't no use telling somebody not to be sad when they were crying, especially a child, so I gave her a minute to cry herself out and calm down.

When she was done, she wiped her snot on my leg and looked up at me. Her eyes were bloodshot, and her cheeks flushed. I walked over and got her a tissue to wipe the rest of the snot from her nose, and when I was on her level, I smiled at her as big as I could, and then talked as sweet as possible.

"Listen here, little girl. It's going to be okay." I didn't believe that, but you didn't have to believe something to say it. "Now, is it still at your house?"

She nodded. "I think so. I heard Mama scream right before you pulled up. I went to help her, but she told me to run. She made me promise, Jess. She made me—"

"It's okay, little girl. You did the right thing." I stood up and pulled my gun from my hip. "Don't you move. No matter what you do, stay quiet. Even if I scream, okay?"

She nodded and rushed back into the kitchen, where she dropped into the shadows. I went out the front door and locked it tight behind me. This was nothing if a horror wanted to break through, but they didn't usually feed randomly. Once it was satisfied, it would move on, but I couldn't wait that long. Not if Rosaline's mother was alive. She made the best casserole.

I heard the sound of chomping as I moved closer to the house. I moved slowly across the verve, trying to avoid any rocks or pebbles that could give my position away. I was the closer of our team, so I was used to delivering the kill shot to the monsters we hunted. Tommy was the distraction, and then we had Ginger for long-distance kills.

My .50 caliber was enough to put down all but the biggest monsters with one shot. I just hoped this wasn't something I couldn't handle solo. I hadn't done a solo mission in a long time, and more people got killed on them than any other in the Shaman States. That's why we had teams of three, for safety.

But then, even the best-laid plans blew up on the battlefield.

By the time I got to the front door and saw it had been snapped in half, the sounds of eating were loud enough to turn my stomach. Not every horror ate human flesh, but those that did were the most vicious.

The horror didn't move when I stepped through the door. It was busy looking at its kill. It ripped another piece of flesh off the lifeless, mangled corpse of Rosaline's father. At least, I hoped it was only her father.

The monster was small enough that I could kill it with one shot, barely full-grown, and yet still a killer.

I raised my gun and took one more step to steady myself; one step too many, as when I came down, I must have caught something, and a snapping sound filled the room. It wasn't loud, but it was big enough to grab the monster's attention.

It whipped toward me as I fired and lunged at me. The bullet went through the wall as it barreled me through the door and into the front yard. I kicked it off me as it swiped with serrated claws.

I fired two more shots, but it was too fast for me to get a clear shot at its head. One bullet went through its shoulder and another into its ribs, but the horror kept charging. I swung around and roundhouse kicked the monster into a tree, but the weight of it was enough to strain my groin.

I reloaded my gun and fired again at the monster but once again missed my target. The horror looked at me with malice. I had seen that look before enough times but always had backup. Now, I was alone, and I feared I would lose. That's what I get for being a hero.

The adrenaline was something they trained you to mitigate, but no matter what I did, my hand still shook violently as I leveled my gun at the horror in front of me. It narrowed its eyes as I aimed my gun, then it lunged forward.

I fired, and fired, and fired again, but the horror kept coming. It kept rushing until—

A shotgun fired out and sent the horror skidding across the lawn. I looked over to see Cindy, Rosaline's mother, at the front of the house.

"Sorry about that," she said. "I can't see these damn things, but I saw where you were aiming and took a shot."

"Thank you," I replied with a nod. "Kindly obliged."

The horror was on the ground, gasping for air and bleeding its noxious blood over the ground. With a dozen bullets inside of it, and the buckshot Rosaline's father used to hunt deer tearing away at its flesh, the horror was a piteous thing.

Still, I did not pity it, but I did take pity on it, lined up my gun, and fired two bullets directly into its temple. The thing didn't even let out a final moan. It simply fell back onto the ground, lifeless.

"Are you alright, ma'am?" I asked as I hobbled over to the woman.

She nodded. "Some scrapes and bruises, but I was able to get into the crawl space before it could get me. Rosaline—I sent her to you. Does that mean—?"

It was my turn to nod. "She's alright, ma'am. Probably a little worse for wear, but I have to ask. Do you know she can see monsters?"

"I knew she was different, but I never wanted to believe it."

"You know what that means?"

"She'll have to become a hunter."

I nodded. "If anyone finds out."

I waited to see if she caught my drift, and finally, after a while, she nodded. "I don't see why anyone would have to know."

"Me either." I looked back at the horror. "I'm gonna call my men to clean this up. I think you should stay at my house tonight."

"I don't think I can ever stay here again."

"Well, we'll take that as it comes." I turned to my house. "This is gonna sound indelicate, but you don't happen to have any of that casserole left, do you? Hunting fills me with a mighty hunger."

"I am not going back into that house, except maybe to burn it," she replied. "But I can order you a pizza."

"Well, that would be mighty fine."

CLOMBARGE

Originally appeared in "Tavern of Dreams"

IT WAS THE dark of night on the coldest eve of the year when the door to the tavern swung open with a great crack. A ghastly cold shot through the room, snapping every neck toward the door in a single movement. Customers entering the inn after dark had a habit of causing trouble, and the rankles on the bartender's neck stood on end as the dark shadow hobbled into the room.

Tonight would be no exception.

Gurlich had never seen a clombarge before, though she had heard tales of it from the occasional lucky traveler who survived an encounter with it. They lived on the edges of the forest, where dreams went to die, and one look at the odd creature told her that it did more than survive in the darkness. It thrived there.

Nobody had ever seen the true visage of a clombarge. None she knew at least, and all tales of travelers who tried to sneak a look under the loose skin that it wore like a union suit met with a horrible end.

This night, the clombarge wore the fur of a mountain lion but wore it strangely. The glassy eyes of the cougar, roaring a final scream of distress, hung limp at the top of the clombarge's body while the rest of the cadaver stretched around like a sheet tied tightly around a bed.

If it tried to impersonate a puma, it was doing a poor job of it, but she knew better than to laugh at the weirdly shaped beast. That was certain death. The only travelers who survived a visit from the nightmare creature were polite and pleasant to it, treating it like a cherished friend.

So, against her every instinct to retch at the foul beast, she smiled at the clombarge when it rolled up to the bar. It did not speak, but deep in her brain, she knew that the creature desired a glass of mead and a bowl of the everything-stew that she had bubbling from a cauldron over the fire. It had been brewing as far back as memory served, and every morning she picked up more ingredients from the market and threw them into the stew.

She had long since lost track of the ingredients.

The clombarge nudged a seat from one of the tables and plopped in front of it. Gurlich had no idea how the being would eat or drink, as it didn't seem to have a mouth, save for the expressionless one that hung at the nape of its body.

However, she knew better than to ask questions from any of her customers.

She poured the stew, sat it down in front of the creature, next to the flagon of mead, and went back to tending the bar. From the back of the room, she heard the chuckle of a drunken man, and the bar turned to it for a moment to get a final look at the poor fool who insulted their odd guest.

The next morning, the man was gone, as was the clombarge, having left the soup cooling on the table. It had found a tastier meal in the insolent drunk, and who was she to blame? She also detested an impolite cur.

THE CASE OF FLOSSIE AND JAMES

Originally a Kickstarter backer reward for my father, RIP

STUART GREENBAUM HATED the dentist. I mean, who liked the dentist, right? They always talked to you in that condescending tone about flossing more and brushing better, as if anybody had the time for that.

"This is highly illogical, Stuart," Timothy said, looking up from his *Highlights* magazine. "I don't see why I had to come with you."

"You had to come because you're my friend and I don't like my doctor, okay?"

"Why don't you find somebody you do like?"

Stuart glared at him. "You really overestimate how much pull I have with my mom, don't you?"

"All I'm hypothesizing is that if you simply told your mother about this, she might let you find another dentist, which would be agreeable to all parties involved, right?"

"Stuart Greenbaum," the receptionist said. We all called her Flossie because she was always flossing. Every time I saw her, she was flossing.

Stuart stood. "I already did. Just wait here." Stuart walked up to the counter. "Yes, Flossie? It is time?"

She shook her head. "It's not about that. It's personal. You guys have a detective agency, right?"

"Yeah. The Gumshoes Detective Agency." Stuart pointed to Timothy. "Me and Timothy run it together."

"Perfect. And you found that Madison girl's father a couple of months ago?"

Stuart beamed. This wasn't the first person to show an interest in his detective work since they found

Madison's father, but it never got old. "We sure did. Cops couldn't have done it without us."

Flossie leaned forward. "I have a case for you. I need you to find my dear, sweet Jim. He's on the lam."

Stuart looked back at Timothy, who was deep into another Highlights. He would want to be consulted because they took on a case. He would be so mad if Stuart just agreed. "We'll take the case!"

*

"You can't just accept cases without telling me!" Timothy whined on the way home. "We are partners. Equal partners."

"I know, Tim," Stuart responded. "But she needs our help!"

"You didn't even get the details of the case before you said yes!"

"No, but we know them now."

The details of the case were these: Flossie's dear sweet boyfriend James Nohelty was arrested for ten counts of contempt of court during a deposition about Donald Trump's violation of campaign finance laws in East Willow.

James, or Jimmy as Flossie called him, racked up ten contempt of court charges in four days because every time they brought him back to apologize, he just screamed more obscenities about how Trump was a "lying, know-nothing, jerk who should be run out of the country on a pike." All he had to do was apologize, but Jimmy wasn't known for keeping a cool head when it came to politics.

"I can't believe they would release him from prison without paying his fines," Timothy said.

"Really? Do you see the ship my dad is running down there?"

Due to a filing error, they let Jimmy out of the slammer. By the time they figured out their mistake, Jimmy was on the lam.

"You have to find my sweet Jimmy," Flossie told Stuart. "Before goons get to him first."

"Do you really want to leave this to the police, Tim?" Stuart asked. "After they bungled up and let him out of prison in the first place?"

"You make a valid point, Stuart. I would not be able to trust the police after such a mistake."

"And that means?"

"It means we have to take the case, I suppose."

"See, I knew you would come around. I just saved you the trouble of hemming and hawing about it. Let's tell Madison!"

*

The Gumshoes Detective Agency had never run smoother since they brought on Madison to help with the planning. Madison was a whiz at making sure everything was perfect. She was about to triple the workload the Gumshoes took on and even get them paid real money. Stuart and Timothy were the brawn and brains of the operation, respectively, but Madison was the heart. She kept everything flowing on time and on budget.

Stuart and Timothy walked into the newly remodeled agency, complete with painted walls and wall-to-wall carpet. Timothy fought against the carpet at first, but even he had to admit it felt wonderful, much better than the splintered wood they had been used to for years.

"We got a new case, Madison!" Stuart shouted when they walked inside.

Madison was on the couch, pounding on her laptop. "Put it in the scheduler."

"But…aren't you supposed to do that?"

Madison glared up at him. "Do you want me to punch you?"

Stuart thought for a moment. He didn't like being touched, but he still had a crush on Madison. A big one. So being touched by her did have some appeal. "I suppose not."

"What is this case, anyway?" she said. "You know we have 23 open cases already."

Timothy sighed. "That is all Stuart. He can't turn a case down."

Stuart threw his hands in the air. "Really? I mean really? For years we couldn't get one case. Now we have 24, and you are complaining? Sorry for being excited that people want to work with us."

"Boys!" Madison shouted. "Is this the time or the place? Really?"

"Well, technically, yes, Madison. I mean, this is what we do here, lest you forget."

Madison shot a look at Timothy. "Fine. But can we get on with it? I just want to get one of these cases crossed off today."

Stuart smiled. "Well, then you're in luck because this is an easy one. This guy Jimmy is on the lam. His girlfriend Flossie wants us to find him. Easy peasy."

"And what makes you think this is easy?"

"He's a paper pusher on the run from a maniacal billionaire. Do you really think he's going to be that hard to find? This isn't James Bond here."

Madison walked over to Timothy's computer. "What do you think, Tim? Can you find him?"

Timothy stared at the cavalcade of monitors in front of him. His fingers glided across the keyboard in front of him. "Well, of course, I can find him. That's not the issue. The issue is convincing him to come back."

"We aren't being paid to bring him in, Tim," Stuart said. "Just find him and bring them together."

Timothy typed furiously at his keyboard. "Well, he's using an Apple iPhone, which means he thinks it's encrypted. However, little does he know there's a developer back door the government forced Apple to include in their new update. If you know the encryption algorithm, which I do, you can quickly hack their back door and…boom. He's at the Little Gravy Goat Lodge."

*

Stuart and Madison sat in front of the Little Gravy Goat Lodge. They had watched the customers walk in and out for over an hour. "This is ridiculous. Why don't we just go inside?"

"Are you kidding?" Madison said. "Trump's goons are looking for him too. I don't want to get shot."

Stuart smiled. "Please, Trump is all bluster. Maybe his goons would threaten, but there's nothing behind his words. He's a big pansy."

"I would rather not find out, alright?"

A tall, bearded man with glasses walked out of the lodge. He was wearing very short running shorts and a vest with about a million pockets. Stuart looked down at a picture Flossie gave him. "That's our guy. Let's go."

*

Timothy sat at his computer, monitoring Jimmy as he walked from the restaurant. Jimmy's phone rang. "He's making a call. I'll patch you through."

"Copy that," Stuart said.

The computer rang and rang until a woman's voice picked up. "Oh, Jimmy. What are you doing, huh? Just come in and apologize. We can be together again."

"I can't do that, Flossie. He's just such a lying jerk. If I get back on that stand, it's just gonna be more of the same. This is the only way, baby. Goodbye."

"Just tell me where you are. We can go together."

"I won't put you through that. Keep flossin', Flossie. I love ya, baby."

The phone cut out, and the blip on the screen turned left and disappeared. "He's headed inside a building. I can't follow him anymore. You're on your own."

*

Stuart and Madison followed Jimmy up three flights of stairs and watched him disappear into room 307. "This is it," Stuart said. "It's time to call up Flossie."

"Wait. We can't do that. You heard what he said. He doesn't want a life on the run with her. He's willing to give up everything to keep her safe. It's sweet."

"That's not the job, Madison. The job is to get them together. That's why they pay us. Not to wrap it all up in a nice neat bow."

"Then that's not right. We can do better."

"How?"

"I have an idea."

Madison knocked on Jimmy's door. "Go away!" she heard from behind it.

"I'm not here to hurt you. I think I have a plan to make this all go away."

Feet stomped on the door. A massive figure towered over Madison when the door opened. "This better be good."

*

Madison walked through the courthouse, past bustling lawyers and clerks. Defendants sat on benches, heads hung low, waiting for their trial. Madison knocked on the chamber door of Judge Edwards.

"Come in."

Madison pushed the door open. In her hand was a file folder stuffed to the brim. "Mr. Edwards, sir?"

"That's Judge Edwards."

"You are the judge on the Trump case, correct?"

"That's right."

"I have something you need to see. It's about James Nohelty."

"If you have something about the case, send it to the lawyers."

"Oh, this isn't about the case. It's about James Nohelty. You see, sir, he really believes Trump is a liar. He can't return to this trial because if he does, he'll make an outburst again."

The judge stood. "If you know where Mister Nohelty is, you are bound by law to tell me."

Madison nodded. "I know, and I will. But first, I brought this to you." She laid down the folder on his desk. "It's a thousand pages of files which show Trump flip-flopping on positions, articles of him admitting to lying, and generally being a bad person. Just look at it. Inside the file folder is Jimmy's address. He'll await your punishment, but he's just telling the truth. Trump is the worst."

*

They arrested Jimmy again. He spent the next day in prison until his trial. They brought him back to the stand. Judge Edwards looked at him. "You realize you are still under oath, right?"

"Yes, Judge."

"Now, before we get to the matter at hand, I would like to say that I looked through several hundred pages of documents related to Mister Trump, and I can't say you are incorrect about him being a liar. There are hundreds of documents showing that he lied and plenty of others where he admitted lying for what seemed like his own amusement. I mean, who would lie about hiring a PR person and pretending to be him? That's certifiable.

"Now, that does not condone the contempt of court charges leveled against you, but I will suspend any penalties as long as you promise never to step foot in my courtroom again. Agreed?"

Jimmy smiled. "Yes, Judge. Thank you, Judge."

"In this matter, James Nohelty's testimony is stricken from the record. Any charges leveled against him are dismissed."

Judge Edwards banged his gavel. James ran through the courtroom and up to Flossie. He went to kiss her. "Wait," she said. She pulled out floss from her purse. "I have something in my teeth."

"Every time, woman. I don't care." He grabbed her arms and pulled her close. They kissed as the floss fell to the floor.

"Ooooh, James."

*

The Gumshoes walked out of the courtroom, a smile plastered on all their faces. "We did good today, huh?" Madison asked.

"You did good," Stuart responded.

"Hey, where do you think all that research came from?" Timothy replied. "I did good too. I suppose you did alright too, Stuart."

"Thanks."

There was rustling in the bushes. "Hey, kids."

They turned around, and an orange-faced, puckered man with a bad toupee jumped out of the bushes. He wore a Trump 2016 pin. It was, in fact, Donald Trump.

"I hear some people have been talking trash about me," The Donald said. "I don't like when people talk trash about me. I use the best words. Other people use worse words. If they use worse words about me, those words aren't good. I don't like those words."

"Mr. Trump," Timothy said. "Is there a reason you are so terrible?"

"I'm not terrible," Trump said. "I'm the best. I'm the best of all the things."

Madison shook her head. "That's impossible. That's why there are three of us. Because none of us is the best at all the things. Are you the best speller? The best speaker? The best landscaper?"

"I can landscape with the best of them. I love Mexicans, and Mexicans love me."

Stuart sighed. "That means nothing. You mean nothing. All your statements are just jumbles of words. You don't make any sense. I think you need to think about your life."

"I'm the best at thinking. I can outthink you. I can outthink anybody."

The Gumshoes looked at each other. It was useless to argue with him. He was the epitome of everything America had become; everything it had become for the worse.

"Can you promise me," Timothy said, "that you won't hurt James or Flossie?"

"They don't have any more words against me, and I have no more words against them."

"So they are safe. Just simply answer me yes or no. Are they safe?"

The Donald nodded. "Yes. They are safe."

The Gumshoes sighed. Their job was done. If they never saw the Donald again, it would be too soon.

THE LAST DEATH OF OSCAR HERNANDEZ

Originally appeared in "Parallel Worlds"

THE LAST TIME I died wasn't much different than the first time, the twelfth time, the thousandth time, or…

…well, you get the picture. I've died quite a few times before, and every single one of them sucked equally.

There was immense, searing pain, followed by a loud snap as my soul disconnected from my body. After that, I floated in the cold, dark, nothingness of space until my soul was yanked into another body. Sometimes, it was a baby. Sometimes, it was a dying adult. Sometimes I was on another planet, acting like I understood R'lyehian or why aliens had three heads.

Those times were few and far between. Most of the time, it snapped into a middle-aged man on Earth, who lost their will to live, and I took over after their soul faded from their body.

I was an anomaly when it came to death, but not in a good way.

For most people, their past lives were wiped from their minds at the moment of death, before they dealt with the void or the agony of rebirth, but lucky me, I got to experience it all, every single time, as if it were my own personal Hell.

I suppose it's possible this was my Hell, and I was condemned to cycle through it until I learned some sort of cosmic lesson.

But the joke's on whoever created this screwed-up universe because I'm a horrible student. I haven't done one worthwhile thing in 3251ish chances at life—I may have missed a couple here or there, and I'm awful at math.

3251 chances at life, and I'm pretty sure I'm not going to get many more chances. Or at least that's what I've been told.

Or, more accurately, that's what I learned through my travels. In my many lifetimes, I've traveled to the tops of the Himalayas and explored the bottom of the Marianas Trench, trying to find answers and unlock the secrets to my plight. Why every time I come back, I feel less tethered to my body.

All I've been able to figure out is that the human soul has a shelf life, like cheese. The longer it sits out, gathering mold, the more it rots.

Rot.

I've thought a lot about rot over the past ten thousand years or so. The rot was more apparent with each generation of humanity.

Sometimes, I would reincarnate on another planet and hope humanity would figure it out by the time I got back, but they never did.

Sure, sometimes they made a breakthrough. Sometimes they banded together to save the planet, but more often than not, humanity rotted with each subsequent generation.

I saw it when we couldn't come together to fight global warming, and the planet destroyed itself. I saw it when a third and fourth World War decimated what little remained of our species. I saw it when we promised to be better, over and over, but then couldn't even keep that promise for even a decade.

I was no better. I felt like I was supposed to become something better than what I was, but every time I came back, I drifted further and further from that person until I was nothing but a shell of my former self, unable to remember what it even meant to be good.

I felt my soul rotting with the rest of humanity, but I didn't want that to happen. I didn't want my soul to rot away.

Not until I could become a hero, whatever that meant. When I was a child, I thought that being a hero meant spandex and capes. After I had died a few times, I thought it meant living as long as possible in this horrible world. A few times, I thought it meant accruing enough power and money that you could pass it on to the next generation.

Now, I've forgotten what any of that meant. Was it doing the most good or the least bad? What about doing bad for the sake of good? Does that count? All the moral philosophers I've read in my many lives, and I'm still not sure.

I don't have any time left, either. It felt as though my soul lost elasticity to this body, like chewing gum that has lost its flavor. It was harder to stick with every reincarnation, and this body was the hardest yet.

Oscar Hernandez. That was my name once when I was born the first time, or at least the first time I remembered. I stopped paying attention to each individual reincarnation and now just focused on my original body. What did I want? What was I here for?

I've still not figured it out, and if I don't do it right this time, there might not be another go around to figure it out.

"Hey, mister?" I heard from across the park from where I sat on a metal park bench. There was not much grass in Los Angeles anymore, not that there was much to start with, even during my first life. This grass was plastic, of course, as were the trees, but the humans playing in the park were real. At least, they seemed real.

I looked up to see a little girl in pigtails waving at me. She wore a polka dot dress that scraped all the way down to her knobby knees. She looked happy, which was something that wasn't normal in this day and age.

We had long since killed the sky and were forced to live inside bubbles of our own design, which filtered the smog outside and made it breathable. Of course, that little girl didn't know any different. She just knew what she knew, which was that this was the way of the world.

"Yes?" I shouted back to her.

"Can you help me?" she replied. "I lost my kite up in this tree, and if I don't get it back, my mom's going to kill me. She traded a week's rations for it."

I sighed. I wanted to say no and brood more, but that's not what a hero would do. At least, that's not what I thought a hero would do.

"Sure," I said, pushing myself up from my seat.

My weary bones weren't what they used to be. I came into this body as a young man, full of vim and vigor, but over the decades, my body deteriorated until it was almost unusable.

Yet, even though I felt like an old man, I was only thirty-five. Not uncommon for the times we lived in these days. The pills they gave us for calcium and vitamin C weren't the same as the real thing, as much as they said they were. I remember lifetimes in my distant memory where I lived until a hundred and fifty years old, and now, here I was, in the distant future, barely able to live to be what they would have called an adult a few thousand years ago.

"It's up in that tree," the little girl said as she pointed up to a pink kite stuck in a fake plastic oak the city council planted in the middle of the park. It would have cost too much, and been too expensive, to plant a real tree, even if it did give off real oxygen instead of the fake stuff I breathed all day.

I stared down at the little girl for a moment as she radiated joy back at me. I didn't spend much time with children anymore. It was too sad to think about their shortened life. The shortened life their ancestors, me included, doomed them to when we forced them to live in a hermetically sealed bubble and eat rationed powders for food. I wished, just once, they could have the joy of a freshly cooked steak. Maybe I should have thought of that before the last war when we had a chance to save ourselves.

"What do you want me to do about that?" I asked, scratching my head as I looked up at the kite stuck in the highest branch of the tree.

"Well, I can't climb it. The limbs are too tall for me to grab. Can you climb it and get it down for me, please?"

The truth was I didn't know if I had the energy to do anything more than exist, but if I wanted to be a hero, it meant occasionally acting as if I wanted to help people. Heroes helped people, if I remembered correctly.

"Sure, little girl."

"Becca," the girl said. "My name is Becca."

Becca was the type of name you heard a thousand years ago, but now names were more likely to be B'c'c' than anything normal that I remembered. I hadn't heard a name I would consider normal for hundreds of years.

"That's a pretty name," I said, walking toward the tall oak tree.

"I hate it," she replied. "Everybody makes fun of me for it."

I smiled at her. "Well, I like it."

She turned away from me. Adults weren't known to smile much, and that was inclusive of me. I hardly ever smiled or emoted in any way. Still, I couldn't help but see something of my past in her eyes, and it almost brought me to tears. It didn't, but it almost did, and that was more emotion than I felt in quite a while.

"I'll get your kite down for you," I replied, latching onto the rubbery tree. "Don't you worry about it."

"Thank you, mister," she replied.

Helping people wasn't normal. Not anymore. There was a time when people liked being helpful and polite, but those days were long gone. Now, people understood their part in the machine and worked to keep it going one moment more. There wasn't joy in a job well done. There was only the satisfaction of having lived another day, whatever satisfaction could be drawn from that, of course.

I pulled my aching body up to the next tree limb. My bones creaked inside me, and they popped as I struggled to climb higher into the sky. There were peacekeepers whose duty it was to help little girls with their problems and make sure the city was running smoothly, but it was best not to engage them unless necessary. If you engaged them, you were seen as causing a problem for the city, and even a minor problem was met with a demerit. Enough demerits and you were labeled a threat to civilization and banished into the wastelands.

This isn't some great science fiction novel, where the wastelands were truly livable, and the city had been lying to its denizens the whole time until a great man stood up and showed them the truth.

I thought that might be the case two lifetimes ago, but when I tested the peacekeepers and was sent into the wastelands, I fried in the heat of the outside in less than ten minutes. Perhaps others lived. That was possible. I don't know. However, I knew I didn't. I knew the threat of banishment was real—all too real.

"How goes it up there, mister?" Becca yelled up to me from the ground.

"I'll be honest," I said, catching my breath as I rose to another limb into the tree, "it could be going better."

I was already winded halfway up the tree, but I kept climbing. It reminded me of my younger days and earlier lives when the trees crackled in your hands and sent splinters deep into your palms. They weren't nearly as spongy back then as they were now when they were manufactured instead of grown. Finally, with a great heave of my body, I reached the highest branch where Becca's pink kite rested.

"Now," I said, huffing and puffing, "I'll ask you not to fly your kite anymore, please, when I get this down. It could get you in a lot of trouble if it got lost again."

"But what's the fun in that?" Becca said, looking up at me as I peered down at her.

"The fun is in living," I replied.

"Oh," Becca said, confused. "But what is the fun in living if you can't do anything fun?"

I shook the branch until the kite floated free, down to the ground, and into Becca's loving arms. "The fun is in not dying."

"That doesn't sound like much fun."

I couldn't argue with her, at least not about that. There was no fun in dying, but there was even less fun in living, especially if it meant living in a world with so little joy. However, that was my job, as an adult, to toe society's line and make sure she grew up to be an adult like me, even if all we gave back was our lives.

I placed my hand on the hollow rubber tree and made my way back down to the ground. When I finally had two feet on solid ground, I turned to Becca.

"Now, you be a good girl, okay?" I said to her.

"What does that even mean?" she asked, clutching her kite tightly in her hands.

"Honestly," I said, with not a hint of irony on my breath, "I don't know. It's just something we say to kids."

"Oh," Becca replied. "I guess I understand that."

I shook my head. "No, you don't, and honestly? I don't either."

A strong gust of wind blew through my hair. I looked up to see a Peacekeeper looking down at me from his shiny hoverbike. As it drew closer to the ground, the wind kicked up faster and harder until I fell over onto Becca, and we both crashed to the ground on top of each other.

A Peacekeeper, dressed all in black, covered in a helmet that hid any semblance of his humanity, swung his leg off the bike and unsaddled himself. In his hand, he gripped a long, electric baton, the preferred weapon of their class. However, his other hand gripped tightly around a laser pistol which could evaporate a person in a matter of seconds, and they weren't above using it with extreme prejudice.

"Citizen!" the peacekeeper shouted. "You have been found in violation of code 124.329. Halt!"

I shuffled to my feet. "And what is code 124.329?"

"Flying a kite without a license and getting it stuck in a tree," the Peacekeeper said, stomping forward. "Please move aside so that we may process this dissident."

"Mister!" Becca yelled. "Help me. I've already got three demerits this year."

"That's insane!" I shouted, stepping forward to block the Peacekeeper from Becca. "This girl didn't do anything wrong. She was trying to have a little fun in this stupid world."

"Yes, she did. She is in violation of code 124.329," the Peacekeeper said. "Please move, or I will be forced to use more aggressive means to force your compliance."

In all my previous lives, I would have stepped aside. I valued my own life above anything, especially if its continuation meant I didn't have to deal with the horrors of death again.

But today felt different. My gut burned with the fire and rage. I had to make sure the Peacekeeper couldn't ruin this little girl's life. Perhaps it also burned with the desire to make at least one of my lives matter, even if this was the last one.

"There's nothing you can do to me that will make me abandon this little girl."

The Peacekeeper didn't hesitate before he dug the electric baton into my side, and I fell to the ground in immense pain as electricity flowed through me. Becca ran toward me as I toppled over.

"No!" I shouted. "Run!"

The Peacekeeper slammed his baton into me again as I screamed in pain. "Stop, citizen!"

As the peacekeeper shouted at Becca to stop, I placed my hands around the baton and yanked it away from him. I slammed it into his leg again, and again, and again.

"You will not hurt that little girl! You will not hurt—"

And just like the last time I died, I felt my soul yank out of my body. The Peacekeeper fired a laser beam into my gut, the same gut that burned with rage a moment ago. Now it burned with laser fire.

There was no remorse toward my death in his eyes as he reached his gun up to fire on Becca.

In my last moment of life, I lunged forward and pulled the Peacekeeper's gun down to the ground as it fired into the plastic soil. Becca ran down an alley and out of sight, just as I faded from existence.

I waited, in the darkness of limbo, for something to pull me back into a new body, but it never did. Instead, a blue light fell from the sky, shepherding me onward. Perhaps, finally, I found out what being a hero was all about. Or maybe, I was even more screwed.

I guess I'll find out soon enough, I thought as I swam toward the light and onto the next journey.

INTRUDER AT THE END OF THE WORLD

"**AT THE BEEP,** the time will be…who the hell cares?
It's the Apocalypse. Stop looking at your watch." I waited a
second. "Beep. And that concludes our broadcast day.
You'll still hear me putzing around because I don't know
how to turn this thing off, but I assure you we are closed."

I stood up from the chair with a smile. I had a smile the
whole week, actually. It was so wide and sustained I
actually hurt my cheeks from smiling so much. I didn't
know that was possible.

I never had so much fun during the Apocalypse, and as
I walked up the stairs to the kitchen, I kicked myself for not
following my gut and getting into radio sooner. I poured
myself a glass of water and pulled out some trail mix I
found in one of the cabinets.

Then, I walked over to the couch and plopped down on
it. When I turned the TV on, it was set to the emergency
station—they were all the emergency stations now–but I
quickly flipped it to aux and turned on the Playstation 4,
not knowing if I wanted to play *Grand Theft Auto* or watch
Half Baked.

Before I could decide, I heard something rustle outside
and leaped from my chair, spilling the trail mix over myself
and the couch. I assumed somebody would come
eventually, so I had prepared by setting traps around the
house while I was off the air. It turned out that having the
high ground and a defensible position was a boon. I
understood a bit better why people clustered together now.

One of my bear traps snapped, and then a male voice
screeched out in pain. I grabbed my gun from the top of the
TV and rushed to the door. When I opened it, I found a guy
not much older than me, with brown hair and a pale

complexion, screaming bloody murder as he tried to pull his leg out of the bear trap.

"That's going to leave a mark," I said, holding out the gun. "Who are you, and what are you doing here?"

"Ahhh!" he screeched. "Please, help me. I'm bleeding out."

"The pressure's keeping the blood in right now."

He whimpered in pain before raising his eyes to me. "You are a psycho. Did you know that? Even for the Apocalypse, you are a psycho."

"You're the intruder here, man." I stepped toward him onto the porch. "If you want my help, tell me who you are."

"Fine!" He grunted in pain. "My name is Pete."

"And what are you doing here, Pete?"

"…I heard you on the radio."

"You…heard that?"

He nodded. "The only thing on the dial for miles. You have a good radio voice."

I furrowed my brow. "I don't buy that, Pete. I never told anyone my address. Heck, I don't even know the address here. How did you find me?"

He was breathing heavily and sweating. "I found a phone book. You know this place is listed in the Yellow Pages, right?"

I hadn't thought of that, but now I was kicking myself. Of course, somebody could use a phone book to find this place. *Idiot.*

"Please," Pete said. "I'm not here to hurt you. I swear. I heard you on the radio, and I thought maybe you were as alone and scared as I was." He bit his lip. "I have been out here by myself since the jump, and hearing your voice was the first time that the pit in the bottom of my stomach wasn't hollow no more." He gritted his teeth. "You know that feeling I mean?"

I did. I hadn't thought about it in a while, but that feeling had become an ever-present part of me. The part that was scared and alone and wanted something, anything, to make sense again. But now that I thought about it, for the past week I hadn't felt that feeling damn near at all.

"Maybe," I said. I couldn't give anything away. "But that's all you're getting out of me."

"I know you feel it. You have to. Otherwise, why would you be broadcasting yourself all over tarnation and back? I swear I'm not here to hurt you. I want to help you."

My eyes narrowed. "And how can you help me, Pete?"

"I was an audio engineer back in the real world, or training to be, down in Florida. I know how to turn off the station. I know how to make you sound better. I know how to add music to your… I know how to do all the stuff you don't."

My face softened for a moment at the thought of having help, but it was too good to be true, and my rational mind quickly took over and hardened me again. "This is a long way to go to rob me, Pete,"

"I'm not going to rob you."

"Then this is the most convenient thing to ever happen to me. That a bloody radio engineer happened to show up on my stoop."

He squeezed his hands. They were turning white. "Isn't it time one convenient thing happened in this world? I know it's hard to trust right now, but there are good people left. This place can be a beacon to them."

"A beacon to idiots is more like it," I replied with a sigh. He had won me over. I was too soft. It was a problem. "You better not try to kill me."

"I won't. I swear."

"We'll see about that." I holstered my gun and walked toward the door. Pete started to panic. "Stay here."

"Where are you going?"

"I saw a first aid kit inside. That wound is gonna bleed something fierce when I pull the trap off, and I don't want you dying on me. I don't need that on my conscience."

NOT TONIGHT

Originally appeared in "The Phone"

NO! NO, NO, *no, no.* This was not happening. *I will not become a widower tonight.*

"Come on, come on, come on," I muttered to myself, swiveling my neck like an owl, searching for the impossible.

All he had to do was get a stupid shot. One stupid shot and none of this would have happened, I raged, reliving the mountains of logic that had failed to convince him. It only got worse the more I pushed. The number of knockdowns, drag-out fights we'd had about whether it was safe—*why do you have to be such a stubborn old mule?*

He did not believe in science, as if facts required devout followers to be real. I swerved to avoid a gurney rushing down the wide hall, nurses barely recognizable beneath the layers of trash bags duct taped around their gloves. The remainder of the gaps in protective gear threatened the stability of my legs. I swallowed the scream building behind my clenched jaw.

He was *really* flatlining now, and science was his literal and possibly last lifeline. Unless, of course, I joined him in believing in miracles. Well, we needed several miracles, and all the others hinged on my ability to find this one in time.

Asshole! He would drag me over to his side of the argument before considering mine. The unexpected realization bordered on comforting, like he was with me in my head as I searched. *Unless it was already*—I slammed the door on the ward's partition.

We'd watched the pandemic drag on, riding out each wave in anxious anticipation of a vaccine, the Phone showing up slightly more predictably around overflowing hospitals. Then there was that time it appeared on the side of a speeding ambulance, flashing lights bouncing off polished chrome like a strobe light as the EMTs barreled toward another stricken home. It had been on the news for days.

Mount Peter Hospital held the distinction of killing the most people in the state before a worldwide pandemic had them turning people away from the overflow tents. I'd begged Charles to move to a better district for years. I told him if we ever needed it, County General had a much better reputation. We would be in superior hands, but he'd taken his refusal to make hasty decisions to an absurd level. Exhaustive examinations of big issues used to be one of his best qualities.

It's too expensive, and we're healthy, he'd said—stupid in retrospect. I should have fought harder against it, but then, my miracle might only appear because Charles dug in his heels. *That would be just like him, to win for losing.*

"Come on, come on!" I screamed, voice wobbling, as I searched frantically through every hallway of the hospital. My logical brain knew it wasn't likely to show up because I willed it to obey me. Running pulled in bigger and deeper mouthfuls of the antiseptic coating every surface, the scent mixing with an aroma of death that no amount of scrubbing wipes clean.

That smell… I always thought it would be rancid, foul, but *that,* I'd discovered, came later. Death itself was actually a bit fruity. Sure, if the body stayed around for a little while, the putrid, rotten odor I dreaded set in, but that first moment of death—it was as unsettling as it was surprising.

I turned a corner. My attention snagged on a scene playing out in a poorly curtained area, a woman crying over an elderly man's body. A doctor stood eerily still, shoulders slumped, eyes unfocused, as nurses and security struggled to pry a middle-aged woman off a body nearly obscured by tubes and machines. Her wail, strangled and broken only by sobs as she flailed her arms, snapped me back to my purpose.

Not me. Not tonight… I would find that accursed Phone or tear the hospital apart in the attempt. But even as I ran, the agony pulling on that woman's chest drew out the memories in mine.

Tears came almost immediately, falling hot against my cheeks like a torrent of rain on a window. The dull screech of my husband's heart monitor ripped through my body like I was still in the room with him. For several precious, wasteful seconds, I'd realized I always knew one of us would die first, *but not yet. We're young, supposed to have a lifetime left still.* That's what I told myself, anyway.

I dodged a crash cart and turned down another hallway, slamming into a set of windows of a waiting area for specialized offices. Heads came up. I looked past the medical staff on a much-needed break. I was gone before the ones who put their food down could stand.

If he dies like this, I won't have time to say goodbye.

Three weeks ago, Charles was 'hale and hearty' as he put it. The first coughing fits brought him to his knees, and he cracked jokes. When the test came back positive, he posted about how he wasn't scared. He was still taunting my worries moments before the convulsions threw him against his sweat-soaked bed. My world became a whirlpool of gloved hands, pushing me out of the room even as the seizure ended and he looked for me. For the rest of my life, I'd have the picture of the door closing between us burned into my mind, of his eyes screaming out to me even as the tubes took his ability to speak.

The squeal of shoes on linoleum pulled me back to my search. An orderly with frizzy hair swept back in a messy bun turned down a hallway with a cart full of cleaning products. My thoughts went back to the woman clinging to the withered body of her loved one. White tents had smothered the grassy knoll of the hospital lawn for weeks. Refrigerator trucks for bodies that didn't fit in the morgue were due to arrive any day. There was no mourning period anymore, it seemed, only an endlessly cruel parade of despair.

"Hey, you!" I shouted to another orderly. "Have you seen the Phone?"

The woman looked at me funny as she shook her head. "I think there's one in the lobby, but—"

"No, not that one. The Phone— Forget it," I said, but I hated her anyway. She was doing her best. Nothing happening was her fault—no one here was to blame. They were heroes. Literal heroes surrounded me. . . and it wasn't enough.

I stomped past her. This was not the moment to blow my cool, and yet. . .

Rose-scented perfume suddenly combined with the death in the air; antiseptic rose from the floor, squeezing my insides until I feared dry heaving. The nurse who looked after Charles wore that scent. I could never smell it again without seeing that masked face looking me dead in the eyes and saying it was over.

Nothing was over. She didn't know my Charles at all. He wasn't just any stubborn old mule; he was my stubborn mule, damn it!

My watch buzzed a request for me to slow my breathing.

It had only been seconds, thirty at most, since Charles flatlined. I had less than seven minutes from that moment to find the Phone before he was beyond any so-called heroic measures. The platitudes of passing staff threatened to overwhelm me. How long could anyone listen to them telling families to remember the good times? Trying to convince fathers, mothers, husbands, wives, and children that there was comfort in knowing their suffering was over seemed like a cruel joke. *How could anything be better than living full lives with loved ones?*

Charles and I had our good times, but they were not enough. I was barely 40, which meant in a decent life span, I had more years to dread without him than I ever enjoyed with him. Maybe it was a selfish thing to want for me, but Charles knows I am selfish as all hell. We had nearly two decades together, and they were by and large good years, even if days, weeks, or months were less than wonderful, but it was nowhere near enough.

I don't care. I want more.

The memories clawed at my insides as one hallway blurred into another. We traveled the world in the before times and enjoyed the cocoon of lockdown in a way we never had in the days after the world stopped.

I will have more!

Yes, it was scary to be locked inside, helpless, as a pandemic raged around us. But we always thought our busy schedules made us appreciate the few precious moments spent together. It wasn't until we were stuck with each other all day, every day, that we realized how much we enjoyed each other's company, even in the quiet moments.

"COME ON, YOU SON OF A BITCH!" I screamed it into the ether, trying to will the Phone into existence. I threw open a set of doors, scanning the crowded hospital wing until I noticed the heads that turned, brows furrowed, eyes wary. In every expression, I saw the reflection of someone who appeared very much like they were coming unhinged. I stormed past them anyway.

So, what if I was completely losing it? My only hope to save my husband's life was a phone that had to come to me. I couldn't imagine a better reason to surrender to every hair-brained idea that crossed my path. I wasn't the irrational one, though. That was Charles, down to his core, at least until these last months. He was always stubborn, but his views were pliable when presented with the latest information until he found a deep vein of crazy on the internet and fell into it.

Charles wasn't irrational at the beginning of the pandemic. He even agreed with the lockdown at first. But the weeks dragged into months, and things at his job fractured, splintered, then blew up completely. His patience wore thin. While I could do my job from anywhere that had an internet connection, Charles worked with his hands on the docks. Without shipments coming into port, the furlough became a termination.

I think he resented me but never said it. Instead, he wore his pain on his face, which spoke loudly enough for a million unsaid words.

When the docks reopened, they hired him again, but for half the hours. It was part of the safety requirements the company implemented to comply with government restrictions. He didn't see that last part, though. In Charles' eyes, his livelihood was being taken from him.

I tried to tell him that his health was more important than money, but the months became a year, our bank account dwindled, and he grew angry. By the time there was a vaccine…he was too far gone to believe it. The government had taken everything from him. The last thing he was inclined to do was believe they had his best interests at heart.

"Where are you?" I screamed through the void, voice shaking, the despair inside me exploding with each passing second.

All eyes were on me now. Two orderlies circled the unit, ready to tackle the crazy person sprinting through it. But I wasn't dangerous. I was desperate. Sometimes that was the same thing, but not today. I could accept death, but just not from him—not after the way we ended things.

Those last days were hard. I got the shot, despite all his consternation. He felt I'd betrayed him. And when he tested positive, he was sure it was because I had brought the vaccine to him. He slept on the couch and pulled away from my touch. His breathing became labored. By the time he had to go to the hospital, we couldn't be in the same room without it descending into a shouting match.

He only eased up when his symptoms took a turn for the tragic.

"It has to be here somewh—"

I tripped over something, twisting my ankle as I slid across the linoleum floor. A familiar shape under the nurse's station caught my eye. My heart leaped into my chest. A mop in a bright yellow bucket nearly hid it completely, but the glint of metal, too well polished for this drab and hopeless place, was unmistakable.

If I hadn't fallen, I'd never have seen it.

"Nobody touch it!" I screamed, rushing to my salvation on hands and knees, distantly aware of the hovering staff suddenly murmuring understanding and having other things to do.

Moment of truth. If I punched in his name and the letters didn't light up, he was still alive. I'd have to repeat my search the next time he flatlined. *How long would it stay around?* Charles's life was still measured in hours if he survived this. There was no way I'd find the Phone twice in that short of time. But if he was dead. . . *How long before the doctor called the time of death? What if my search had taken too long?*

The receiver was in my hand before I knew I'd grabbed it. I watched my shaking hand as if it belonged to someone else, unable to breathe until I pushed the last letter. A moment later, my favorite name in the world glowed warmly from behind the buttons. A blanket of welcoming silence seemed to wrap around me.

"Charles?" I couldn't help asking as the terror consuming me erupted in full force. "CHARLES! Do you hear me? Get the fuck up. You will not leave me like this. You are not a quitter. I don't care if your body is broken. You get back inside of it and open your eyes. Gods damn it! I've watched you do the impossible before, Charles, and you will do it again. Come back to me right this minute. You are not getting away from me that easily."

I took a deep, ragged breath, struggling for focus, determined to find the right words. "Charles, listen to me."

This is a one-way conversation, I reminded myself, closing my eyes so he couldn't see me roll them, *my favorite kind.*

"Do you remember when you sprained your knee free climbing up Half Dome and still insisted on making it to the top? And you did, you stubborn mule. Sometimes I hate that about you, but I love it too. Watching you do the impossible gives me the strength to do things I never dreamed of. You're kind in a way I was never kind before I met you. I'm a bitch, I know that about myself, but you loved. . . you promised to love me anyways. And you taught me how to love other people almost as much as I love you. This isn't supposed to happen. Not to us. Charles—I need you to come back to me. I will not do this without you. I can't. I won't. . ."

I swallowed hard, gathering myself.

"So, get your ass up and come back to me. Be the stubborn mule I know you are. I love you so much, Charles. Please—I can be better. I will be better. I swear if you come back to me, I'll stop putting my feet on the coffee table. I know you hate that. I will be good. I won't complain when you want pizza for the tenth day in a row. I'll eat it with a smile on my face—okay, no, we both know I won't do that, but I'll choke it down anyway, and I won't say a word about it. You can have anything you want. Please, Charles, just come back to me."

I paused, waiting for a sign, for any kind of reaction from the universe signaling that he understood me. But in that weighted silence, anger bubbled up inside of me. I squeezed the handle of the phone so hard that my palm ached.

"Goddamn it, Charles. Why did you have to be so stupid? Why couldn't you just listen to reason?" I looked around at the beds surrounding me, with the eyes of doctors, nurses, and patients staring at me. "Why couldn't any of you listen to fucking reason? It was right there in front of you. Hundreds of millions of people have taken this fucking vaccine, and they're *fine!* Ninety-six percent of deaths are unvaccinated people. This hospital is overflowing with you idiots. Do you think it's fair for them? Is your selfishness finally worth it?"

The smell of rose perfume wafted closer. I bit my lip. An image of Charles helpless, limp, half obscured by tubes, surrounded by monitors, machines, and medicine filled my vision. I pressed my thumb and fingers into my eyes until they swam with stars.

"Look at the faces of these poor doctors and nurses. They look like death. They've been working non-stop for months because you selfish sons-of-bitches are too up your own asses to see what's right in front of you. We live in a society, Charles! We do for others; that's the whole point. That's the whole reason we survived for so long. We give up a little of ourselves, so we can all thrive. You used to believe that, Charles. What happened?"

I swallowed; the crushing devastation suddenly impossible to avoid. The air felt thin, like I was shouting from a mountain top with only the wind to hear me.

"What did I do?" I said, distantly aware of the whimper in my voice. "Where did I go wrong? What could I have done to make you see the truth? How am I going to keep going on without you?"

I sighed loudly. "I won't. I'll simply shrivel up and die. I'll simply…I can already feel myself falling away, Charles. The biggest part of myself, the part you love, is vanishing into the ether. When it's gone, nothing but a dark hole will remain. That's what I am without you, empty."

I hesitated, hearing my own words, absorbing the truth of them for the first time. For a second, I wondered if this was what it was like to die, to feel yourself dissolving into a shell, a shadow of someone who could only remember love but no longer felt it or anything else... I slammed my free hand on the base of the phone. The hospital came back into focus around me, but the edges of my vision remained blurry.

"They want me to accept it, Charles, but I can't. We fit together perfectly, and that is so rare. I won't give it up, and I won't let you give us up, either. You're the part of me I always felt was missing, but it's not missing anymore, Charles. It's right there, in your room, waiting for you to go back to it. So quit being a fucking bastard and open your goddamn eyes!"

Suddenly, the sound of the hospital rushed back in around me. The glowing letters spelling out C-H-A-R-L-E-S in the letter wheels on the Phone blinked once, grabbing my attention moments before they went dark. The call was over.

What happened? It wasn't supposed to hang up until I slammed down the receiver. Did it work? Or did I break it?

I dropped the receiver, shaking uncontrollably as I slumped against the wall in defeat. The cold floor I sat on, mop and rolling bucket at my back, barely registered. Dozens of eyes stared at me from behind all the layers of protective gear, but I no longer cared.

Then there was something else; a soft hand on my back, and I turned. It was the nurse, the same one who pushed me

out of the room when Charles left it. She was reaching out
to help me up.

"Mister Johnson!" the nurse said, pulling me to my feet.
Rose perfume filled my nose. "You need to come with me
right now."

I followed the woman through the halls like I was
floating through someone else's dream. She stopped, and I
finally noticed the absence of screeching alarms.

"You have no idea how incredibly rare that save was,"
the nurse said as she pushed open the door to the room. "He
was gone, to be sure, and then he wasn't. I've only heard of
that happening one other time, and it was years before you
or I were born."

I dropped to my knees as I heard the sweetest sound my
ears had ever heard; the heart monitor that once harkened
my love's doom beeped loudly. His chest rose and fell in
time with it.

"Charles." My voice quaked when I realized he was
breathing. "He came back?"

The nurse nodded. "He's not out of the woods yet, but
you must have a guardian angel. Welcome to Mount Peter's
legend board. We're all going to be talking about you two
for a long time."

I barely believed it. *Had it really worked?*

I leaped up to his side, protocols be damned, and
grabbed his hand. "He'll make it. He's a stubborn old
mule."

Nothing was okay, but for a moment, just one moment
in all the shit of the past two years, it felt okay enough to
get us through today.

LITTLE WIFI GIRL

*Based on the short story "The Little Match Girl" by
Hans Christian Andersen*

A DREADFUL CHILL whipped through the girl's face as she stood on the corner of a darkened street deep in the heart of the cruel city she called home. Ash fell on her face like snow, but it never snowed in the Dregs. Snow was a privilege for those who lived in the thousand stories above her; those who saw the light of the sun instead of the shadows cast by the buildings that towered over her, blotting out the warmth of its rays.

She had never seen the sun or felt the warm rays on her face. Instead, her life was consumed by the cold. Even on the hottest day, the wind whipped through her tattered clothes. She was the youngest of ten children, and they insisted she was one of the lucky ones, as six of them hadn't survived to their eighth year of life as she had.

Lucky wasn't the word she would use to describe herself, though. Nobody was lucky in the Dregs. How could she be lucky when she couldn't feel the tips of her fingers that poked out of her thin gloves? How could she feel lucky when her stomach howled, begging for a hot meal? It would be her turn to eat in three days…unless she could sell some of the precious gifts she had been given.

That was what her father called it, at least—a gift.

To her, the wifi that had been implanted in her head as a toddler amounted to little more than a splitting headache, and a life on the streets, begging for connection. How could she be lucky if she never knew anything but pain?

Only twenty percent of children survived the procedure, and while some might consider them lucky, she thought they were the fortunate ones. They never knew suffering, hunger, or cold.

If she could sell just one connection to the network, she might be able to eat tonight—she might be able to afford a bundle of kindling from the garbage pickers that dug through the dump looking for anything that burned.

She closed her eyes and took a breath. She was not supposed to connect to the network on her own. If anyone found out, they would punish her, but what punishment could be worse than how she felt at that moment? She would only stay a moment, she told herself. Just enough to forget the cold that drilled deep into her pores.

Her face flinched as the circuit in her cerebellum flickered, and then, relief. The lights—red, green, blue, and yellow—flashed in front of her. It was Christmas in the towers above her. She had never known Christmas, save for the clips of movies she scoured from the internet.

To be given a gift, instead of having everything they had stolen from her, would be a wonderful kindness. Kindness was a rare thing in the Dregs, and she couldn't remember the last time it had been bestowed on her.

A pain in her shoulder roused her from the fleeting warmth of her connection. When she woke from her circuitous dream, she lay prone on the ground. A man looked back at her and scoffed, rubbing his right knee. He hadn't been paying attention when he turned the corner and crashed into her. Instead of helping her up, he cursed at the little girl before turning up an alley out of sight.

It was one of the dangers of connecting to the network. You lost all sense of yourself as the system enveloped you. Many have fallen prey to the welcoming glow of the web and lost themselves, often forever.

That was one of its great joys, too, though. For a few moments, you could forget your lot in life and be truly free.

She was too poor to afford a connection, and the price rose every day. There was a time, years ago, when the poor of the Dregs would buy a minute here or an hour there, but as the fees rose over time, the poor were driven out of the connection, and the little girl hadn't had a customer in a month.

It was for the best, the company that owned the connection decided. A short-term reduction in revenue was worth not having "those types of people" connected to their precious network anymore. They never thought about the little girl who would go starving in the darkness of the Dregs. No, they never thought about people like her at all.

It was so bitterly cold, and the soles had worn out of the little girl's shoes long ago, leaving her only the thinnest barrier between her foot and the frigid ground below.

"Excuse me, miss," an old woman sang sweetly from behind her. "Are you the little wifi girl?"

When she turned to the woman, she was illuminated with an ethereal white glow, so brilliant that it washed over her eyes and made them tear. Behind her, a beautiful black hovercar idled in the street that only came into view when she acclimated to the brilliant light.

"Yes," the little girl said. "I am."

"I can't bear watching you sit out here anymore. Would you like to come with me to warm yourself and fill your belly?"

Nothing had ever been so grand as the lady's kind eyes, and she could barely say yes before the woman scooped her up in her arms and lifted her into the car, and they flew together, away from the Dregs, toward the sky high above, and as she closed her eyes, she felt the light of the sun for the first time in her little life.

When she didn't come home that night, her father went searching for her and found the little wifi girl leaning against the wall of the building where he had left her earlier that morning—ice cold, frozen by the chill of the air.

She was peaceful in death, and a smile crested on her face as if her last moments were peaceful ones, lost in the bliss of the forbidden internet that was at once her curse and her salvation. Perhaps now, she truly was one of the lucky ones.

AKTA'S ICE HEADACHE

Prequel story to "Hell"

"WHERE ARE YOU going?" Akta shouted at Sir Cleybourne as he made his way down the long hallway past King Odgeir's throne room toward the castle's massive wooden doors. He hadn't worn full battle regalia in many years, and his breastplate slid down his thin frame.

"To the front lines!" he replied.

Around them, the castle walls shook and shuddered. Akta flittered her wings until she was in front of him and dug her thick boots into the ground. She'd learned long ago that she needed big boots to weigh her to the ground and give her the leverage to stop monsters much bigger than Sir Cleybourne.

"You're not going anywhere!"

Sir Cleybourne flung his arm toward the nearest window. Outside, a sixty-foot-high frost giant rampaged through the town. "We've already lost half of our best knights fighting this thing and have gotten nowhere. They need me!"

"No, they don't! They're all gonna die anyway! Let them die without you!"

Sir Cleybourne pushed past Akta. "If that's the way you feel about it, then I've taught you terribly."

From the time she was a little girl, Sir Cleybourne taught Akta everything he knew about fighting. He was once the greatest knight in King Odgeir's army, but time was a battle no knight could beat, and eventually, he slowed with age.

Few knights made it to old age, so those who did were revered. The King made Sir Cleybourne the High Guard of the Kingdom and appointed him to train monster hunters and knights alike. Akta was his most challenging task to date.

Not just because she was stubborn, either, but because she was a pixie, which meant she could fly and disappear at will. No other knight had that power, and that made training her difficult. Still, Sir Cleybourne drilled into her head all he knew, and Akta became a great monster hunter, far surpassing even Sir Cleybourne's skill.

She had captured the great Dragon of Abanzta and returned its riches to her kingdom. She had fought off the blubbering blob of Ringa and saved King Odgeir's prized iron mines. When there was a monster no other knight could defeat, the kingdom turned to Atka.

And yet Sir Cleybourne treated her like a child.

"Let me go instead. I can fight, Cley!" Akta shouted after her teacher.

"You fulfilled your mission admirably. Every man, woman, and child we could find is safe within the castle keep. You should be very proud." He slowed for a moment and looked over his shoulder. "This is not your mission."

"I'm glad the people are safe, but I can still be useful to you!"

Two guards swung open the castle door, and Sir Cleybourne strutted outside, where a hundred knights and cavalrymen flanked either side of his horse. "You are to stay in the castle and protect the king. That is an order. Do you understand?"

Akta nodded begrudgingly. "Yes, sir."

Sir Cleybourne hurled his foot over the horse's saddle and rose atop his steed. He once looked like a proud knight riding into battle, but now he looked like an enfeebled fool, and Akta knew deep in her bones he galloped to his death.

"I wish you good stead, knights," Akta said, nodding slightly to them.

Sir Cleybourne cracked a slight smile and nodded back. "Until our return. Heya!" He dug his heels into the horse, and it dashed forward. The King's banners rode next, followed by row after row of glittering knights, riding off to their doom.

Akta turned back to the castle, the sound of arrows twanging from the top of the keep following her. Their arrows would do nothing, nor would the cavalry. Akta posted up at the closest window and watched as Sir Cleybourne galloped through the winding streets of the town toward his fate.

"I can take care of myself, you know," King Odgeir said, walking up to her.

"Yes, my prince." Akta caught herself. "Sorry—your grace."

King Odgeir smiled. "You don't have to apologize to me, Akta."

King Odgeir the First died peacefully in his sleep three years before. He had been like a father to Akta. He found her when she was a baby, discarded and left for dead, and took her in to raise as his own, despite her being a monster and different in every way possible.

Akta was a pixie, which meant she came complete with wings and hollow bones like a bird; it also meant darker skin and a higher voice than anybody she knew. Nobody in town or anywhere in the surrounding countryside looked like her, but that didn't matter to the King. He treated her every bit as well as the crown prince, which made her love him all the more.

It also created a special bond between King Odgeir the Second and Akta. The two of them were as much family as she was a subject to her lord. The moment he put on the gold crown and picked up the scepter, many things changed, but nothing weakened their bond. She could no longer joke with him as she once did, and they didn't spend lazy days walking through the pastures anymore, but there was still respect, admiration, and deep love between them.

"I don't want them to die," King Odgeir said. "I hope you know that."

Akta bowed her head. "I know, my king."

The castle shook again as the ice giant slammed his fist on the ground and took out a dozen knights charging at it.

"I fear it may look as such, as I sent them out there when we have no hope of winning."

Akta choked back tears. "No, my king. It does not look as such."

"Even now, my keep shakes, and my people cry in fright. Those knights are the last in the kingdom. My reserve. They are old and feeble, knock-kneed and frightened. My best men, they've all died already or have been wounded beyond repair."

"Then why fight?"

"Because without those men, my people will be lost. They will surely all die. My hope is that whatever time those knights buy is enough for us to come up with a plan."

"Then let me help buy them time. Don't keep me here. Let me do what I'm best at. Let me fight and die for you."

The king raised an eyebrow. "Sir Cleybourne specifically asked—"

"Screw him! You are the king. Are you going to listen to a doddering old buffoon over your adopted sister?"

King Odgeir breathed deeply. "It is specifically because of my love for you that I don't want you to go."

"What is my life compared to the life of all your people, my king?"

King Odgeir turned away. Tears swelled in his eyes, and he didn't want Akta to see them. "Go, if you must."

"Thank you, my king."

Akta burst out the front doors to the castle and soared into the sky. One of the advantages of being a pixie was that she could fly as high or low as she wanted, at speeds no mortal could reach. Another advantage was a never-ending supply of pixie dust, a magical powder that allowed her to appear and disappear at will.

She wouldn't deny that between the dust and her wings, she had an unfair advantage over the rest of the monster hunters in the kingdom, but she didn't care. She used everything in her arsenal in every battle. In some fights, that meant relying on her prowess with daggers, in others, it meant her agile footwork, and still, other fights forced her to use her magical abilities to her advantage. She would be a fool not to use every opportunity to gain the upper hand.

Akta tossed a handful of pixie dust into the air and vanished as the arrows shot around her. She reappeared in the face of the giant, right between its eyes.

"Hi!" she shouted to it.

The monster crossed its eyes to see the tiny pixie. It raised its arm and swiped at her, but she disappeared again into a cloud of pink and purple smoke, reappearing at the giant's ear.

"It's not very polite to hit people," her voice echoed inside its cavernous ear canal. The giant

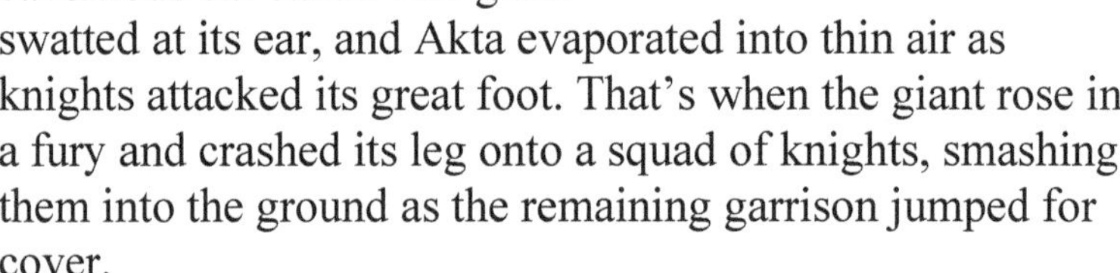

swatted at its ear, and Akta evaporated into thin air as knights attacked its great foot. That's when the giant rose in a fury and crashed its leg onto a squad of knights, smashing them into the ground as the remaining garrison jumped for cover.

"I can't stand for this," Akta said.

She pulled out her daggers and dug them deep into the giant's neck. It screamed out in pain and smashed its hand down toward Akta, who disappeared at the last moment.

When she materialized on the other side of its neck, she dug in her daggers again. Like a wasp, she needled in her weapons repeatedly until the monster recoiled backward.

"It's retreating!" Sir Cleybourne shouted. "Attack!"

No, you stupid fool, Akta thought. *Head back to the castle!*

But it was too late. The last of the garrison charged at full speed, brandishing their weapons like ants upon the great giant. Their attacks would do nothing, and Akta could not hope to defeat the giant, either. Everything they did was a stall tactic.

"Stop!" Akta zipped down to the ground and placed herself between the charging men and the giant. "You're all going to die!"

"Back away, you fool!" Sir Cleybourne shouted back. "You are hindering our advance. We have the upper hand now!"

"Your advance will do nothing but lead to your deaths. Don't you know that?"

"An honorable death is nothing to fear!"

"What about a foolhardy one?"

Akta and Sir Cleybourne argued so intensely that they didn't notice the giant's foot rise again or the other knights jumping out of the way. It wasn't until the last second that Akta saw the foot's shadow fall on Sir Cleybourne's face. Instinctively she jumped away, leaving her teacher to bear the brunt of the attack.

"Cley!"

A moment later, the foot lifted. Akta shot forward, gathered Sir Cleybourne into her arms, and flew them to a desolate corner of the city.

"Cley! Cley! Cley! Don't be dead. Please...please."

Sir Cleybourne looked up at her and smiled. Blood trickled out of the sides of his mouth as he struggled to breathe. "Do you know what I remember at the end?"

"This isn't the end. It's not the end." Akta rocked him gently and wiped a tear from her cheek.

"I remember our first hunt when you saved me from that troll in the woods. Do you remember how you kicked that fiery pot into its face and scalded him good?"

Akta cried and cried. "I remember."

"I very much liked that. Giants really hate fire, don't they?"

The life faded from Sir Cleybourne's eyes until he stared blankly into the great abyss, and his arms fell limp on the ground. Akta pressed her head against the old knight's chest and cried

until the ground shook from the giant's foot. She looked up to see the frost giant advancing on the castle. There wasn't time to grieve.

Sir Cleybourne's last words gave Akta an idea. Frost…Ice…*Fire*. Of course, fire melts ice. She bet that ice giants hated fire as much as trolls did, and she could use it to drive the monster out of town. Perhaps she could even melt the giant! Why had they not thought of it before?

First, she had to distract the monster. Akta gritted her teeth and picked up Sir Cleybourne's sword. He would not die in vain. Akta disappeared into the ether and reemerged right in the monster's face. She turned the sword over and flung it into one of its gigantic eyeballs, temporarily blinding it. Both arms flung up to its face as it tried to pull the sword out.

Akta soared through the town until she found a blacksmith shop with a roaring fire. She grabbed some loose rags from a nearby bench, lit them ablaze, then flew back to where the monster was still digging at its eyes in pain. "I hope this works," she muttered to herself.

Akta dropped the flaming rags upon the giant's arm. The fire melted into the frozen limb, and water dripped onto the ground. The frost giant cried out to the heavens until the water from its wound quelled the fire.

"That's *it*!" Akta shouted.

Akta flew back to the archers in the castle. "Everybody, douse your arrows in kerosene and tar. Light them on fire before you shoot them!"

"That's crazy," said Frederick, captain of the guard, through his comically bushy mustache. "We'll burn down the whole city!"

"Of course, it's crazy!" Akta said. "This is all crazy, but any minute now, that monster is going to be at our gate, so we can try something or do nothing. Your choice."

Frederick thought for a moment. "I will find a light."

"Good man."

Akta disappeared, and a second later, she was inside the castle. Quakes rocked the walls as King Odgeir sat on his throne, nervously stroking his long beard. He looked regal even in the darkest moments, and this was surely the darkest his kingdom had ever experienced.

"I have a plan, good king," Akta said.

"I won't like it, will I?" King Odgeir smiled.

She shook her head. "It will destroy the town but save its people."

King Odgeir weighed this. "How certain are you it will work?"

"It's risky, but I do believe it is our best chance. The knights, including Sir Cleybourne, are dead. The archers have proven ineffective. This is our last effort. If it fails, we will all be doomed."

King Odgeir looked up at Akta. There was a weariness there she had not noticed before. "Do what must be done to save my people."

Akta nodded and flitted away, then rematerialized on top of the castle. Dozens of archers lugged kerosene and tar across the rooftop between stations. They doused their arrows in the fuel and lit them with great torches before letting them loose into the air.

"I need to borrow this," Akta said, disappearing with a clay jar full of kerosene.

Akta reappeared on the battlefield in front of the giant. It had finally pulled the sword out of its eye and now lumbered toward the castle with nothing to stop it. The flaming arrows that fell on its icy skin were little more than a nuisance. Each arrow burned for a moment and melted a small piece of the giant, but the barrage could never stop it in time.

Only lighting the town on fire could do that.

Akta took a deep breath and floated into the air. She tilted the kerosene jar and drenched the houses with it, creating a circle around the great beast.

She disappeared again and threw the last of the kerosene into the blacksmith's fire. She lit dozens of rags on fire and flew upwards with them, dropping them on the thatched houses below her.

The houses caught flame almost immediately, and soon the fire raged around the giant while fire continued to rain down from the archers. The entire town went up in flames, with the giant caught in the middle. Within moments, the ice monster began to melt.

Akta disappeared to the castle and reemerged with more kerosene to keep the fire raging. Everywhere the giant stepped, an immense fire consumed it until all that remained of the once great giant was a river of water to wash away the fire.

The arrows from the castle stopped, and Akta surveyed her damage. She had destroyed the entire town and cremated Sir Cleybourne and the rest of the soldiers that died valiantly in battle, but she was alive, and so were the townspeople. She had saved the day. She had saved everybody.

Now, she would help them rebuild a better town from the ashes. From that moment on, Akta was a legend. At eighteen years old, she would go on to fight a hundred more battles before her untimely death at twenty-seven, but this is the only one that would become song and lore for all eternity.

GAMESMANSHIP

PEOPLE THOUGHT I came up from Hell to take their souls, but that couldn't be further from the truth. Well, that's not entirely accurate. I supposed thinking that I was a bowl of soup would be further from the truth, but not by enough to matter in this particular instance.

I was not evil, but people believed the worst about me. I'm not even the one that killed people. The gods and their flawed design handled that for me. I was just there to pick up the pieces once humans shed their mortal coil. It was the gods who designed you. Humanity should be mad at them instead of me. I was just the middleman. Yet, I always got the blame, while the gods got the adulation.

"Boss!" my secretary, Charise, shouted from the other room. There was a time when I handled every death by myself, but as humanity infested the world like locusts and ballooned up to seven billion people, I was forced to take on additional help in the form of secretaries and an army of reapers. "Phone call for you!"

"Take a message!" I replied. "Tell whoever it is that I have a headache."

"Used that one yesterday."

"I can have more than one headache, Charise. There's not a finite amount of them, as opposed to cares I have to give, of which I have none left."

After a moment of silence, Charise let out a sigh. "It's the big man. He said you need to take it, being as you haven't answered any of his numerous messages."

Charise had left several hundred Post-it notes from God on my desk over the past century, but I didn't have the energy to call the omnipotent one back. God was pure drama, and I had no interest in stoking his fire or stroking his ego.

"He says that he knows you've been avoiding him!" Charise added.

"Of course he does!" I replied, picking up the phone. "What kind of omniscient being would he be if he didn't know I was avoiding his call? Patch him through."

I put the receiver up to my ear and smiled the fakest smile I could muster. The smile was fake, but even a fake smile sent real endorphins to your brain. It didn't work as well as whiskey, but it did the job in a pinch.

"You've been avoiding me," God said in a booming voice that was equal points monotonous, authoritative, and peevish. "I don't like being ignored."

"There is no way to reply to that statement without making you angrier, so I am hopeful we can move on to the point of your call."

"An apology would be nice."

I rubbed the bridge of my nose with my fingers. Talking to God really was giving me a migraine. "You know I'm not sorry, so in what way would that be a productive course of action?"

God was a petulant child when he didn't get what he wanted. Luckily, the gods prevented him from harming me with his temper tantrums. The same couldn't be said about humanity, which he seemed to enjoy torturing every few centuries.

"We have a problem," God said.

"There are always problems," I replied. "No matter how hard I try to get away from them, they keep following me everywhere I go."

"This one is about a woman."

"They usually are," Charise said into the receiver. She had been listening this whole time, as she often did, but she usually had the good grace to keep her phone on mute. "Sorry."

"Is this about the Greta Bunchen incident?" I replied.

"Yes. Has it been resolved yet?"

The Greta Bunchen incident. One hundred years ago, one of my best reapers went to collect her soul from Earth. She challenged him to a game, as mortals often did, and were within their right. The problem was that she won, which was less common. Even less common still was that every time one of my reapers went to collect her, she won again, and again, and again. It was not abnormal for one of my reapers to lose once or twice, but Mrs. Bunchen had an unbeaten streak of 3891-0.

"I'm afraid there is nobody left to challenge her in my employ. If you would approve my budget overrun, I could hire more and—"

"This is unacceptable!"

"I'm sorry," I replied. "But there's nothing I can do."

"So what? I am supposed to keep bending the laws of time and space because of your reapers' horrible gamesmanship?"

"Yes?" I said in a huff. "You wrote the laws, not me. It's not my fault they are stupid."

"Watch yourself, Carl," God bellowed to me.

"I prefer it if you address me as Death. I don't call you Bacchus, after all."

"You'll get the respect of your position when you earn it."

"You're all-knowing. How about you tell me how to fix it then, Mr. Smarty Pants?"

"Gladly," he replied. "It seems there, when going through our records, we found one reaper who has yet to try to collect Mrs. Bunchen's soul."

"That's impossible. Who could it—" But I knew the answer before he said it.

"It's you."

I stood up and started to pace across the room. "You must be joking. I haven't been back to Earth since the Great War."

"Then this is a perfect time to make the trip. Get her soul, Carl, or we'll see what happens when an immortal gets snapped out of existence. I am ever so curious."

I sighed. There was no arguing with the alpha or the omega in him. "Fine."

"I knew you would see it my way."

"You literally know everything. That's not a great accomplishment!"

He snapped his fingers, and I was gone to Earth, the backwater cesspool of the galaxy. I was so excited I could drop dead that very minute.

*

Greta Bunchen lived at the end of a long lane in a small house that sat on a large patch of grass. During her lengthy life, she married and had children, and those children had children, and those children had children. She had a rather large lineage, yet she didn't ever see them for fear they wouldn't understand her elongated lifespan.

So even though her great-great-great grandchildren roamed the earth, they didn't know she existed. To prevent suspicion, every few decades, she moved to a new house at the end of a new lane and kept mostly to herself.

Her house was small but clean. She had a fresh coat of paint on the single-story ranch house, and her front yard was meticulously groomed. She paid a local handyman to come twice a month and take care of any unseemliness in her yard. For his service, he was paid handsomely in the form of cash, which was placed under her front mat—a bland, dull cat print with *Welcome* written on it in block letters—and he never had any interaction with her. His instructions were to complete the tasks assigned until the money no longer appeared.

I walked up to the front door and rang the bell. Five miles away, an awful man was having a heart attack, and one of my people would pick him up. However, now I was focused on the singular case of Greta Bunchen.

"Go away!" Greta scowled behind the door.

"That's not very nice. Your mat says I'm welcome. Is that a lie?" I asked.

"It's not a lie, but it's not the whole truth either. You are welcome to piss off is what you're welcome to do."

I banged the brass knocker in the center of the door. "We have unfinished business, ma'am."

"I'm all paid up on everything," she hollered at me. "You need something? Take it up with my accountant."

I leaned my head against the door knocker. "I'm afraid this matter falls outside the realm of your accountant's purview."

Her feet shuffled toward the door, scraping against the floor as she went. I suppose I could have walked through the door if I were so inclined, but the rules of polite society are there for a reason and must be observed, lest there be anarchy.

The lock flipped, and the door creaked open. In front of me stood a legend, and though I should have been furious at how she manipulated the system, I couldn't help but admire her a little. She had a will to live unmatched by any other in the history of humanity.

"What do you want?" she said as the door flung open.

"I believe you know what this is about," I replied, gesturing to my black robe.

There was no dress code among reapers, but I quite enjoyed the tattered cloak that had become associated with me over the centuries. It gave me a sense of gravitas in any situation and made it so that I rarely had to explain myself.

"Oh," she said without a hint of fear in her eyes. "It's you. I was wondering when you would show up again."

"Yes," I said. "Well, it took several years for us to find somebody whom you hadn't beaten yet."

She pulled her old, wrinkled hands out of her apron and waved me inside her humble home. God had bent the laws of space and time to accommodate her impressive winning streak against the forces of death, but he could only do so much to halt the ravages of old age. "Come in, come in. Let's get this over with."

The inside of her house smelled of stale cheese and mothballs. However, it was surprisingly well maintained. This was because every fortnight, she allowed a maid to clean her house from top to bottom. They never interacted. While the maid cleaned, Greta sat in a crawl space in the back of the house to avoid any suspicion. The maid was to come promptly at ten am on every other Tuesday and leave promptly at noon, or she would not be paid her bonus, which was a hefty sum, nearly double what she made at any other house on her route.

"I suppose I should expect that you would like to play a game," I asked.

"Well, it is my custom, isn't it?" Greta replied. "But I don't get many visitors, so I thought maybe we could chat for a minute. After all, you and your reapers are the only ones who know the truth about my life, and it would be nice to have an honest conversation for a change."

"Very well," I said. "I suppose I could use a spot of tea if you have any lying around."

Her droopy mouth creased up on either side. "I have some hot water in the kettle and some Earl Grey if that will do."

"That would be lovely," I replied, sitting down on a brown sofa in her living room.

Once a week, Greta paid a boy to bring her groceries from the store. She would leave the money on the table for him, and he was never to stay longer than fifteen minutes, which was what it took to unload two bags of groceries and leave her house. Like her relationship with the maid and gardener, they were never to interact.

"You have a lovely home here, Greta," I said, admiring the artwork hanging on her wall. "You've built quite a life for yourself."

"Oh, it's something all right," she said, walking out of the kitchen and handing me a cup of tea. "Wish somebody could hear all the stories I have to tell, but if they did, they would just think I was crazy."

I took a sip of the tea. "Oh, that is lovely." I took another sip, and it warmed my cold, immortal heart. "If it makes you feel any better, you are quite the legend around my office."

She smiled again, returning from the kitchen a second time with her own cup of tea. "Really?"

I nodded. "Oh yes. No other human has come close to beating your winning streak against my reapers. You are the stuff of legend. There's a whole chapter on you in the training manual."

"I would very much like to see that," Greta replied, sitting across from me on a high-back armchair.

I took another sip of tea. "I believe we could arrange that if you were willing to come with me."

She tittered girlishly. "You're more charming than the others; I'll give you that."

I nodded. "I hope so. I've been doing it quite a long time."

Greta leaned in toward me. "Then why haven't I ever seen you before?"

"I don't come to Earth anymore, except in special circumstances."

Greta chuckled, slapping her leg enthusiastically. "I'm a special circumstance?"

"I should think so. God himself called to complain about you. And thus, here I am."

"Isn't that something? You and God talked about me? Little old me?"

"Yes. He was none too pleased that you found a loophole around mortality."

Greta placed down her tea on the maple coffee table that separated us. "And what about you? Does it piss you off, too?"

I shook my head. "Oh, no. I don't care one way or the other. Frankly, that you could rankle God's britches endeared you to me even more."

"I like you," Greta said. "You're more fun than the others. Why don't you come down to Earth more often?"

I cracked a wry smile. "Who has the time? I have an afterlife to run, after all. Not to mention, you humans are dreadful."

"Oh, I don't think we are so bad."

"Please, you've been at nearly constant war with each other for centuries. You've given my staff nothing but heartache. The more you multiply, the more you kill each other. It's a vicious cycle."

"Sure, but there are good things, too."

"Are there?" I asked. "Are there really?"

She nodded. "There are. I believe that. It's one of the reasons I stayed around so long. I wanna be here to see it all."

I placed my tea on the coffee table in front of me. "Well, if you beat me, then you'll get your chance since there are no other reapers to challenge."

"Does that mean I could be immortal?"

I nodded. "It appears that way unless we find some other loophole, of course."

"Of course," she said, pulling a deck of cards from her apron. "I suppose we should begin then."

Greta shuffled the cards in her hand and dealt seven to me and seven to her before placing the rest of the deck in the middle of the table. When she did, I realized they were not a normal deck of cards at all but an Uno deck.

"Uno?" I asked.

"I've been obsessed with it since the late 70s. Unfortunately, I haven't been able to play much recently, but I always keep a deck on me, just in case." She flipped over a red eight from the top of the deck. "As the guest, you can go first."

I played a red three on top of the red eight. "Seems like a simple game to play for your soul."

"Simple games are the best. They allow you to control all the variables."

She played a red nine on top of my red three, and I countered with a blue nine. "Is that how you won so many times? By playing the game so much, it gave you an unfair advantage?"

Greta played a blue skip a turn and followed it up with a blue seven. "That's one way, of course. Reapers don't get challenged often, and even when they did, they couldn't be experts at every game in existence. Or at least, that was my bet."

I looked down at my hand. I didn't have any blue cards, so I pulled a card from the deck. I got a red six on my first pull, a yellow four on my second, and finally a blue two on my third, which I played. "That was a good bet. You are very good at this game. I didn't even know there was any skill involved with Uno."

"Every game has a skill," she said, placing down a yellow 2. "You just have to play it enough to develop it."

I put down my yellow four. "There are so many luck variables in Uno, though. To develop any skill with it, you would have to know the whole deck every time and then exactly what I was going to play."

She smiled. "I'm sorry to do this to you." She placed down a draw four. "Actually, I'm not. Blue."

I grinned at her. She was a pain in my eternal behind, but I couldn't help but like her, even as I drew four cards, including the blue eight I played. "You're very good at this."

"I know." She played a blue three. "Uno."

"Already?" I said.

"As you said, I'm very good."

I played a yellow three and prayed she didn't have the right card. She did, though.

She placed down another draw four card and grinned. "I win."

"How is that possible?"

She stacked the cards into a neat pile. "I told you. I know the game better than anybody. Of course, it helps that I cheat, too."

"You cheat?" I scowled. "That's not allowed!"

She laughed and stood up. "Actually, it's nowhere in the rulebook."

I scoffed. "How could you possibly know that?"

Greta walked over to a bookcase behind her chair and shuffled through a shelf of old, leather-bound books. After a moment, she pulled one out and brought it over to me. "The first time I beat your reaper, I won fair and square. She was so angry, she stormed out, forgetting this in the process."

She handed the book over to me. It was titled *The Rules of Death*. I recognized it because I wrote it before I hired my first reaper. "Of course."

"I studied it extensively, and nowhere did it say I couldn't cheat. So, I did."

I couldn't help but laugh. "That is quite the loophole you found. I will be sure to rectify it in the next edition."

"I have always been good at exploiting loopholes," she said, sitting back down. "Can I ask you what it's like, up there?"

"It's much like anywhere else, I suppose. Nicer than Flagstaff, not as nice as Paris. Traffic is abysmal, as you can imagine, with so many billions of souls roaming around."

"And Hell?" she said. Her voice shook as she said the words. "What of it?"

"That crack in your voice tells me you are afraid? Is that what you fear? Going to Hell?"

She nodded. "It's what I have always feared. I wasn't always the best person in my life. Every time I beat one of your reapers, I promised that I was gonna change, but then life happened, and I never got around to it."

"I'm afraid I can't tell you what will happen after you die. It is outside of my purview. I bring souls in for processing, but after they arrive in the afterlife, I only know whispers of what happens."

"Well, that's a shame," she said, shaking her head. "I am old, and I am in so much pain. I would very much like to see what is beyond this life, but not without knowing what will happen."

"Perhaps a deal could be struck, though, which could circumvent the system. What if I offered you a job?"

"A job? Like, as a reaper?"

"Why not? You know more than any person in history about grim reapers. You've met over 3,000 of them in your time here. And you know how to win a game, which is something I   desperately need help teaching the rest of my staff."

"This is a trick, isn't it?" she said. "To get me to leave this place?"

I shook my head. "No, I am not a trickster. I am a helper. You beat me, so that means you can stay here forever. Immortality can be a blessing, but it is also a curse. You will not be able to leave Earth, ever. Even when the sun burns through the Earth, you will still be here."

"That's a long time."

"It is. Even as long as you have lived, it will feel merely like a moment by the end of time. Think carefully about what you want," I said. "I have studied your case extensively, and while you have a life here, what kind of life is it, really? You have not had a real conversation with another human in twenty-three years."

"The cable repairman who installed my modem. He was nice."

I stood up from my chair. "I am offering you a chance to start again, to forge a new life for yourself."

Greta pushed herself up and walked toward me. "You know, for years, it was fun to beat you all and cheat death, but the more I did it, the less fun it became. I watched everybody I love die, and then I was alone. There were plenty of times I thought about losing, but something stopped me. I have to say that in the long intervening years when you didn't come, I wished you would. I wished you would come, and I wished you would beat me."

I held out my arm for her. "I am here now, Greta. I am here to take you away if you choose."

"And it's really nice up there?" she said, grabbing onto my arm.

"It's better than here; I promise you that. You'll have a nice desk and everything. Maybe even an office plant."

"Can I look out over the clouds?" Greta asked.

I smiled. "I think that can be arranged."

And thus ended the curious case of Greta Bunchen. She stepped into the great unknown with me, and together we went off to eternity.

BULLETINS AT THE END OF THE WORLD

"THIS IS A mad idea," I said to Pete as he ate a bowl of breakfast cereal next to me on the counter. He preferred the sweet stuff and mixed Lucky Charms and Fruity Pebbles into a monstrosity, while I preferred Raisin Bran. He called me boring, and I called him a child, but other than that, we got along just fine.

"It's not, though," he replied. "It makes perfect sense. We're about to run out of food, and unless you want to get on the road again, we need help."

Pete and I had been broadcasting together for three months, and every day he tried to get me to use the broadcast to invite other people to join us using a series of cryptic clues that he set up around our broadcast area and would eventually lead them to our location, but only if they cared deeply about finding us.

"You understand people could find me the way you did, right? All they have to do is pick up a phone book."

He shrugged. "Yeah, but it's been months, and nobody has. Maybe they are waiting for an invite."

"You think people are being polite in the Apocalypse. You really are a child." I chuckled at him. "We're opening ourselves up to marauders and criminals if we do this."

"And we're also opening up to people who want to help and desperately need a place to call home."

I shook my head. "You think better of the world than I do."

He wrapped his arms around mine. "You opened your heart to an outsider once."

"Yeah, and look where it got me." I looked up into his eyes and smiled. Then I kissed him. "Just kidding." He kissed me back and then pulled me in for a tight hug. "This is the first time in my life I have ever been happy. Not sure I'm ready to give that up."

"You give up a bit of yourself to live in a society, but you also get so much in return. We could find people to sew our clothes, hunt for meat, or do any number of things we can't or won't do. You want to gut a rabbit?"

"Absolutely not, I don't." I poked him in the stomach. "Alright. I'll do it if you promise to stop your sanctimonious speeches."

"Deal." He kissed me on the forehead. "Let's get on it then."

We put our bowls in the sink and walked downstairs. I took my position at the microphone and looked over at him. He gave a thumbs up and flipped a switch. The room came alive with activity, and the red light lit up the room.

"Good morning, chillins," I said into the microphone. My radio voice was much better these days. "It's Sammy Chops, and you're listening to 89.7 on the low end of the dial. Today we're doing something I think is absolutely mental. My engineer Pete has convinced me that there are people out there that need a place to call home: a safe place where we can try to rebuild a better society than the one we left. I think that he's asking for marauders and monsters by offering, but I love him quite a bit—" he mouthed 'I love you, too' when I smiled at him "—so I'm willing to give it a shot.

"Here's the deal. Hidden out there in listener land are clues that will lead you here, to this radio station. If you try hard enough, you can find them, and when you get here, we'll welcome you with open arms. No judgment and no reservations. The only thing we ask is that you contribute what you can when you can. In return, we'll protect each other.

"This might be a terrible idea, but we're hoping you want this station to keep broadcasting more than you want to rob us. Only time will tell if that's a good idea or not.

The first clue is in the next song, and then we'll be back with a story. We'll keep making these bulletins every chance we get. I look forward to meeting you soon."

The red light went dark, and I turned on "Peaches" by The Presidents of the United States of America. It was the only CD Pete had on him when he got here, and when he played it for me, I looked into his eyes and knew right then that I loved him.

"It's going to be great," Pete said with a smile.

"We'll see," I replied. "I hope you're right, though."

"I am. Just know it."

THE HORRORS OF VENDING

Originally appeared in "Cthulhu FhCon"

"YOU'RE NOT REALLY doing this show, are you?" my wife asked as I loaded the last box from the garage. She waved a green flier around in front of her. "This flier doesn't even seem like it was written by a human."

I placed the box of books in the truck and turned to her. "We talked about this, Harriet. If we want to put a down payment on our own place, then I have to do every convention that comes my way."

She looked down at the flier. "But Cthulhu Fhcon? That doesn't even make any sense. And it's on that old, creepy island off the coast…"

I smiled as I walked up and grabbed her shoulders. "How bad could it be? Remember that holiday con two years ago?"

She chuckled. "You mean the one where all the attendees were off playing Magic all day, and there were only like ten vendors?"

I nodded. "And I still made a couple of hundred bucks. Besides, if it's really that bad, I'll complain, and they'll probably give me my money back. I don't like using that trick, but I can be very intimidating."

"You do know how to beat a dead horse, my love."

I feigned offense at her. "Me? That doesn't sound like anything I would have ever done in my whole life. How dare you?"

After that, she smiled and kissed me softly on the lips. "I have a bad feeling about this."

I tapped my forehead against hers. "I have a bad feeling about every convention, but if I'm ever going to be Neil Gaiman, I need to sell a bunch of books. The only way I know how to do that is at conventions."

"I know." She sighed. "Just come back in one piece, okay?"

I raised my head and kissed her on the forehead. "If that's the bar, then I think I can hit that."

"Famous last words."

I walked to the car and closed the trunk. "I love you."

"I love you, too."

I understood Harriet's concern. I had been running the convention circuit for two years full time, and they were mostly bad these days, with some terrible sprinkled in for good measure. In my first year, I did a lot of business, but recently I had been barely breaking even on table fees, let alone gas and printing costs.

That's one thing people didn't understand about conventions. Fans assumed you were a guest of the show when they came to your table, but more often than not, you were stuck paying your own way. Even if they somehow comped you a table, you had to get yourself to the show, including your room and even parking.

It was not an easy life. I thought becoming a full-time author would be different. I grew up on movies where authors wore tweed coats, lived in lake houses, and only wrote one book a year. I was sold a bill of goods, and the reality was much different than that. It was a lot of supply chain management, bookkeeping, and heavy lifting. If I knew how much manual labor was involved in being an author, I would have worked out much more when I was younger.

The road to Havenhurst Hotel was cracked with potholes, and the bridge over to the island hadn't been properly maintained in a coon's age. I'm not saying we had great roads and bridges two hours south of where I lived, but these ones seemed built to keep people out. And yet…dozens of cars were on the road up to the old hotel, which made my old heart smile a bit that I hadn't chosen a terrible convention in an awful location instead of being with my pregnant wife back at home.

That was always the worst part of conventions; the loneliness of it. My wife tried them a couple of times, but she hated crowds and abhorred capitalism, which meant conventions were her worst nightmare. She still came every once in a while when I went out of state, but even when she was there, Harriet spent most of her time wandering around the city, seeing the sights, and having a grand old time, while I was stuck with the bill. I didn't begrudge her since she worked hard, but my margins were abysmally thin even when she didn't come.

The songs of Jason Isbell blared from the radio as I waited to unload my car and head into the convention. They promised free parking, which was a huge hold, as a weekend show could set you back $50 in parking fees alone. I recognized some of the cars and trucks in front and behind me on the road, and we waved at each other as we waited for our chance to get into the show. It took a special type of crazy to willingly spend all your time selling stuff to strangers, and those who ran the circuit became friends, at least by association.

An hour after starting across the bridge, I finally pulled up to the front of the hotel. The siding was cracked with age, and the paint was peeling off every surface. Perhaps the ancient gothic building was beautiful once, but those days were long gone, like a Hollywood starlet lying on her deathbed.

A young man in a red blazer waved at me when I stepped out of my car. "Ye're for con'ven'tion, sir?"

I nodded. "I am. I'm a vendor. I have a trunk full of stuff to—"

He didn't let me finish before snapping his fingers to signal a bellhop in a red cap and a tarnished gold cart to rush up to me. "Sh'va'na he'lp."

"Thank you." I turned to the woman with her hair pulled up in a bun that the cap covered. "Shavana. It's nice to meet you."

"Sh'va'na," her voice croaked.

The man in the red blazer pulled a box out of my car. "She doesn't speak much, but she'll get you where you need to go."

He helped unload my boxes and then held out his hand for my keys. Before I could reach into my pocket to pull out a tip, he was around the car and hopping into my driver's seat. Sh'va'na clicked her mouth several times and began inside, walking as if she had never been on dry land before.

"How long have you worked here?" I asked before I remembered she didn't talk much, so I became content to just follow her through the lobby, where a dozen men, women, and families checked into the hotel. I hoped this meant the weekend would be a success.

Every convention had a rhythm to it, and the hardest part was doing one for the first time. You never knew how much you would sell, so you had to steel yourself away for making almost nothing. My books were pretty good sellers at horror conventions, and they are all influenced by Lovecraft myths, so I had high hopes but low expectations.

I had been lost in thought, looking at the worn wallpaper that curled at the edges, for at least five minutes when I realized we had been zigging and zagging through hallways that didn't seem to make any sense—not unless the hotel was a hundred miles long, at least. All convention centers were circuitous and hard to navigate, but I had never seen one as confusing as this place.

Luckily, Sh'va'na knew exactly where she was going, and eventually, the hallway broke into a wide show floor. I worried that nobody would be able to find it, but my fears were partially alleviated when I saw my friend Tim setting up his booth a couple down from where Sh'va'na led me.

He never did bad shows and was the one who told me about this convention.

"Oh, thank the gods you're here, buddy," I said, shaking his hand. "I was worried you wouldn't make it."

"Are you kidding me, man?" he replied with a southern twang in his voice. "We need a new dishwasher, so I can't miss out on a way to make some money."

Tim sold old comic books and trinkets, so his sales were always good no matter where he went, as long as the people that came to the convention had a sense of nostalgia about them…and they always did.

It was easy to set up my booth. I had only published three books in my Cthulhu Howard, P.I. series, so I had a tablecloth, some books, and a few stands to set up around my table, along with a free print for signing up for my newsletter and bookmarks to draw people over to the table.

"Do you wanna go exploring?" Tim asked when I was done setting up. "Or do you still need to check in?"

"Both, but it doesn't matter to me. Maybe one and then the other."

Tim thought that sounded like a good idea, so we set out back into the hotel, waving and chatting with the other vendors as we passed. I brought my own food from home, but Tim always liked having a drink at the hotel bar after set-up, so I said I would join him. I had no idea where we were as we darted left and right, but Tim seemed to be an old ham at navigating the windy corridors.

"I loved this place as a kid, man," he said when we finally reached the bar in the lobby. "My mom was a maid here before we moved down south, and I guess the directions just stayed with me, wandering these halls as a kid."

"It reminds me of *The Shining*," I said as a bartender brought us two beers.

"You're not wrong. Kubrick stayed here once, and it never left him."

"You're messing with me."

"Nope. I met him once. Weird guy. I got these," Tim said, pulling a twenty out and sliding it to the bartender. "Keep the change."

Tim was a generous man. He took pity on me when I started out, and showed me the ropes of conventions, helped me hone my sales pitch, and made sure I was choosing the right shows so I didn't lose my shirt. He also knew how tough it had been for me lately and was the one who told me about the show in the first place.

"I just hope it's a good show, man," I said to him. "I can't have another bad one. It feels like each one is worse than the one before it."

"You'll get your mojo back," Tim said, taking a sip. "We all go through dry spells. I have a good feeling about this place. You're a great writer, and I'll bet your fans show up this time."

I didn't have many fans, outside of the few I met at conventions at least. I made decent sales online, but the only real money was at shows for me, and that money was drying up fast.

"Yeah," I sighed, chugging my beer. "I hope so, but I'm not as confident as you about it. Maybe I should go back to selling shoes."

"Yuck. Don't do that. I think it'll be different this time. This is the one that'll turn it around for you. I mean, it's a Cthulhu convention, and you sell a Cthulhu book. If you can't clean up here, you should get out of the selling books business."

He said it as a joke, but it dug into my gut because that was what I feared. Tim had staked me for this show, and I owed him my table fee if I made it back, but it had been a long time since I cleared three hundred dollars at a convention. I was running out of money for buying tables, and we were already barely scraping by with two, let alone a third mouth to feed in a couple of months. If things didn't turn around soon, I would have no choice but to stop chasing the dream.

After finishing our beers, I said goodbye to Tim and went to check in for my room. The crowd had died down, and I could walk up to a dark-skinned woman who was itching her skin. "Hello, I'm checking into my room. Shadrack Magilicutty. I booked—"

She held up her finger. "Sh'ad'rack."

I nodded. "Magilicutty, yes."

She looked at me for a long moment, and I swore I watched her eyes blink sideways before she looked down at her computer screen and typed very slowly onto it. "Sssss-hh-aa-ddd-raaa-ck."

"It's probably under Magilicutty," I replied, but she didn't seem to care.

"Eee'ar'ly," she groaned out to me when she finally looked back up.

I nodded. "Yes, that's right. I know I'm early, but I was hoping to check in with my bags before the convention started and freshen up. If you don't have a room…"

"Fi've. Th'ree. Se'e'ven." She reached down and slowly scrawled it on a piece of paper and then turned and pulled an old, thick key off the wall. When she turned to me again, she screeched into the air. "Sh'va'na."

Sh'va'na rushed forward and took the key. She pointed ahead and then started to scuttle along toward the elevator. "Sh'va'na."

The halls were nowhere less confusing upstairs, but at least the rooms were numbered. I took notes of them while we walked, and soon enough, I was at my room. Sh'va'na opened the door with the key and left it in the door for me. "Sh'va'na."

I walked inside and went to hand her a tip, but by the time I turned around, she was gone. Weird people worked here, but at least they were nice. I pulled the key and closed the door before falling into the bed.

I shouldn't have even gotten a room. Two hours wasn't that far to drive every night, but Tim told me I had to do it, and after he staked me for the table, I felt I owed it to him, so I said yes. Now, I regretted it.

I threw my clothes into the ancient dresser and watched the wallpaper peel as I texted Harriet and told her I was in the room and everything would be okay. However, I wasn't sure anything would be okay. Harriet had a decent job that paid for our mortgage, but with every weekend that passed, the baby came closer and closer. How could I let my wife care for a baby while I pursued some stupid dream?

I talked to her often about giving it up, and she constantly told me that I would be miserable doing anything else and that our child should know that her daddy loved his life…but did I love this? Did I love being gone every weekend, begging people to try my books out, watching them walk around with $20 cups of root beer they would consume in ten minutes and telling me my book was too expensive? Looking through me with dead eyes like I didn't even exist? Was this really better than selling vacuums or cell phones? At least then, I didn't take it personally when people rejected me.

I must have worried myself to sleep because the next thing I knew, it was dark, and there was a banging on my door. I opened it to find Tim on the other side, smiling at me. "Come on, buddy. It's just about time."

I looked down at my watch. It was 7 pm. *Oh crap.* I had missed a whole day at the convention. This was not good. "Oh my god. I can't believe I missed the whole convention. Harriet is going to kill me."

"You didn't miss much," Tim said. "The real convention starts in ten minutes."

I cocked my head to one side. "I don't—the flier said it started at 11 am. I was just coming to lie down for a minute, and I wasted the whole day."

"Oh…yeah…" he said. "That's not the convention I wanted you to come to. Follow me. You've gotta see this."

He pulled me out of my room, confused and bitter at myself. We zig-zagged through the halls again and made it back to the lobby. There was an eerie green glow about the whole place that was amplified by the fluorescent lights everywhere. Convention-goers muddled through the halls, talking to each other, and a tightness grew in my stomach.

I had blown it.

When we got to the convention floor, I was confused to see all the vendors still at their tables, talking to each other, chit-chatting and ready for something I had no idea was coming. Usually, when the convention floor closed to attendees, the vendors rushed to the doors.

"I don't understand." The doors slammed behind me, and it made me jump. "What's happening?"

Tim slapped me on the back. "The best convention ever is about to start. Get to your table."

I did what he said, shaking my head for a few minutes until a huge light shot from atop us and then turned into a calming blue. At that moment, the doors to the back of the convention floor opened, and hundreds of maids and bellhops wandered inside. They all moved uncomfortably in their skin as they ambled around toward the tables, looking at the tables with a little amusement.

I watched as Sh'va'na walked through the door and strolled up to me, looking at her feet. She reached into her purse and pulled out all three volumes of my book and a pen. "Sh'va'na."

"She wants you to sign them, mate!" Tim shouted, and I was very confused. "She's your biggest fan."

"How is that possible? She didn't say a word to me except her name. And how do you understand her?"

"We'll talk about it later." Tim waved me off. "Just sign the dang books."

I turned back to Sh'va'na and complied with her request, signing all three of her books. Then, she looked down at my table, pointed to all three of the books there, made a five with her fingers, and then nodded. "Sh'va'na."

"You want five of each?" I asked.

She nodded and made a signing motion with her hand. "Sh'va'na."

I smiled and counted out five of each book. I signed them, and she gladly paid me for them with a big smile on her face. Her teeth were sharp, like those of sharks, but her excitement was palpable. Her eyes were wide with wonder, and I swore I saw her eyes blink vertically instead of horizontally, but she was exceptionally happy. When she had paid and scooped up her books, she turned to a group of other bellhops and showed them the books, pointing at me.

The other bellhops' eyes went wide. They rushed over to me, growling and clicking to each other. They pointed to my books and made signing motions with their hands.

"What is happening?" I mumbled to myself.

"I told you, you just had to find your audience, bud," Tim said. "You're famous in certain circles. You just had to find them."

I sold out of all my books in the first two hours and had to dip into my excess stock in my suitcase. Once I was done with the day, I had a hundred pre-orders for books I had to bring back the following morning and had my best day at a convention ever by a wide margin.

When the bellhops were gone and the maids had cleaned me out even more, I walked over to Tim. I handed him three hundred dollars for the table. "I think this is yours."

"Good day, then?" he asked with a wide grin.

"I have no idea what just happened."

He looked at my table. "Looks like you'll have to go home tomorrow and get more books."

"I absolutely do," I said. "Who are those people?"

"They're your fans," he replied. "And they're my people. I showed your books to my mom, and she passed them around. Everyone loves them here. You're a really talented writer."

"I swear I saw their eyes blink vertically, man, and their teeth—I don't think they are human."

I watched as Tim pulled out a tooth from his mouth to reveal a sharp tooth underneath. Then, I watched as he blinked horizontally, and then vertically, and then horizontally again. "Is that a problem?"

"I—" I looked down at my wad of cash. "I guess not. Their money spends just like anyone else's."

"That's the right attitude. I thought you would be cool with it." He leaned forward. "You'll have to excuse Sh'va'na and the others. They haven't been on land long. They'll learn how to be human more as they get to know the surface."

I placed my hands on the table. "Are they—" an idea crossed my mind, too crazy to express to anyone but Tim, "—Deep Ones?"

He winced. "We don't like that term, but let us just say H.P. Lovecraft revealed many things he shouldn't have."

"Was—he a De—one of you?"

Tim placed his hand on his lips and nodded. "Luckily, people think it is just myth and legend. We have done a good job of that."

My eyes furrowed, but I only had one question left. "Are there other cons like this?"

He chuckled. "Oh, so many."

It was a revelation. I couldn't believe I had found a group that loved my books. I didn't even care that they were monsters. They treated my work with reverence. They rushed to me and they ran off to read the books with glee and gusto. Were they really even monsters at all, if they could make me feel like my work had value?

"How about dinner?" I asked Tim, holding up my cash. "I'm buying."

I couldn't wait to show Harriet. She would never believe it. I barely believed it, but I wasn't going to turn up my nose at the best con day ever or the best group of humans I ever met…even if they were not human at all.

THERE ARE NO JOBS ON A DEAD PLANET

Originally appeared in "After the Fall"

THEY ROSE FROM the deep on a Wednesday. Disgusting, soulless creatures from the bottom of the ocean. The USA was the last government to fall to their rule. They lasted until Friday. Since then, for the last twenty years, we have lived under their constant watchful eye. Every move dissected. Every minute cataloged.

If you were a good boy and cowed to their rule, then they kept you fat and docile. If you worshiped them, they showed you mercy. Mercy for the frogs meant you became like them. There was no bigger compliment.

Most were captured or served voluntarily, but some of us, the lucky few, escaped their reign. We lived in the trees. We did not play by their rules. We became the hunters.

Their flesh was rancid and vile, but they had destroyed the ecosystem and salted the earth. There was no food left except that which they provided their followers, so we made do with what remained. The Deep Ones, they are called, but to us, they were dinner.

"Hazel!" a young, brunette boy shouted at me as he waved his arms toward me. "Come on. We're going to be late."

That was Tyler, my boyfriend. I grew up in the trees, and so did Tyler. We were born after The Rise, as my father called it. He died two years ago. My mother died ten years before that. We are the only two children of the tree who survived until adulthood. The rest of the young in our tribe died long ago.

I pushed myself to my feet and looked down at the canopy below us. The Deep Ones feared heights, so the only way to be safe was to live high above the ground, in the highest trees we could find.

"I'm coming!" I shouted back to him as I ran across the rope bridge that connected our bungalows.

There were few things we enjoyed in this life, but Tyler and I loved the hunt. I loved to send my arrows through the neck of Dagon's minions. I relished killing them, and so did Tyler. They took our parents. The least we could do was take their lives.

"We're going to be late," Tyler said, grabbing my hand and dragging me along across the canopy toward the main bungalow where the rest of our hunting group gathered.

We might not be the last of humanity, but that was how it felt. Once the frog god welcomed you, your body morphed to become like him. Your eyes bulged out of your head. You became scaly. Gills grew out of the sides of your neck. You ceased to be human.

Perhaps other tribes of humanity survived throughout the world, but for all we knew, we were the last of the humans living on a dead planet.

I poked my head into the bungalow and surveyed the night's hunting party. Every night it got smaller and smaller. Tonight, there were only four of us, including Tyler and me.

"Thank you all for coming," Jill, our commander, said. She was a mortgage banker before the Rise. Everybody was somebody else before the Rise, but like my father always said, "there are no jobs in a dead world".

Her eyes were once a bright blue, but I watched them fade with time as the dark circles filled in under them. We used to be two hundred strong, and now we were less than 20, and every time she lost somebody, it weighed on her conscience more and more.

Next to her stood Otto, who lived for hunting, even before a hunter's life was forced on him. He was a nothing before the Rise, and now he was second in command. He may be one of the few that benefited from the Rise, if you can call living out your masturbatory survival fantasies benefiting from the end of the world.

"We're going to hit a sector we haven't hunted in a while," Jill started, pointing to the corkboard where we kept a map of the forest. "The frogs are getting restless. It's becoming harder and harder to hunt without getting caught."

"They're closing in on us," Tyler muttered to me.

"That's correct," Jill replied. "But we're not going to let them find us. With any luck, we'll gather enough food tonight to last for a couple of months. Then, we can plan our escape."

Jill had talked about our escape for years now, but it never materialized. It was hard to move on from this place. We were warm here. We knew the land. We knew the frogs in Innsmouth as well as we knew ourselves. Who knew what waited for us beyond the horizon?

Still, we couldn't stay here much longer. The frogs knew who we were and that we were a problem. Frogs didn't like problems. They liked to be in control of everything, which made us a threat, and every day they came closer to eliminating us.

"We'll break up into two teams," Jill continued. "Hazel, you and Tyler take the east. Otto and I will take the west. With any luck, we'll be back by sunset."

Frogs liked the darkness. Their eyes still hadn't grown accustomed to life on the surface, so the cover of light was our best defense against them.

"We're ready," Tyler said, nodding.

"We won't let you down," I added.

"You never have before," Jill replied.

Tyler and I ran from the main bungalow into the munitions tent next to it. When we were stronger, we spent days raiding Innsmouth for weapons. As our numbers dwindled, so did our need to restock. There were enough guns and ammo in our munitions tent to survive for decades.

I didn't like guns, though. I preferred a bow and arrow. They were silent and just as deadly if you used them right. I picked up my trusty bow and placed a quiver of arrows on my back.

"Your love of that arcane tech is going to get you killed one day," Tyler said.

"Maybe," I replied. "But it didn't help any of the others survive."

"Morbid."

"True, though."

We didn't talk about the dead much. We tried to stay focused on the living and on moving forward, but it was hard not to think about them, especially in the dark of night, when the frogs scattered below us, when they were so close you could hear them breathe.

Why was I still here, after all? Better men and women than me were gone. Was there a reason for me to be spared while I watched them be torn limb from limb?

Not likely. It was probably dumb luck. Dumb, stupid luck. I turned left at just the right moment, or I chose not to go out on a raid when hunters attacked the wrong frogs. We all had stories of why we survived, and we all carried the guilt with us of the fallen dead.

Of my mother.

Of my father.

Of the love of my life.

"Let's go," Tyler said. "I wanna kill some frogs already!"

"Alright," I replied with a chuckle. "There will be plenty of chances. They're multiplying like crazy these days. Seems like every time we go out, there's more and more."

"Probably are," Tyler said, walking along a rope bridge toward the bicycles which let us drop below the canopies. "New ones come up from the deep every day."

My father designed the bicycle elevators we used to descend below the canopy. Thick ropes looped around each tire frame, and the bike acted as its own pulley to bring you above and below the canopy. All you needed to do was take your feet off the brake to descend and pedal again to rise. My dad was a genius that way.

He was a genius in a lot of ways, but that didn't stop him from getting killed.

Nothing could stop you from being killed when it was your time. I watched the greatest warriors in our pack fall while meek children lived. I watched the young perish while the old remained. I've seen the healthy ripped to shreds while the feeble continued with their lives. It was random. It was chance. That was what we had to tell ourselves.

"Are you alright?" Tyler asked me as I hopped onto the bike elevator, which would take us down below the canopy.

"Yeah," I replied as I kicked off the brake and started to descend.

I lied. I wasn't alright. I had been on the hunt a hundred times before, but never on the anniversary of my father's death. Before, they would rotate out shifts of hunters, and I always asked for this day off.

That was when we had enough hunters to have a rotation. We didn't anymore, so I was always on the prowl.

The pedals flipped backward on the bicycle as we descended under the canopy and landed on the platform designed to hold our bikes while we hunted. Without the bikes, there was no way back up above the treeline.

"You ready?" Tyler asked.

I wasn't ready, but I couldn't let on that I was hampered by my thoughts. Tyler lost people, too. His mother. His father. The love of his life. We were the same in that respect. We understood each other. I knew in my heart that he didn't love me, but I didn't love him either. We were just the best each other could do given the circumstances.

"I'm fine. Let's get this over with."

The canopy hid much of the light from the sun. Even in the light of midday, frogs were active under the trees. However, the day was when most of them slept, so it was easier to hunt without being caught.

The branches of the old forest twisted and turned into each other, allowing us to move freely from tree to tree with ease. In the beginning, many of us fell to our deaths navigating the trees, but that didn't happen anymore. The only people left had excellent balance.

We hopped across tree limbs for over a mile. We didn't hunt near our base. That was how we survived for so long. The frogs didn't know where we were. They only knew we came like the night and left just as fast.

"Hold," Tyler said in front of me after a half-hour scampering through the trees. "I see one."

The trick of hunting frogs was to find one patrolling alone. They usually traveled in packs of two, even more so these days, so finding a lone frog was somewhat of a rarity.

"How close are we to a lift?" I asked.

Tyler scanned the trees to triangulate our location. When I was a child, the trees confused me, but once Daddy taught me what to look for, they became easy to navigate, even without a map.

"300 meters, give or take."

"Go," I replied. "I'll make sure it doesn't get away."

Tyler gave me a peck on the cheek and ran off through the canopy. It didn't take long before he disappeared through the thicket.

Hunting frogs was always a two-person job. One hunter stayed in the canopy as a lookout, and the other took a wooden elevator down to the ground to retrieve the carcass.

Given a choice, you always wanted to remain in the tree. Most of our men died on the ground, retrieving a fresh kill.

Usually, we drew straws to see who would take the rope elevator to the ground, but tonight Tyler volunteered. Maybe it was because he knew it was a tough day for me. Maybe it was because he felt like doing something nice. Either way, I was grateful.

I eyed the frog on the ground as it knelt to tie its shoe. Tyler needed to hurry. I didn't want to take a shot until I knew he was on the ground, ready to retrieve the body. The longer the carcass sat, the greater chance it would be found by another patrol.

Soon, I wouldn't have a choice, though. I couldn't let it disappear into the brush. I pulled my bow from behind my back and took out an arrow from my quiver.

Tyler didn't like the bow. He said it wasn't accurate, but he didn't train with it, either. I was deadly accurate with it. I could hit a quarter from a hundred meters nearly every time.

I stepped forward onto a sturdy branch until the target was right below me. I watched as the frog reached into its pocket and pulled something out.

It was a phone. The screen lit up, and it slid its slimy fingers over it. My father told me about phones and how he used them to communicate with people all over the world. He told me you could do all sorts of things with one, like use the dictionary and read books. They sounded magical.

The frog reached into its pocket and pulled out a pair of white headphones.

Music.

It was listening to music. I knew about music. Sometimes, my father would sing to me. Sometimes we would sing together, but we could never listen to music on command. The frogs stole that from us.

Frogs had taken everything and left us with nothing. Now, this one was listening to music, just as if it were human. No, not like a human, not like us, better than us.

Fire fueled my belly. I placed the arrow in my bow and pulled back until the string grazed my ear. I wasn't in a rush. I could take my time. The frog was right out in the open. It didn't have a care in the world.

I took a deep breath and steadied myself. My heartbeat fell, and a calm washed over me. I never felt bad killing a frog. They weren't human. They were evil.

I released my finger, and the bow snapped back. The arrow flew through the air. My aim was true. Before the frog could look up, the arrow embedded into the top of its skull, and it fell over, dead. Frogs died just as easily as people.

I looked up to see Tyler run across the grass toward the frog. I feared I struck too soon, but I had timed it perfectly. I knew Tyler's movements. I knew how long it took him to reach the ground.

And I was right.

That was the benefit of working with somebody for so long. You started to know their movements. It wasn't love, but it was appreciation, and there wasn't much more we could hope for in these dark days.

Tyler looked up at me and gave me a smile. His smile was warm and soft. He threw the frog around his back and disappeared again into the darkness. Tonight was a success. We did our job, and we did it well.

I rushed across the canopy to find Tyler. Tonight, we dined on frog. Tonight, we ate well.

THE BLACKSMITH

Originally appeared in "Wailing Blade"

THE BLADE WAS never meant to be a bringer of death but a symbol of peace. That is why it wails when it takes a life. It cries for the blood shed by it and for those that tremble before it.

Before recorded time, two gods sent the whole galaxy into a terrible war, one that pitted tribe against tribe and brother against brother. It was ceaseless and unyielding, lasting a hundred generations, until one day, a humble and lowly blacksmith lost his only daughter in battle and went about constructing his greatest weapon ever, The Wailing Blade.

He poured into it all his grief, anger, and sadness and then traveled across the galaxy to deliver a message to the wicked gods who took his beloved child from him. The journey was perilous, and he nearly died a hundred times on his trek, but eventually, he reached the battle line. He offered the gods a choice—end the war or face his blade.

They laughed at the weak, frail, trembling man who dared threaten them. With this last insult, the blacksmith gripped the blade tightly and became the first executioner.

His might was so great with his newfound power he destroyed both gods in a single battle. With the treacherous deities dead, he declared the war over and that peace would reign over the galaxy from that day forward.

He ruled over the greatest era of peace in the whole history of the galaxy, but even great men die, and when the blacksmith went into the great beyond, the peace could not hold. Corrupt men took the blade and twisted its aim, subjugating whole planets under their thumb…killing each other to grasp its power…until it ended up here…and we were cursed with the incredible power held inside its cutting edge.

One day, the righteous will wield the sword again, and there will be peace. Or at least that's what I heard.

OUT OF THE FRYING PAN

Originally appeared in "War for Monster Earth"

"CAN YOU DESCRIBE the monster, please?"

Chip Willaby was used to driving up and down Queensland handling insurance claims. After all, he had been doing it for the past twenty years. He remembered the day, fourteen years ago, that the "egg," as they called it in the trade, set down on the Gold Coast, decimating Robina and Burleigh Heads in its wake.

He had mentally prepared for the possibility of it opening, or so he thought, but when a giant hippopotamus emerged from the egg and started to rampage west across the country, leaving a path of destruction, he realized there was a difference between being mentally prepared and actually prepared. It turned out that he was not, in any respect, actually prepared.

Australia had its own monster, of course, just like those from other countries, except theirs was a monstrous koala. It had a habit of swimming in the ocean, which made it even more dangerous-looking than its hundred-foot frame. A dry koala could look cuddly, adorable even, but soak it with water, and it was horrific and blood-curdling in its ferociousness, as if all its flurry fur hid murderous intent underneath, much like his first wife. He was lucky he had only encountered the beast three times in his life, and it was from hundreds of yards away each time.

"Well, it was a giant hippo, wasn't it?" the woman said, exasperated, as she hopped from one foot to the other.

Maria McCormick had lost her home to the Coker monster, which was their official name. Dissemblers warned of them for decades, but Chip always found them silly. His brother was a believer, but even after the five eggs landed on Earth and everything the Dissemblers had predicted started to come to pass, Chip couldn't bring himself to do anything but chuckle when his brother spouted their gospel. It seemed so far-fetched, so absurd, and yet, it was all true.

"Not a koala?" Chip asked. "You need to be very sure, ay? It's very important that you are positive."

The eggs hatching threw everything Chip knew about the world into stark relief. What if the Bible was true, too? What if there would one day be an actual rapture, and the antichrist returned to roam the world? What if the entire universe danced in the mind of an ancient Aziolith, and if it woke, reality would crumble upon itself? His mind went to dark places when he spiraled, which was why he preferred to keep busy. There were plenty of new claims across the country, and Chip took as many as he could to ease his troubled mind in these dark times.

"You think I don't know the difference between a hippo and a koala?" Maria McCormick fumed. "I got two eyes, and that frigging monster was a hundred feet tall. I'm telling you it was a hippo." Maria took a long drag of a cigarette as she looked back at the pile of kindling that used to be her house. "Eleven years I was in that house, and some monster came along and destroyed it all in the snap of my fingers."

Chip didn't like to deliver bad news, but it was part of his job. In his experience, there were only two options when people heard bad news: either they broke down into a heap of tears in front of him, or they rose up in a fit of violent rage. He sized Maria up for a moment and didn't know what to make of her, so in an abundance of caution, he inched back toward the black Holden Commodore he won for having the highest clearance rate in the whole company three years ago.

Maria was older, and her legs were heavy with a lifetime of inhaling junk food like it was oxygen, while Chip kept in decent shape in case he needed to make a quick escape from a furious customer. He slipped his hand into his pocket and held his finger over the button which would unlock his car in an emergency.

"I'm sorry, ma'am, but seeing as you don't have comprehensive coverage, your property is not covered."

She narrowed her eyes at Chip. "What do you mean, comprehensive coverage?"

Chip swallowed his fear. "Well, see, our base policy covers you against Kota—the koala monster, as you know—but it doesn't cover any other monsters, like the hippo that ravaged your home. Had you upgraded to our comprehensive policy—oh, it looks like you did have that policy, but you let it lapse several years ago."

"We ain't never had any monster but Kota since I can remember. Why would I need to pay more for something I didn't need?"

Chip stepped back again. "Well, for exactly this scenario. We tried to reach out to all our customers when the egg—or the Coker Object to be more formal—landed, and we have been running ads for years touting the benefits of being protected with a compreh—"

"So, what the heck am I supposed to do?" She waved her hand at the pile of broken wood that was all that remained of her home. "You telling me I ain't got no home now?"

"What I am saying is that any damage is entirely your responsibility at this time."

"You arrogant little—"

Maria took a long drag of her cigarette and advanced toward Chip, who spun nimbly on his feet and lunged for the passenger side door. When he was safely inside his car, he locked the door and crawled over to the driver's seat.

"I'm afraid this is not the problem of the Noble Insurance Company. If you feel as if I've made an error, you can file an appeal, but I promise I am very thorough. I am sorry for your loss."

"Get out here!" Maria said, cigarette in mouth, smashing against the window. Chip turned the key in his ignition, but instead of the pleasant sound of an engine turning over, he heard a shriek rip through the air. He looked over to Maria on instinct and saw her looking up into the sky, the cigarette barely hanging on to her bottom lip.

Chip squinted and looked up into the air, where he saw an enormous black bat blot out the sun and soar past. As the shriek dissipated into the distance, the whirling of three helicopters followed close behind, and a bad feeling sank into his stomach. Luckily, there were plenty of other claims to tamp down his anxiety.

* * *

Dr. Nozomi McClaren hadn't slept in two days, except for a few moments in the Eagle before it landed in Brisbane. She kept herself awake from a combination of coffee and energy bars, which tasted like somebody from another planet was told what food on Earth tasted like, then made their best guess based on their limited data set. It was sorta kinda food, but barely.

She had been on the phone constantly since leaving London, and when she wasn't on the phone, she was working with Dr. Clark Bennett to run predictive models on the best course of action. It was one thing to have the buy-in from the nations of the world and quite another thing to coordinate a global response to the Coker Objects in real-time.

Still, after hours of planning, she was ready to enact phase one of her plan. She wasn't supremely confident with it, but it was the best twenty hours could muster. Think tanks had been running models for years about what to expect when the eggs opened, and Bennett had plugged all their data in and combined them with his to run their analysis.

She chose Australia as the first prong of her plan because the interior of the country was sparsely populated, and funneling the giant hippo that emerged from the Coker Object on the Gold Coast into a relatively uninhabited part of the country would be easier than doing so just about anywhere else on Earth.

If the monsters could contain the threat as she expected, then she could create bottleneck funnels all over the world and isolate the Coker monsters until they could find a way to kill them.

"We're coming up on Uluru now, ma'am," the helicopter pilot told her as it flew across the Australian outback. They left Joe Bantam at the airport to await their return, along with their suitcases, save for a small go bag that contained computers, vials for collecting fluid from the monsters, and other essentials, and picked up a helicopter pilot to take them the rest of the way to the temporary Army base outside of Uluru, which had been constructed with ruthless efficiency.

McClaren always enjoyed coming into the desert and getting lost for days at a time. However, this time she would be surrounded by coalition forces from Australia, the United States, Japan, and Vietnam.

The Vietnamese didn't have much of a military, but they insisted their people be involved if they were to use the country's Shrieker to fight against the hippo. McClaren had a theory that while the hides of the Coker monsters were thicker than even the many monsters she had dealt with in her career, perhaps they would be susceptible to soundwaves, and she needed the Shrieker to test her theory.

As she saw the great plateau of Uluru break across the horizon, she chuckled at the idea that all of science was little more than guesses and hunches. There was no good reason the sound should work against the Coker monster, except that animals were often sensitive to it. She could have just as easily started with any other senses, but she had to start somewhere, and her gut screamed to try sound first. If she was right, she might be able to cut the Coker monsters down early, but she could have just as easily been sending the Shrieker to its doom against a more powerful monster.

"How much further?" McClaren asked, her voice already hoarse from talking non-stop for the past day.

"We'll be passing the blockade in about three minutes," Bennett replied from the seat next to her.

The rest of her team was spread across the world, working to contain the other monsters and coordinate the laboratories where she would send samples once she could gather some from the hippo. Bennett, though, McClaren trusted above the rest, but more importantly, he filled in a gap for her, and a big one. She held degrees in biology, chemistry, and physics, but her weak spot was engineering and statistical analysis, which was exactly Bennett's strength.

"There!" Bennett said as a sea of soldiers rose on the horizon. The armies of the world were more accommodating to using their military assets than their monsters, and within hours of her leaving London, super weapons from around the world were flooding into Australia until they had an arsenal that could kill any monster on the planet. Similar stockpiles were being accumulated around the world to fight the other monsters, and McClaren hoped that Bennett's new specs could help an unknown foe.

Five minutes later, McClaren and Bennett were running from the dust kicked up from the helicopter as it settled on the ground. General Octavius Johnson stood at attention and gave an enthusiastic salute when they finally cleared the helicopter.

"Good to see you, Dr. McClaren," he said gruffly as if he gargled with the coarse desert sand. "I wish it were under better circumstances."

"Me, too, General. Are you set up?"

The general turned on his heels and nodded. "Yes, ma'am. We have enough firepower here to blow the world to bits several times over." His head cocked toward Bennett. "Thank you for the new specs. Our boys have been working around the clock to meet them. Let's hope they work."

"They'll work," Bennett said confidently before a worried look washed across his face. "I think they'll work. I hope they'll work."

McClaren had been working with Bennett long enough that she knew when he needed saving. "Where are the monsters?"

"Kota was walkabout in Papua New Guinea, but he made landfall earlier today. He'll be here shortly, but not until a few minutes after the hippo arrives."

"That's not good news," McClaren said. "What about the Shrieker?"

"Seemed to have a mind of its own for a while," The general replied as they reached a tent city in the desert with hundreds of men and women in army fatigues rushing around to their assignments. "However, our soldiers finally got it on track. It's flying across Queensland right now. It should be here soon after Kota. Luckily, that crazy bat is three times faster than the hippo."

The general ducked into the tent, but McClaren didn't follow. Instead, she looked out on the horizon, where the shadow of a giant hippo lumbered toward them. Hippos were the most dangerous animal on Earth when angered, and that was just what they planned to do. It was about to start, and all her theories would be put into practice, and either she would be right, or she would be responsible for a lot of death and destruction.

It was in moments like these that she hated science as much as she loved it.

* * *

"With any luck," McClaren told the general, "we'll be able to hold the hippo up for a little while."

"How long is a little while?" General Johnson replied.

"It's hard to tell. If we're lucky, a couple of days. It all depends if we can tire the hippo out quickly. We're hoping it has the same metabolism as a normal animal in its class, but—"

"And what if luck's not on our side?" the general said. "Lady luck has never been kind to me."

Bennett pulled a laptop out of his carrying bag and slid it onto the table between them. He typed furiously and then spun the computer toward the general. "I've run thirty-six thousand scenarios plugging in every imaginable power level for Kota, the Shrieker, and the hippo. Even in the worst-case scenario, we should be able to stop the hippo in its tracks and stop its rampage. If we can even hold it up for a few hours, the towns behind us can finish evacuating."

The general chuckled. "I have found that usually, the worst-case scenario becomes the best-case scenario when shit hits the fan."

"All we have are our predictions right now," McClaren said. "If the Dissembling are to be believed, then nothing on Earth can stop these monsters, and if that's the case, we're all doomed. So, while I respect and appreciate what you're saying, General, I prefer not to go into any situation thinking the worst unless the worst is called for."

"And if it is?"

"Then may God have mercy on our souls."

The general stood up and nodded. "First contact with the enemy is always the worst. Once we have a handle on what we're dealing with, we'll recalibrate and regroup, but for now, I suppose you are right, Doctor. All that's left to do is fight the battle."

He walked over to a makeshift wardrobe and pulled out a metal helmet that fit over his head and made him look like the spitting image of General Patton. "I've had this helmet since 'Nam. Three tours of duty and not a scratch on her. Let's hope that continues through today."

"I hope so, General," McClaren said. She looked over at Bennett, but he had nothing to say. When the general was gone, she narrowed her eyes at Bennett. "You didn't tell him the worst of it."

Bennett pushed up. "What's the need? If it goes tits up, then the whole world has a lot more to worry about than my stupid predictions."

"They aren't stupid," McClaren said. "In ten percent of the scenarios, the hippo tore through Kota in a matter of minutes. That's not an outlier."

"Which is why we brought in the Shrieker, right? When both of them were attacking together, that number went down to less than one percent. They just have to make sure not to attack without the other one, and we should be fine."

McClaren sighed, bowing her head. "You know it's not that easy to control monsters."

"I know you quite literally have the world on your shoulders, but no matter how this goes, you are doing the best you can." Bennett touched McClaren's shoulder, and a deep sadness rolled through him. If this really was the end, he wanted to tell the woman he loved for as long as he'd known her about his true feelings, but he couldn't bear to add more to her already overburdened mind. So, instead, he simply gave a comforting squeeze and let go. "Do you want to watch?"

"No," she said, faking a smile. "But what choice do I have?"

She watched Bennett push the flap on the entrance away and walk outside, and while she wanted to move forward, her feet felt like lead as she tried to raise them. Every bit of the fear she felt in her gut had cemented her to the ground.

"It's going to be okay." She didn't believe it, but sometimes just saying the words were enough to trick herself. "It's going to be okay."

She took a deep breath, and her leg lurched forward, then the other, until she was standing outside the tent, the bright sun of the Australian outback glaring down on her.

"Care to give the order?" the general asked, holding the phone out to her.

"No," she said. She couldn't imagine calling in the order that sent so many into danger and perhaps to their deaths. Somehow, she convinced herself that if she didn't make the final order, she wasn't culpable if her plan went pear-shaped, but of course, simultaneously, her logical brain knew that she was uniquely responsible, possibly the most responsible in the whole world. Everyone was looking at her, and, summoning all her courage, she lunged for the phone and grabbed it before the general could put it to his mouth. "On second thought…" She placed the phone to her lips. "Initiate the attack."

Once it was done, she dropped the phone to the ground and covered her mouth. Her stomach heaved, and a bit of bile gurgled up into her mouth, but she swallowed it down. She had always been so confident and in control of every situation, but now, at the end, when it was all on the line, she doubted everything she had ever done.

Now, she could do nothing but watch, and she hated being so helpless. The general picked up the phone and brushed the sand off from it being dropped. "You heard the doctor. Start the attack."

McClaren wanted to turn away, but as the cannons and tanks began to fire on the monster approaching over the horizon, all she could do was stare forward as the barrage found its target. The one thing about the monsters of the world was that they were easy to hit. They stood as tall as skyscrapers and moved slower than molasses.

She knew, though, that the attack, even if it were successful, would infuriate the hippo, and when angry, they were maniacally vicious. The explosions rocked all around the monster and plumed dust high into the sky. The cannons fired a second and third round, the ground shaking with every explosion from their mammoth guns. McClaren placed her hands over her ears at the sound of the explosions, and the general handed her a bright orange pair of earphones that muzzled the sound tremendously.

When she turned back to the battlefield, the smoke and dust were clearing, and her stomach dropped back to her feet as she saw the hippo stomp forward as if the attack hadn't registered at all.

* * *

"Fire again!" the general screamed into the phone, and the barrage of cannons exploded again, hurling their payload across the outback. "AGAIN!"

Bennett knew that the firepower of the cannons would not likely stop the hippo, but he hoped it would be enough to slow it down. However, the hippo barely seemed to stumble at the retrofitted specs from his newly improved weaponry. Of course, when it came to ammunition, it took time to manufacture and process new parts and more powerful ammo, which meant that he had a lot of constraints when it came to designing the new weaponry.

He wasn't reliant on just old tanks and cannons, though. Since the Coker Objects landed, scientists had been trying to find a way to penetrate the surface of the objects, and while they all failed, laser technology had improved by a million percent in the past decade.

"Time for the big gun," Bennett said to the general.

The general nodded and twisted the phone tight in his hand. "Time for Project Star Wars."

The military had more than a little contempt for lasers. They didn't go boom, and they didn't explode, so they were far less fun than their bombs. Still, they were extremely effective for certain purposes, and Bennett thought one of those might be piercing the hide of the Coker monsters, especially once the objects opened and he got a look at the synthetic material that made up the interior.

The ground rumbled underneath Bennett as he watched a long, silver monstrosity of a gun roll toward the front line. Even though he had seen blueprints for it, he couldn't help but laugh at the sheer audacity of the laser existing in real life. Unfortunately, there were only a half dozen in the world. If it worked, he hoped they would be able to build more, but for now, it was precious even before his modification, and if his calculations were off even slightly, it could vaporize everyone in a two-mile radius. Of course, if he was right, he hoped it could cut through the monster and give them an early victory.

"I hope you're right," the general muttered as he watched the silver gun glisten in the sun. He raised his hand into the air, and the giant laser stopped. "Go!"

Unlike the cannon, there was no explosion when the laser fired, just a crackling in the air as the invisible beam sizzled through toward the hippo. It was completely unsatisfying. Unlike the movies where red and green light shot through the air, the heat from the laser was invisible, but he knew it was working when the hippo wretched a terrible scream into the air.

"It's working!" Bennett shouted.

"NO! Look!" McClaren said, pointing at the monster, who was now charging forward even faster. "It's just pissing it off!"

"Turn it off!" the general shouted. "Turn it off!"

"Well, that didn't work," Bennett said.

"Call in the airstrike!" McClaren shouted. "Now!"

"Are you sure?" the general asked.

"Unless you want to die!" McClaren said.

The airstrike was the third and final phase of the plan to stall the monster. It involved dropping napalm and enough bombs to destroy any city in the world ten times over on top of it. Even for a bloodhungry general, it seemed excessive, but they didn't have any other choice, and within two minutes, a fleet of bombers streaked past the front lines toward the monster.

McClaren held her breath as the bombers dropped their payload around the monster. The napalm flashed and burned across the sand, and the cloud of smoke was large enough that it could have been mistaken for a nuclear explosion. That was an option, of course, but McClaren decided that nuking the planet was a line even she couldn't cross, at least not until she exhausted all other options.

Again, the smoke cleared, and when McClaren squinted through the dust and soot, she saw the hippo on its knees, winching and coughing. They had done it. They had stopped the hippo from advancing, if even for a moment. Still, when she realized just how much they had to use to stop the monster, her eyes went wide, and then her jaw dropped when she saw the monster rise onto its hind legs and screech into the air, barely fazed by the encounter.

"I think we made it madder," Bennett said.

"Yeah," the general added. "But look."

McClaren craned her neck toward Uluru, the mesa that was the most sacred spot in Australia, as Kota, the monstrous koala, soaking wet, crawled on top of it and looked down at the hippo. Australia was on Kota's turf, and Kota was territorial. McClaren had never seen the Australian monster in person, and she didn't expect to be filled with terror when she finally did but watching the koala's wet fur stick to its hideous skeleton as it roared into the distance, the air left her lungs, and she was awestruck.

Kota surveyed the battlefield in front of him for a moment, then leaped down from the great mesa, thundering the ground for miles, and rushed the hippo, ready for a fight.

*

McClaren knew the odds were against Kota if they came to blows without the Shrieker to help him. Bennett might have blown off a ten percent chance of catastrophe, but she couldn't discount it nearly as easily.

"We can't let them fight!" McClaren said. "That hippo will destroy Kota."

"I don't know what to tell you," the general said. "Those two are pissed at each other, and I know better than to get between two furious, hundred-foot-tall monsters."

"Well, I don't," McClaren said. "Get me into the air."

"You can't be serious!" Bennett shouted. "You're not really going out there."

"You're damn right I am." She clutched her go bag tightly. "This whole plan goes to pot if we can't keep them apart." McClaren turned to the general. "What do you use to keep that thing under control?"

"There's a female koala call that we pipe through the speakers of our helicopters, and it hypnotizes the old boy."

"All helicopters? Including the one I took to get here?"

The general nodded. "We have them fitted to every chopper just in case."

"I'll lead Kota away," McClaren said. "You keep that hippo trained on you."

"That's suicide!" the general shouted.

"No," McClaren replied, running off. "That's war."

The helicopter pilot who brought McClaren to Uluru was sitting outside her chopper, laughing with two other pilots. When McClaren rushed forward, the pilot stood at attention. "Ma'am, what can I do for you?"

McClaren pointed to the impending battle. "I need you to get me out there and lure that big koala away from the hippo."

"That's insane," the pilot said with a smirk. "Alright. Let's do it."

As McClaren turned away from Kota, she saw Bennett running up to her. "Go back, Clark."

Bennett stomped forward. "No way, if you're going to do something stupid, then I'm coming with you."

McClaren ducked into the helicopter. "That was an order."

"Luckily," Bennett said with a smile, "I'm not in the military, so I don't have to follow orders."

"You're still my subordinate, and I need you here."

"Why?" he said. "Being here is gonna be just as dangerous if they can draw that hippo's attention."

McClaren couldn't argue. There was no good place to be, honestly, so she nodded tersely and slid to the other side of the helicopter, bringing her go bag with her. "If we die, I'm gonna be so pissed."

Bennett slid into the back seat and put on a helmet. "I have no doubt you will take it up with my corpse."

The helicopter jerked into the air, kicking up sand as it rose toward the clouds. Once the chopper was airborne, McClaren grabbed onto the seat in front of her and pulled herself up to the pilot. "Get me a direct line to the general."

"Yes, ma'am." The pilot flipped several switches and then nodded. "You're good to go."

"General!" McClaren screamed into her headset. "We need an airstrike between those two monsters right now, or they are never going to stop."

"Roger," the general replied through the crackling speaker.

Two fighter jets appeared out of the sky seconds later and dived-bombed toward the battlefield. As they neared the ground, the jets laid down two rows of machine gun fire across the desert in front of the hippo and Kota, causing them to pull up from their full-speed sprint.

"Good!" McClaren said into the mic. "Now, bring the full squad in to distract the hippo while I get Kota out of there."

There was no response, but out of the clouds, ten more jets appeared, along with a half dozen bombers, and they encircled the hippo like flies. The hippo swatted and swiped at the jets as McClaren neared Kota.

"Pilot!"

"It's Gibbons, ma'am," the pilot replied. "Thought you should know that if we're about to die."

"Alright, Gibbons," McClaren said. "I need you to get close enough to blast Kota's mating call to distract him."

"You think that's going to work?" Bennett said.

"I don't know, but the only thing more powerful than the drive to kill is the drive to mate, so let's hope so." The helicopter slowed down when it got into audio range of Kota. "Ready?"

"Ready!" Gibbons replied. She flipped two switches, and a piercing call came from the speakers.

Kota's ears perked up, and his head swiveled toward the helicopter. When it caught the sound, McClaren tapped on Gibbons's shoulder. "Take it around Uluru, slowly. Make sure Kota follows you."

"Got it."

Gibbons moved the stick around and turned the chopped toward the great mesa behind her. She pushed the stick forward, and the helicopter moved forward slowly. As it did, McClaren looked out the side door, watching as Kota spun toward them.

"Come on, big guy. Come on." Kota cocked his head and took a wobbly step forward toward the ship. "Good, good."

The chopper made a slow turn around Uluru as Kota stumbled behind them. Koalas were not the most coordinated creatures in the world, and they were dumb as rocks, with the smallest head-to-brain ratio of any mammal. They were also mean as sin, which most people didn't realize, having only watched them at zoos, but in the wild, they were exceptionally mean and could fight like the dickens, which was the only reason Kota would have any chance against the genetically modified hippo, and even then, it wouldn't have a good chance alone. McClaren's job was to give it the best chance to win.

Meanwhile, back at the base, the general hadn't lost grip on his phone. He had grown tired of losing jets to an overgrown hippo and was ready to launch an offensive, especially now that Kota was a safe distance away.

"Get out of there!" he screamed into the phone, and the jets began to rise into the air. When the airplanes were a safe distance away, the general turned to his cannons. "Unleash Hell!"

The cannons ground to action, and a successive volley of three rounds echoed across the desert toward the hippo. When they exploded on the hippo's body, the general went back to his radio. "Fighter squadron, fire everything you've got left."

The jets swung down in formation and fired every rocket in their arsenal at the hippo, causing dozens of direct hits, and still, the hippo was barely fazed. As they rose into the air again, the general went to his third wave of attack, knowing it would do little more than anger the hippo.

"Fire the laser!" he screamed into the phone.

The laser crackled to life and fired into the desert. The hippo screeched into the air, first in pain and then in anger, spinning around and dropping back to the ground. It charged at full speed to the front line, and the tanks shot their payload, along with the cannons, at it as the hippo barreled toward them.

"This may be the end," the general mumbled, but then, as he was saying his last goodbyes, Kota smashed into the side of the hippo and sent it skidding across the desert.

The radio crackled to life. "I'm sorry, General. I couldn't let you sacrifice yourself. Not yet, at least."

"You idiot!" the general screamed. "That's what I was trained for. Now, what do we do?"

"Hope the Shrieker will get here soon. Fingers crossed that lady luck is on our side."

* * *

"No, no, no, no, no," McClaren muttered under her breath while she watched the hippo charge the Coalition troops from a hundred feet above the safety of Uluru. She didn't know why it tightened her gut to watch the inevitable battle. It was exactly what she wanted, wasn't it? But witnessing men about to be sent to their death was different than ordering it.

"They're going to get slaughtered," Bennett said, leaning forward toward the window.

"I know!" McClaren barked back to him.

"Do something, Zomi!" Bennett shouted.

There was nothing to do until—Yes, that was it. She pressed the headset close to her lips. "Gibbons, how far out is the Shrieker?"

"Not sure, ma'am," Gibbons replied, flipping several switches on her intercom. "Whiskey Tango Foxtrot, how far out is the payload?"

The radio scratched and crackled to life, and the silence was maddening. Every second they waited was more slaughter brought upon the troops.

"Hurry up!" McClaren shouted.

The radio finally crackled to life. "It'll crest the horizon in two minutes. We're breaking off pursuit. See you on the other side."

McClaren bit her lip. It was a huge gamble, but if she could reinforce Kota's attack with the targeted Coalition bombing, then they should easily be able to hold off the hippo until the Shrieker arrived.

"Let Kota go!" McClaren shouted to Gibbons.

"Are you sure, ma'am?"

"Not at all, but do it anyway."

"The odds are—" Bennett started before McClaren cut him off.

"I know the odds!" McClaren eyed Gibbons. "Do it."

Gibbons nodded, and with the flick of her wrist, the screeching coming from the speakers stopped, and seconds later, Kota shook off his lovestruck stupidity and screeched at the helicopter, rattling it back and forth.

"Let's get out of here," Bennett said.

"You don't have to tell me twice," Gibbons replied, pulling back on the throttle and rising higher into the air.

As the chopper vacated the space in front of Kota, the koala caught sight of the hippo charging the base. It leaped atop Uluru with one jump, and then with a deep growl, the monster took off across the plains, charging at the hippo at full speed.

"Please," McClaren said under her breath, hoping she made the right choice, risking one life to save hundreds.

The hippo was mere feet from the Coalition forces when Kota smashed into it at full speed and sent it rolling across the sand with the force of a major earthquake until it finally skidded to a stop a hundred yards from the front line.

"Yes!" Bennett said. "Now, get that Koala some support!"

"Right," McClaren said, clicking the mic on her helmet. "General, we need air support on that fight!"

"Pilots are all out of ammo," the general replied. "They had to come back to restock."

"Then lay down tank blasts," McClaren said. "Without the Shrieker, Kota is a sitting duck."

Kota cut an imposing figure on the horrible plains, covered in sand, still dripping wet from the ocean, his mouth open, screaming in rage, jagged teeth ready to attack. It stomped the ground once, then twice, as the hippo staggered to its feet.

The hippo wobbled for a moment, finding its footing, and then let out its own ferocious scream that drowned out

Kota's and could be felt in McClaren's helicopter over a mile away.

"Uh oh," Bennett said. McClaren shared his trepidation but couldn't show it on her face, even to one of her oldest friends.

"It's going to be okay," she said, mustering whatever confidence she could from the bowels of her soul to mask her fear.

Kota kicked off from the ground, and the massive monsters sprinted toward each other at full speed, quaking the Earth and swirling dirt from the ground into a giant dust storm that masked them.

"We lost them," the general squawked. "Without a clear shot, we can't risk hurting Kota."

"Then find a clear shot!" McClaren screamed. "We have to help that koala until the Shrieker gets here."

"If we fire without a clear shot, then we'll be doing more harm than good," the general barked. "I will not risk this mission because you made a mistake."

"She was saving your life!" Bennett shouted into the microphone.

"And I'm trying to save the world!" the general growled. "That's why they don't send civilians to do the military's job!"

"Enough!" McClaren said. "I don't care if you agree with my decisions, but you will respect me. Now, do what you can to find a clear shot. We only have to buy a couple of minutes. Got it?"

"Yes, ma'am," the general said, disrespect and petulance oozing off every word. "We'll do what we c—"

A hideous howl cut through the air, not one of anger but one of pain, and Kota flew out of the dust, skidding across the ground, a massive gash on its right arm. Seconds later, the hippo appeared, blood dripping from its jaw and fire swelling in its eyes.

Kota pushed itself to stand, but before he could get to his free, the hippo's head smashed hard into the koala's side, and Kota let out another howl as the hippo charged it hard into the side of Uluru. When Kota smashed hard into the edge, McClaren heard a crack echo through the sky.

"That can't be good," Bennett said.

"Dislocated shoulder at least," Gibbons said. "Sorry, I have five brothers. Heard that exact sound before. Poor Kota."

Kota was supposed to hold the hippo off for hours at least, and it was barely able to withstand five minutes of assault from the giant beast, who didn't have a scratch on it and showed no sign of slowing.

"Does this thing have any weapons?" McClaren asked Gibbons.

Gibbons nodded. "Missiles and guns."

"Then fire away!" McClaren screamed. "We have to give Kota a chance to get out of there."

Gibbons didn't reply. She simply turned the helicopter to line up with the hippo and smashed her hand on the red button on the front console. Missiles on both sides of the chopper flew toward the hippo, exploding on its back as Gibbons fired a stream of bullets into it.

The hippo looked back and sneered, but it was clearly there for Kota and turned itself back to the koala, rising up and smashing it into the side of Uluru with all its incredible force.

The life drained from Kota's eyes, but as the hippo rose up for a killing blow, a shriek cracked through the air, and the hippo fell off Kota into the trees around the great mesa.

McClaren turned to see a giant bat flapping its wings in the distance. The Shrieker had arrived.

* * *

"Are those birds ready to fly yet, General?" McClaren asked, staring out at the massive, red-eyed bat that hovered above Uluru. "We're going to need them."

"First squadron is taking off right now. All jets will be in the sky in three minutes."

McClaren looked back at the base to see four fighter planes soar into the air. How could they have gotten it so wrong? This was a massacre. Kota would be lucky to live out the day.

"I guess those worst-case scenarios really were generous like the general said, huh?" Bennett said, trying to eke out a slight smile but finding it hard even to feign anything but sheer horror.

"These Coker Monsters are like nothing we've ever seen before. Every prediction we made, every single one, miscalculated their strength by at least tenfold." McClaren looked over at the hippo that was rocking back and forth to stand. "That's why we have experiments, though. We can feed the new data into the program and develop a new plan."

"Sure," Bennett said. "But how are we going to save Australia? We can't let Kota and the Shrieker sacrifice themselves for nothing."

"We're not going to have them sacrifice themselves at all," McClaren replied. "We're going to get them out of here. Step one, get Kota up and walking. Step two, get them away, and step three is to move the hippo toward the water, somehow, and away from as many civilian casualties as we can."

"That's a hell of an optimistic plan," Bennett said. "But just look at Kota."

McClaren didn't want to look, but she forced herself to reach over Bennett to look down at Kota. He was bloodied from the nose down to his chest. He was breathing, but barely, and blood clumped on his soggy fur. A low groan escaped his lips as he tried listlessly to stand. She held back a tear. Even though they were monsters, they were living things, too, and while Kota wasn't the most powerful monster on Earth, watching it lie helpless filled her with both pity and dread. If a Coker monster could do that much damage in a couple of minutes, how could they ever hope to defeat it?

"The hippo is standing, ma'am," Gibbons said from the cockpit.

Bennett and McClaren twisted their heads behind them to watch the hippo lumber to its feet. The one positive was that if they could knock the beast over, it needed time to get back up, and it was as good a chance as any to get Kota to safety. All they had to do was knock it down again.

"General," McClaren said, "the new plan is to get that hippo on the ground again so that we can pull Kota to safety."

"How are we going to do that?" the general replied. "That thing is a hundred feet tall and weighs over 30,000 kilos. I know you care about these monsters, but we'll lose a lot of troops trying to save it. Is that what you want? After all, you just nearly blew this mission to save those same soldiers."

"No, I don't want that!" McClaren replied. Her plan had gone out the window in the time it took to devise it. "What do you recommend?"

"Pull back the troops. Live to fight another day. Make a stand in Mongolia, where we have more monsters, more troops, and more resources."

"And what? Let Australia burn?" Bennett yelled.

"Absolutely," the general replied without hesitation. "Risk the few to save the many. With any luck, this monster will be stuck in Australia for the duration."

"Um…" Bennett replied. "You realize hippos can swim, right? That's kind of their thing."

"Well, let the whales deal with it then. Better them than us!"

"You're right, General," McClaren said. "Start the withdrawal."

"You haven't even seen if the Shrieker can be more effective than Kota!" Bennett screamed. "You are all just going to give up on the plan that easily?"

McClaren snapped her neck to Bennett. "You're goddamn right we are. This plan was flawed from the start. We didn't know how flawed it was, but it was disastrously so, and we can either sacrifice more men to the cause, or we can regroup and restrategize with the data we have. I'm not going to be stupid just because I have some deep attachment to this plan."

"That's not fair," Bennett said. "I'm not—"

"I don't care!" McClaren said. "You are here at my discretion, and if you want me to relieve you, I will."

"You need me."

"I need people who get with the program, not undermine me. Either be with me or get gone." McClaren went back to the microphone. "How much time do you need?"

"As much time as those monsters can give us."

"You're just going to let those monsters die, aren't you?" Bennett asked.

"No," McClaren said with a snide sneer. "But if they die, that's just a casualty of war, isn't it?"

"That's right, ma'am," the general said. "That's the price of war."

"Oh, my god!" Gibbons said. "Look!"

They all looked out the window at Uluru, where Kota dragged himself to his feet and stumbled toward the Shrieker, just as the hippo readied to charge.

"Fire as much as you can at that hippo, General," McClaren said. "But then, get out of there. Leave the ammo. Save the troops. Get everyone out as fast as possible."

"Yes, ma'am," the general said through the earpiece. This became a rescue mission faster than anyone imagined, and now McClaren had to hope Kota and the Shrieker could buy enough time for the base to be evacuated.

* * *

The giant bat shrieked through the air, and the lumbering hippo was too immobile to dodge, so instead, it had no choice but to take the brunt of the blow, which sent it tumbling backward. With the hippo off its feet again, Kota leaped into action, jumping onto the hippo and tearing at its stomach with his one good arm, tearing at its flesh like the wounded animal that he was.

"Go, Kota!" Bennett exalted, pumping his fist in the air. "Go, go, go!"

The hippo swiped its paw and knocked Kota off it, causing the great koala to tumble onto the ground and knock against its dislocated shoulder.

"Get up in the air over that hippo!" McClaren screamed. The helicopter rose into the air, and McClaren looked for any sign of damage but saw none. "What does it take to hurt this thing?"

"Airstrike incoming!" The general screamed. Gibbons moved the helicopter out of the way of the bombers that sprayed napalm down the stomach of the horrible hippo beast. Once they were clear, the fighter jets made a bombing run and dropped hundreds of bombs onto the belly of the hippo, but when the dust cleared, there was nothing but a charred stain where the bombs had it. They did considerably more damage to the treeline around the hippo than to the monster itself.

The hippo rocked again, but Kota wasn't done with it. Instead of going for the belly, Kota grabbed the hippo by the mouth and stomped on its jaw, pulling its mouth apart until the jaw unhinged.

Poor Kota. That kind of attack would have worked for a koala, but a hippo can open its mouth wider than just about any other animal, and when the hippo's jaw snapped back closed, it collapsed upon Kota's foot.

The koala screeched into the air and clawed at the hippo's mouth, but it would not open. Instead, the hippo swung its head from side to side, slamming the koala into the ground violently.

The jet fighters made another run, this time laying machine gun fire onto the hippo's snout and causing it to sneeze. The sneeze quaked the ground, and its jaw unhinged. Kota pulled himself away, hobbling and barely breathing.

With one more rock of its gargantuan body, the great hippo lurched onto its feet and rose into the air, ready to smash Kota, but the Shrieker laid a sonic blast into the monster's stomach and pushed it back until all it did was smash harmlessly on the ground.

"How is the evacuation going, General?" McClaren said.

"Halfway done. We've got most of the troops on transports now. We are about to take off with the first group. One more transport to go, and then we'll be clear. Meanwhile, watch yourself. Tanks incoming, with a truck to bring them back home after dumping their payload."

Bennett looked on the ground to see a division of tanks driving toward them, with a truck transport behind them. "Unleash Hell, boys."

They didn't need permission, though. They unloaded a hail of bombs onto the hippo as it worked against the Shrieker's sonic blast.

"Aim for the mouth!" McClaren shouted.

The hippo's mouth was open in a monstrous scream when the next round of bombs unloaded from the tanks, and this time, when they connected, the hippo howled in tremendous pain.

"That worked!" McClaren said. She moved her headset to her mouth. "General! Do your jets have any bombs left?"

"Absolutely."

"Then do one more run, and give that hippo's mouth everything you got!"

"With pleasure."

Less than a minute later, the jets swooped down in line with the hippo. They laid down a hail of machine gun fire, and when that caused the monster's mouth to open, they fired every weapon in their arsenal at it.

When they exploded in the mouth of the hippo, it lurched up into the air, squirming in pain. For a moment, McClaren thought she had something, but then the hippo landed, licked its lips as if it were trying to get the taste of blast out of its mouth, and turned to the tanks, who let off another round of shells, and charged its attackers. In a final fit of ferocious bravery, Kota leaped onto the back of the great beast and grabbed onto its jaw, stopping the hippo dead.

"That's the best shot we're going to get!" McClaren said. "Give it everything we have left!"

The tanks unleashed the last of their arsenal, and more than half of their rounds found the back of the hippo's throat. If the bombs wounded the creature in the mouth, then they just had to redesign the plan, not abandon it completely. If they were only indestructible on the outside, then they could find a way to win this battle.

However, all her hope was drained when the hippo shook off the attack after only a few seconds. It snapped its jaw closed with another mighty howl, and Kota rolled off the top of the monster's head onto the ground. He was right under McClaren's helicopter when it came to a stop, and Kota was only letting out shallow breaths. It was whimpering in a lot of pain, and when the hippo closed in, Kota didn't even move to defend itself.

The hippo grabbed Kota with its huge jaw and shook him up and down until his back snapped in three places. When the hippo dropped Kota again, all the light was gone from his eyes. Kota was dead, and with that, the hippo turned its attention to the Shrieker.

McClaren, for one brief moment, had a ray of hope, but that was gone. Now, she had to hope they could live to fight another day.

* * *

McClaren watched as the last of the tank division loaded into a truck transport, and it sped across the desert toward the makeshift army base.

"How much longer do you need, General?" McClaren asked.

"Once the tank division gets back, we'll load them up and be off. You should get back here."

"There's one more thing I need you to do, General," McClaren said. "I need you to shoot that laser one more time to distract the hippo and give the Shrieker enough time to escape."

"I'm already ahead of you," the general said. "I'm going to do that myself. Then, I'll take a hilo out."

"Godspeed, General," McClaren said, turning her attention to the giant bat shrieking across Uluru.

"You should get out of there, too," the general said before his mic went dead.

"He's right, you know," Bennett said. "We should go."

McClaren looked down at the dead mega-koala below her. "Even if we can't get that thing to bleed, there's spit and bodily fluids from that monster on Kota. We have to recover and analyze it. I'm not going anywhere until we do."

"That's stupid, but I'm here with you until the end."

McClaren smiled. One would think she would be smarter, having so many advanced degrees, but she found following her gut as valuable as following her brain, which was what set her apart from most of her colleagues.

McClaren turned back to the base. She had watched the first transport take off three minutes ago and was waiting for the last transport to get off the ground before they could turn their attention to saving the Shrieker for another battle.

Even through the helmet and earplugs, the shriek from the Vietnamese monster was grating. It made her heart palpitate, and her jaw tighten. Still, it seemed to be effective against the hippo, and she couldn't discount anything when it came to saving the world. She couldn't risk a valuable asset being destroyed.

The hippo charged the giant bat. While the koala went headfirst into battle, the Shrieker spun and avoided the hippo easily. Though it was not as powerful as the Coker Monster, simply by using evasive maneuvers, it had lasted longer than Kota did. That had been the original goal of the mission—not to destroy but simply detain the monster until a better plan could be devised—one based on hard science and real data instead of guesstimates and hearsay.

"Come around so you can give the base a direct shot," McClaren said. Gibbons moved the helicopter out of the line of fire from the base, and as she did, the Shrieker moved directly into the place where Gibbons had just vacated. "Nicely done."

The giant bat let out another great shriek, but it was nowhere near as powerful as the others. Something nobody talked about with these great monsters was that they needed to refuel and recover, just like any other animal, and using their powers drained them even more than their normal lives. The Shrieker must have consumed close to a million calories a day, and it hadn't had anything to eat since it landed in Australia. Bats usually spent close to 20 hours a day asleep, and the Shrieker had been up for at least a full day. She hadn't noticed it before, but the bat was listing in the air, struggling to keep itself afloat, and with a final wail, it had no choice but to land on the ground, gasping loudly.

"Come on, General!" McClaren shouted into her headset.

"Eagle two is lifting off!" the general yelled into the helmet. A few moments later, McClaren watched as the transport took off into the sky. She would have leaped with joy if it wouldn't have rocked the helicopter. She valued human life, but no single life was as important as protecting the monsters, especially one as valuable as the Shrieker.

"Get me a clear shot!" the general screamed. "That bat is in the way!"

"Gibbons!" McClaren screamed. "We need to get that bat away from the hippo so the general has a clear shot!"

Gibbons laid a layer of suppressive fire at the bat's feet, but the bat didn't move. It was blinking furiously, trying to stay awake. McClaren twisted her head to see the hippo begin to charge.

"LIFT UP!"

Gibbons pulled the helicopter into the air above the giant beasts just as the hippo slammed into the bat. It had tried to scream, but its voice was shot, and even as it fought the hippo, scratching its back and side, it was no match for the hippo.

"NO!" McClaren screamed, but it was no use. The monster opened its jaw and slammed it closed around the bat's frail body. The Shrieker let out one final screech and then fell, limp, as the hippo shook it violently from side to side.

"I've got a clear shot!" the general screamed. "FIRING!"

The hippo screeched and rose into the air at the laser attack, only to slam down with the intent to destroy the base. As it rushed toward the base, McClaren held her breath until she saw another helicopter rise up from the base, and the radio crackled to life.

"Safely lifted off," the general said. "And I think you will enjoy this next part."

A few seconds went by with the hippo rushing forward, and as it disappeared into the base, a massive explosion rocked the base, its flames rising high into the air. The Coker monster flew into the air and landed with a huge crash, kicking up dust and soot all around it.

"Is it dead?" Bennett asked as Gibbons flew closer.

The dust cleared, and the hippo wobbled to its feet. It was alive, but pouring from its shoulder, McClaren saw something that made her smile for the first time all day. The hippo was bleeding. It was just a tiny cut, barely anything, but its blood leaked out onto the ground below as it hobbled off beyond the base to lick its wounds.

They had failed in almost every way, but they at least left their defeat with something that they could use in the future not to have such a loss again.

* * *

Gibbons landed the helicopter, and Doctor McClaren exited, followed by Doctor Bennett. She grabbed her go bag and pulled out two test tubes. From the sky, the blood looked tiny, but it cut a swath of red in the ground a hundred yards wide. McClaren knelt and placed some of the blood in one of her test tubes and then another, carefully trying to keep as much sand out of the test tube as possible.

"Do we count this as a win?" Bennett asked, walking over to McClaren.

"No," McClaren said, popping a rubber stopper on the second vial. "But it's not an unmitigated disaster, either."

"Were those the two options?"

"Well, if we didn't get any blood, then maybe it would have been." McClaren realized his question was more personal. After all, he had a large hand in putting together the war game scenario that they used. "It's not your fault, you know? At least, not entirely."

"I know that intellectually, but it's impossible for me to get over it emotionally." He turned to the Shrieker, who was a half mile away. "What do we tell the Vietnamese prime minister?"

"The truth," McClaren said, walking toward the Shrieker. "Their monster died, saving a lot of lives. It fought bravely and valiantly, and in its death, we learned more about the Coker Objects that we collectively knew before."

"Do you think that will be enough?" he asked, solemn.

McClaren shook her head. "No, but I'll make sure they are well compensated for their loss. It won't heal the wound, but it will soften the sting."

The Shrieker was covered in slobber from the hippo, which made it sticky and gooey. The giant bat's glassy eyes shone a red reflection of McClaren as she passed it. She hadn't been close to a mega-monster many times in her life, even though they defined her career.

"The Dissemblers claim this whole thing is meant to save humanity, but save it from what? There are plenty of horrible things that we've been responsible for, from world hunger to greenhouse gas emissions, to war. Why is this the thing Coker thought would set us free?" Bennett went to answer her, but McClaren held up her hand. "Don't. I'm not looking for an answer. Not really. It's just so stupid and senseless."

She scooped up some of the hippo's saliva into another test tube and then turned to Bennett. "Get a team out here to comb this place for as much DNA evidence on that creature as they can find. Meanwhile, we have a meeting in Mongolia."

Gibbons flew them back to the rendezvous point where the general was waiting for them. "Have you been able to track the hippo?" McClaren asked when they finally arrived.

"Of course, the thing is massive," the general replied. "It's headed to the ocean, we think. With any luck, it will just float out there for a while. It's done enough damage here."

"Good," McClaren said. "Disburse your troops to the other Coker Objects and coordinate with the other generals. I want one garrison left here, just in case, but we finally have something, some shred of evidence that we can use to sequence those monsters' DNA, and we're gonna figure out how to bring them down. I swear that, General."

"I learned a long time ago not to promise more than you can reasonably offer." He nodded tersely to McClaren. "But I appreciate your optimism. It's gonna be needed before the end."

McClaren had never considered herself an optimistic person, just a pragmatic one. They knew more now than they knew before, and any data was good data. It was how you manipulated it that determined if the outcome was a good one or a bad one, and she was determined to make it a good one once this was all over.

VISITORS AT THE END OF THE WORLD

"ARE YOU SURE I have to take down all the traps?" I asked Pete as I dug into the ground to remove the bear trap that once caught him by the leg.

"I'm sure," he replied. "You can't be inviting to people if you ke—"

He stopped mid-sentence, and when I looked up, his face was frozen in confusion. "What are you looking at?" I turned to see a young woman in a thick red coat walking toward us.

"Hi!" she said with a smile. "I'm Cheryl. Is this the…radio station? 87.9, the low end of the dial?"

"Umm…" I didn't know what to say, so I just stood and walked toward her with a crooked smile on my face. "It is, I'm—"

"Sammy Chops, right?" she said with a hint of reverence. "I listen to you all the time."

I chuckled. "That name is so stupid. I started with it and just never got around to changing it. You can call me Stephanie."

"Nice to meet you, Stephanie."

She stuck out her hand, and I shook it. "Same to you, Cheryl."

"One of my best friends in grade school was named Stephanie. I love that name. Love the name Sammy Chops, too, though." She pulled a bit of her loose hair behind her ear. "It's perfect for radio. Reminds me of the DJs by my house. Jugdish and the Beav. They were cheesy, but I loved them."

"Hey!" Pete said, walking up behind me. "That's exactly what I say about Steph."

"Shut up." I elbowed him lightly in the stomach. "So, you found all the clues then? It's been two weeks, and I was starting to think we made it too hard."

"Not too hard, but you do know people could look you up in the phone book, right?"

"Yeah?" Pete said, feigning ignorance. "Who would have thunk?"

"I didn't, though, for the record," Cheryl said, holding up her hands. "I played the game straight just like you wanted, but I did look it up to make sure I got it right in the end. I didn't want to come here after cheating. Didn't seem like a good first impression."

"That's very good of you, Cheryl," I replied. "I like that you followed our rules. It bodes well for our time together."

"I hope so." She pointed to the road behind her. "Well, I have about twenty changes of clothes and a bunch of jams and jellies I canned before I left Nebraska. Is it cool if I bring them in?"

"Of course," I said with a nod. "We're running low on supplies."

"I thought you might be."

"Let me help you." Pete jogged toward her. "Just be careful before you go inside. We still haven't taken down all the traps."

"I…will…just follow you."

"Probably a good idea," Pete said.

Cheryl was a dynamite cook and took control of the kitchen immediately. After Cheryl, a pair of hikers with long beards came a week later. They helped us cut down trees and build homes so that we had enough places to stay when there were too many people living there to fit in the main house. Pete and I didn't think about ourselves.

Then an older man came who helped us till the land and decide what to plant for the next season. One by one, little angels came out of the woodwork. Some monsters, too, but we handled them in our own way.

We started to ask questions about where people found clues to make sure they were following the rules of the game. If they couldn't, then they would never fit in with us. We didn't lie or cheat, ever. That was our most important rule. Every month, Pete even took a group into the woods to move everything around so the game didn't get stale and people couldn't cheat.

After a year, we had three dozen people working the land, along with a fence and security of our own, just like the marauders I ran from.

We weren't like them, though. We were careful not to take more than we needed.

By the end of the second year, we grew everything we needed on the land. There was plenty around, too, and we expanded as needed into the surrounding area.

There were plenty of cows, pigs, and chickens around that nobody was using, either because they were raptured up, dead, or moved on. So, we were well-fed pretty soon after setting up our sanctuary. Pete talked about hunting, but we never thought to simply look at other farms for what we needed. We needed an outside perspective for that.

They weren't all good days, but they never were terrible. Monsters attacked sometimes, and people could still be cruel, but it helped to have people to lighten the load. That's what a community can do for you. It will never take away all your pain, but it can spread it around, dulling the ache.

There were marriages those first years and even children. Some people chose to leave to strike out on their own, while others doubled down and helped recruits learn the skills we needed to survive.

Somehow, I started to look forward to the future, which was something I didn't even do in the before times. Eventually, Pete even put a bun in my oven, and I looked forward to showing my child what you can do when you work together.

You can create joy, even out of misery.

AUTHOR'S NOTE

I AM VERY proud of the breadth of the stories that appeared in this collection. Often, people stick to a single universe or a single theme when it comes to their shorts, but I have stories all over the map, from cute to funny and everything in between, which is ironically one of the major selling points for my comics anthology series, *Cthulhu is Hard to Spell*.

I always thought of anthology pieces as ways to explore new themes, styles, and ideas that are present in your longer works, and I think you can see that in how I designed this book.

When I started my career, I couldn't pay people enough to let me into anthologies, so most of the unplaced work in this collection was from the beginning of my career, when I was writing mostly short stories set in the Godsverse to build out that universe.

Funny story about those Godsverse stories. I forgot any of them existed until I went collecting stories for this anthology. When I found them, it was like discovering a long-lost treasure or reconnecting with old friends. I was actually in the middle of writing the interstitial scenes when I even remembered that one *Katrina Hates the World* existed, and I was shocked that it was over 10,000 words long.

Speaking of the interstitials, how did you like them? I absolutely love the idea of Stephanie setting up a radio station and finding a family for herself, but I didn't think I had enough for me to write a whole novel about it. I'm so excited that I was able to write that story for this collection. It had just enough meat on its bones to work for this kind of weird purpose.

The original inspiration for Stephanie's story and this collection came from *The Graveyard Book,* which I loved because it could be read in any order and still make sense. Obviously, that's not how this book turned out. Reading Stephanie's story out of order makes no sense, but I think the bones of that inspiration undergird the whole of this anthology.

I can tell you now that the reason I didn't want to make this into a book was that I didn't want conflict to ruin it. I just wanted to tell a rather sweet story set in the Apocalypse about found family, and writing a whole book means conflict and bad things will happen. I only wanted good things to happen with Stephanie. Who knows, maybe if you love her, I will bring her back for a full story in the future.

Moving forward from this book, I want to have more cohesiveness in my short stories. I should really be using them to support the series that I love so much, and I'm going to make it a point to do that in the future when I can. It won't always be possible, of course, because sometimes you get asked to write a short monster story starring Frankenstein as a Hellboy-like paranormal investigator in the 50s, and you absolutely can't say no to that, but mostly I am planning to keep things inside my existing universes in the future.

Although with the pace I write shorts, maybe there won't even be a second anthology before I'm kicking up rocks.

I've been saying this for a while now, but I think this anthology really closes the door on the first decade or so of my career, at least on the prose side. Everything I've written from the first decade of my career is either out or soon will be, and if I'm smart, I will have been working on the next thing to take me through my 40s by the time you read this.

Sometimes, I'm not very smart. I know when I wrote this, I had some cool covers and a couple of interesting ideas, but they hadn't all gelled together yet. I hope future Russell figured it out.

Talking about myself in the third person reminded me that I was a character in this book, even though I never showed up on its pages. I was very excited to be able to make myself a character in my own universe because now I can really live forever in the Godsverse.

Now, I've got some special bonuses for you. Things I didn't think I could fit in the bulk of the story. I almost didn't include the Akta pieces, but I thought they were more historical, so they worked well enough, and there are books about Akta, as I referenced in *Ruin.*

I couldn't, however, put the short *Katrina Hates the World* in the bulk of the book because it takes place on the first day of the Apocalypse, and I couldn't figure out how to stuff it into the rest of the book without needing a deep explanation from Stephanie. This is a Godsverse story at the end of the day, and that was too meta even for me.

I wanted to include it since Katrina is such a big part of my career, so you will find it next, along with some comic scripts I wrote for anthologies that either got rejected or never completed for some reason. I really liked these stories. I hope maybe somebody reading this will want to make them so they can still come out in their original comic form.

I hope you enjoy them and enjoyed this anthology as a whole. If you haven't checked out the Godsverse yet, I hope you go back and read it from the beginning. However, if you just want the Apocalypse stories, then you can check out *Death* and *Darkness* for other tales set during this time period.

If you have already read them, then you should go back and read them again. I think it's worth it.

Of course, I'm biased. Bonuses

KATRINA HATES THE WORLD

Prequel story to "Death"

THE WORLD ENDED today, and I didn't even wear my good shoes.

It was destined to be a shitty day, regardless, since they've all been kind of shitty recently, but because the world ended, it immediately leaped over every other day and became the shittiest day in a rather shitty life.

Okay, maybe that's not fair.

My life wasn't really shit. A shit life was living in Sudan, getting traded like a slave, eating asshole for nickels. If your life was shit, Sally Struthers came to your village while Sarah McLaughlin played a dour song.

I knew, intellectually, it wasn't a shitty life, but not being able to bitch about it made things all the shittier.

Sure, my parents loved me, and they still loved each other. I had my own place and a job. Sometimes I ate Whole Foods, and sometimes I ate junk food. I could go to dark bars and hear crappy music like a good yuppie, but my life was far from good.

It's all about perspective, after all. Where I lived, in this small town in Northwestern Oregon, working as a bike courier wasn't really the high life. It rained every day, they paid me peanuts, and the hours sucked. If I had known how shitty my life was about to become, though, I would never have dared complain about living in a foul-smelling apartment with a deadbeat mooch of a roommate.

I woke up in my lumpy bed, surrounded by a mountain of clothes and miscellaneous junk, just like any other day—kinda shitty. I was a bit of a hoarder. There wasn't a piece of clothing, toy, or movie I didn't secretly desire. Since I was a bit of a klepto, too, I had lots of useless crap strewn about my room. My roommate threatened to move out if I didn't keep my shit out of the common area, and I couldn't afford the rent alone, so I basically lived in a garbage dump.

I kicked through the piles of shit and swam toward the bathroom. I'm not gonna go into what happened in there, but I went in dirty and came out clean. I pulled my wet, shoulder-length brown hair up in a towel to dry. It generally took me less than ten minutes to shower and fix my hair—it was straight, and I didn't put much product in it.

That didn't mean I got ready quickly, though. I just reallocated the time spent not fussing with my hair for more time at my vanity. I loved makeup. I know that makes me sound like a diva, but I don't care. We all had our things, and mine was makeup.

Once I slathered on my war paint, I got dressed. I liked to be comfortable when I rode my bike, so I wore cargo pants and a t-shirt, then wrapped myself in a leather jacket and threw on my bike gloves. I know the bike gloves are a little…stupid to most people, but the grips wear on your hands, so fuck you for judging me.

I called it my uniform, but the uniform was really a bright red helmet that said "Speedy Delivery" on it, featuring a man so chipper he must've been on speed when they drew him. When I'd finished putting myself together, I walked into my living room and saw Barry, my roommate, sprawled out on the couch, in his underwear, eating cereal straight from the box and watching cartoons.

"Jesus Christ, Barry!" I shouted at him. "What the fuck are you doing?"

He looked up at me, smiling. His bloodshot eyes glazed over. "Just…chillin' out, man."

Barry was nicer than he was smart. I've heard a lot of "terrible roommate" stories in my life, so I really couldn't complain. He was the best roommate I knew, though that wasn't saying much. At least he didn't steal from me, blare music at all hours, try to sleep with me constantly, or gossip behind my back. He was always late with the rent, but aside from that—and his penchant for roaming around in his skivvies—he was acceptable. Plus, he always had weed. Lots of weed. He paid for his rent in weed. I went and sold it to some of my customers for triple what he owed in rent. Besides, he was my best friend's brother. All in all, it was a workable system.

"Can you put on some pants by the time I get home?" I asked.

Barry took a chomp of his cereal without taking his eyes off the TV. "No guarantees."

I walked out of the house. I wanted so badly to get my own place, but I needed a better job to make that happen, and prospects were slim in East Willow. I needed to get down to Portland if I was going to turn it all around, but to do that, I needed a car, which meant that I needed money. To get money, I needed my job. The cycle continues. You always need money, a job, and a car.

Unfortunately, all I had was a little ten-speed bike my mom gave me for Christmas when I was twelve. I'd been using it for sixteen years. I hopped on and pedaled toward work. East Willow wasn't big, but it was large enough that I got a workout traversing it back and forth a dozen times a day.

When I started at Speedy Delivery, we only delivered packages, but in the last couple of years, we became the go-to delivery stop for every delivery service known to man. There were a thousand different apps that picked up and delivered things for people, and we were plugged into all of them. We delivered everything from booze and food to office supplies. Hell, we'd even pick up your dry cleaning for you.

I preferred the good old days when there was a package or two a day. By the time the world ended, I was on my bike constantly, bopping back and forth everywhere—from laundromats to Barry's Diner—picking shit up. Just so you know, it's hard to balance a one-hundred-scoop sundae on your lap while it's raining outside. The scenery was usually decent, at least.

East Willow wasn't a bad town to grow up in, but it was boring. Even the "wrong side of the tracks" in West Willow, where the homes were shittier and the smells fouler, wasn't bad. I'd never felt unsafe on that side of town, but I'd never felt unsafe anywhere in my entire life.

I arrived at work ten minutes later than my shift started. Luckily, Connie was already there. Connie was my best friend in the world. We went to school together from elementary through high school. We worked the same shitty jobs in the same boring town, and we both hated the same type of things. We had just about everything in common, except Connie was willing to rock a mini-skirt to work, and, well, I wasn't.

"Hey, girl!" Connie said with a big smile, staring at herself in the mirror and tying her bushy hair off into pigtails. "I clocked in for you."

I smiled. "Thanks, buddy. I appreciate it."

"You always do."

"I would do the same for you."

"If you ever got here on time."

"Why would I do that when I have you?"

She slammed the locker door closed. "Old Man Freeman is on the warpath. He's got a mountain of work for us today."

"Shit."

"Hey, Katrina," I heard from behind me.

Connie's boyfriend Dennis sauntered toward us. Dennis and Connie had been together for about three months, and they were just about the most perfect couple in the entire world. It was sickening, really. Connie didn't hate things as much anymore because of him. It gave us less to talk about, and I didn't like that.

Still, Dennis was a nice guy. A little stiff in bed. Yes, I'd slept with him. Everybody slept with everybody at Speedy's. It was one of the benefits of working there. I didn't sleep with him after he got together with Connie, though.

"Hi, Dennis." I gave him a friendly punch in the shoulder.

He wrapped his arms around Connie's stomach and kissed her neck. "You have time for a quick workout before your shift starts?"

Connie spun around and kissed him. "You know I would, sweetheart, but your quickies aren't that quick, and I got a lot of work to do today. Tonight, though. When I'm all hot and sticky."

Dennis kissed her again. "Can't wait."

"You two are sickeningly sweet," I told them.

"You're just jealous cuz I stole him away from you," Connie said with another kiss.

I laughed. "Yeah, that must be it."

I was happy for them, but I was scared Dennis was gonna take Connie away from me. There weren't a lot of people I could talk to in the world. I hadn't made a lot of friends growing up, and the few I did ran away as soon as the ink on their diplomas dried. It didn't help that I'm kind of a jerk, too.

"Katrina!" Old Man Freeman bellowed through the rafters.

He stormed up to me, his bald head dripping with sweat. Pit stains coated his shirt in a disgusting, putrid stench. A massive golden crucifix swung from a gold chain around his hairy neck. "What time do you start?"

I blinked my eyes and flashed an innocent smile. "Nine a.m."

"And what time did you get here?"

"I don't know. I would have to look at my card, but I'm guessing like, eight fifty-five."

"I know your friend punches you in. I know it in my bones. I've watched you stroll in late over and over again. You are lucky this is a shitty job, and nobody wants it. Otherwise, I would fire you."

"No, you wouldn't." I bopped him on the nose. "You love me. Customers love me. Everybody loves me. I am loveable."

Freeman sneered. "That is the biggest load of horseshit I've ever heard." He slammed a clipboard into my stomach. "Here are your assignments for the day."

I looked down the list. Perfect. My first client bought weed from me all the time. I was light on cash, and he could make my rent with one order.

* * *

I complained about being a courier, but sometimes it wasn't so bad. Sometimes, you caught a perfect day. The sun wasn't too hot. The wind wasn't too cold. There was just enough cloud cover so you didn't burn your pale skin, and on those days, you held out your arms and soared. It's the little things in life that make all the difference.

I pulled up to my first client's house, Archie. He was a good, God-fearing Christian with just enough restraint, not to mention I was going to burn in Hell and cool enough to smoke a bowl with me whenever I popped over.

Today was no exception. After he paid me two hundred bucks for a bag of kush, he dutifully packed a bowl and handed it to me. "You get first hit."

I smiled, taking the pipe. "You're a true gentleman."

"Fuck that. I wanna see if you gave me good shit or not."

I took a hit from the pipe and coughed immediately. I coughed so hard I had to hold on to the table so I wouldn't fall over.

Archie smiled. "Yeah. That's good shit. Come on now, cough it out. Cough it out."

I couldn't stop coughing. "Water." I gasped. "Water."

"Alright. Alright." He got up, laughing. "You are a real pussy; you know that?"

"Water!"

Archie disappeared into the kitchen. I heard him pouring the water, and then a flash of blue light exploded from the kitchen. The glass crashed to the floor.

"Archie!"

Blue lights flashed all through the apartment complex. I stood up and looked out the window. Across the street, a woman held a man's jacket, staring dumbly into the Heavens. Further down, a little girl cried alone in a stroller.

I ran into the kitchen. Archie was gone. There was nothing left of him but a robe sopping up the water leaking across the kitchen. I backed out of the apartment and ran toward my bike, pedaling to the courier station as fast as possible.

What had been a beautiful day when I left the depot had turned into a gloomy, cold one. People stood outside in a haze, holding bits of clothing and hollering names. "Carl!" "Kim!" "Edward!" "Becky!"

Hundreds of names echoed into the sky in a jumbled mess. After a while, I couldn't distinguish one name from the other or differentiate them from the incessant sobbing coming from every house.

I kicked up the stand of my bike and ran into the station. "What is happening? What's going on? My first client disappeared right in front of me."

Connie turned around to me. She held a clipboard and Freeman's necklace in her hand. "Yeah. I saw Old Man Freeman vanish into thin air in a sea of blue light. All he left behind was this clipboard and necklace."

"Shit. That's what happened to Archie, too."

"Goddamn it," Dennis said. "I liked him."

I suddenly became aware of the TV blaring a loud hum. "This is not a test." It was the Emergency Broadcast

System. "This is an emergency. Please stay tuned for instructions."

The broadcast cut to a young reporter, barely out of school. She sat behind a news desk, shaking. "Moments ago, thousands of people around the world witnessed friends, loved ones, and neighbors disappear in beams of blue light. We have no idea where they went or where they are. We do know that they are gone. Please stay calm. We are working very hard to find any information."

There was a moment of silence. A stage manager brought the reporter another piece of paper. She read it in horror. "We have new reports of multiple earthquakes erupting…off the Richter scale…all over the world. These rifts have been reported outside Chicago, New York, Orlando, Dallas, and Reno. Reno has been sunk into the ground. Hundreds of thousands presumed dead, all in an instant." The poor young woman was visibly trembling, and her voice became nearly unintelligible when she announced they had managed to patch in a live feed on location somewhere.

On screen, a jumbled, shaking video clip showed a city in chaos, split clear in half by a steaming fissure groaning as it widened, swallowing trees, vehicles, and entire buildings. People were running and screaming, unsure where to go.

"What the…fuck…" Connie dropped the clipboard and necklace. There on the screen, we watched dark figures pour out of the gigantic crevice. Some of them moved unsteadily, like zombies. Others zipped past the camera with their twisted, contorted bodies. There was one final humanoid shriek before the monitor went black.

The broadcast turned off. I spun around to Connie and Dennis. "I have to find Mom and Dad."

"On what?" Connie scoffed. "Your bike?"

"You got a better idea?"

"Girl, I do have a car."

"Oh, right." I nodded. "Let's use that then."

* * *

Connie didn't care much for her parents. Her dad was one of those Uncle Ruckus black guys. The type that hated their own people and yelled about how much they sucked. He was truly disgusted he married a black woman and that together they had black children. I don't know what color he thought the offspring of two black people would be. Her mother knew better than to stay around and conveniently died when Connie was seven, leaving her and her brother Barry alone with him.

Her dad hated everything about his lot in life—his job, his family, himself. The only thing he didn't hate was God. The dude was hyper-religious. The kind of religious that evolved into fanaticism. There were more crosses and rosaries in his house than most churches, and he prayed on them every chance he got. Because of his deep devotion to the church, the church loved him, even though he was the fucking worst. He was a deacon, a golden child, and led the bake sales. It didn't matter that he was quite the little monster at home.

He was always very pleasant around Dennis and me, too. Maybe because we were both white, or maybe because he knew better than to insult guests, but he showered us with compliments. We despised him even more for that. It'd be one thing if he were just an overall prick, but that his pettiness began and ended with Connie was really messed up. He didn't even have the same venom for Barry. We figured it was because his son was lighter-skinned. Somehow that made it even worse.

"I hope he's dead," Connie said as she drove her beat-up yellow jalopy down the road. "I hope that blue light got 'im, and he's rotting in Hell right now."

"I guess you don't need to check on him, then?" I asked.

"Fuck no. Mama Cam and Papa Joe are more important."

Those were my parents. They took Connie in and treated her like family from the day we met. She had dinner with us most evenings and spent the night when her dad was on a bender. She loved my parents, and they loved her. She had a key to our house, for Christ's sake. Often, I came home from school to find her making food and watching TV with my mom.

"I'm sure they're fine, Connie," Dennis said, stroking her arm from the passenger's seat. Dennis didn't have parents. I mean, not anymore. They both died when he was young. I never heard him talk about them, and I certainly never asked. Connie had enough stories about her father for them both.

Connie pulled her rattletrap up to the house and slammed the car into park. My parents lived in the nicest spot in town. They had a big place on a quiet street that ended in a little cul de sac. I swear to god if you pictured the perfect 1950s house, that was my parents' house.

My father used to be an engineer at the hydroelectric dam that powered the town. He was also the only person alive who could call me "Katie" without getting a fist to the throat. I hated that name, except when it came out of his mouth. Mom worked part-time as a school nurse. Both of them retired a few years before and spent most of their golden years saying they were going to move into a smaller house but never actually doing it.

We ran inside, frightened to death that my parents wouldn't be there, that we would never have a chance to say goodbye.

"Mom!" I shouted. "Dad!"

I didn't hear a response, but I saw them staring in shock at the TV. "Mom! Dad!"

I wrapped one arm around each of their necks and held them, squeezing my eyes shut while I caught my breath.

They didn't hug me back. They didn't move. I felt my mother's gentle sobbing. "Mom? What's wrong?"

Connie pointed at the TV. "That."

The young reporter was still sitting at her desk. Next to her was a picture of blue light with the word "Rapture" under it.

"We are now getting word…scientists believe we have just experienced the biblical rapture. Churches and homes emptied out as beams of blue light filled the streets of every city in the world."

The television image transitioned to an old, nerdy man with glasses. "Yes, well, we have no scientific basis for this. However, we have analyzed several of the sites and believe there is no man-made substance alive that could have caused these people to vanish so quickly. Combine that with the fact monsters rose from what appears to be Hell, and the biblical apocalypse is the only logical conclusion. I am not a man of faith. I am a man of science, so I take no pleasure in saying this, but it seems we have reached the end days."

The reporter came back on the screen. "For more on this, we turn to our religious correspondent, Pastor Eugene Wells."

A heavyset blowhard in a narrow tie popped onto the screen. "We all gonna die, y'all. God is pissed off. I told y'all for *years* that the sinners must repent. That we was dealing with hedonistic times, and if we let the gays marry, this shit was gonna happen. Look at it now, y'all. We gonna *die*."

"And Pastor," the reporter said, "why do you think you weren't raptured?"

"Cuz somebody gotta be down here telling y'all how to live right now. I am God's messenger on Earth."

The reporter smiled. "Oh, and here I thought you were just as bad a person as the rest of us. We'll be right back."

The rapture. The fucking rapture. It happened. It finally fucking happened. All the religious nuts had been right all along and were raptured up to Heaven. Well, fucking A. We didn't have one piece of religious junk in our house. My parents never took me to church. I wasn't baptized. I wasn't confirmed. I was outside all the rules God had set for me to enter Heaven.

Mom blew her nose. "We're so sorry, Katrina. We should have forced you to go to Sunday school. We should have been better Christians."

"Fuck that, Mom," I replied. "Any religion that's gonna rapture people just because they go to church, even if they're bastard-covered bastards, isn't one I give a shit about."

I was surprised how little I cared about being stuck in the apocalypse and not being raptured. I was feeling pretty matter-of-fact about the whole stupid thing.

And then, I caught eyes with Connie. It clicked for both of us at once. If God raptured people that went to church, Connie's dad was already gone. "Fuck!"

Connie balled up her fists. "If that son of a bitch got raptured and I didn't, I swear to God I'm gonna kill somebody."

"I understand what you're saying, Connie." I held up my hands. "But just remember, if you kill somebody, that's probably gonna get you into Hell."

"Who the fuck cares about that? There are no rules anymore, Katrina. We can murder anybody we want. This is already Hell."

Mom broke out the mom-voice. "Nobody will be murdering anybody! Not today! Not ever. Is that understood, young lady?"

Connie looked down at the floor. "Yes, ma'am."

"Good. Now…Harold, what do we do now?"

My dad looked at her and then at us before he simply shrugged. "I don't know, Grace. I don't know."

"First things first," I said. "We gotta make sure Connie's dad didn't get raptured. Then we gotta find Barry. Then food. Then guns."

"What are the guns for?"

"Ma, put your pacifist leanings aside. People are gonna be pissed as hell. They're gonna loot, then they're gonna pillage. It's gonna be bedlam. People are in shock now, but soon they'll flip a switch and go fucking nuts. We need to get supplies."

Connie put a hand up. "I dunno who you think I am, but I don't have a clown car. We ain't fitting all these people in my hoopty."

Dad stood up and smiled, a new purpose written all over his face. "We can take the minivan!"

Dad had kept the minivan from my youth. Mom asked him to junk it dozens of times, but he always said he was gonna need it one day. He practically skipped to the front door and pulled out a pile of keys. "I told you, Katie! I told you, Grace!"

Mom pressed her fingers into her temples. "Yes, dear. You did."

* * *

Connie's dad lived about a mile from us. His house wasn't quite as nice as ours, but he had a respectable job as a computer technician that afforded him a better salary than most people in East Willow. While our house was a two-story single-family home, he lived in a three-story townhouse closer to the pool. Connie and I became friends, mostly because we didn't have to leave the community to see each other. We would run into each other at the pool, school, and playground. Familiarity bred friendship for us even as it bred contempt toward everybody else in the universe.

Connie didn't wait for the minivan to stop before she slid open the door and rushed inside. She didn't have a key anymore, but her dad didn't believe in locking the door.

She pushed it open and ran inside. I leaped out of the car with Dennis and followed behind her.

"Stay in the car!" I shouted to my parents. "We won't be long."

Connie was known to have violent outbursts when it came to her father. They fought a lot, and often it led to blows. Back in the day, her father won those battles, but as Connie aged, she immersed herself in Krav Maga. She dragged me along, and we both got good. Good enough that her dad couldn't kick her ass anymore. Quite the opposite. It was the only thing that kept him in line.

Dennis and I ran inside. "Connie! Connie! Connie," I shouted.

"FUCK! FUCK! FUCK! FUCK! FUCK!" I bolted upstairs as Connie threw a mirror across the room. "Fuck!"

"Connie!" I shouted. "Chill out!"

"He's not here. He's not here. That little fucker got blue-lighted! That little fuck!"

"You don't know that, Connie. You don't know that."

She held up a rosary. "This was in the middle of the floor with a pair of socks. He never went anywhere without it. That fucking fuck!"

Dennis stepped toward her carefully, his hands up. "Easy, baby. It's okay."

"It's not fucking okay. That fucking prick gets to go to Heaven because he went to church and I'm stuck down here rotting away! What the fuck did he ever do to deserve Heaven?" Angry tears streamed down her face, and the three of us were quiet for a few moments.

I kicked at the broken glass from the mirror and said, finally, "I get it, Connie. I really do."

"Fuck you do."

"Oh yeah?" I threw my arm toward the window, pointing. "Look down at that fucking car. Both my parents, both of them are still here. They raised me, loved me, and cared for me. They cared for both of us. They are the two most caring people in the fucking world, and look at them. They are down there instead of up in Heaven. You think I'm not fucking livid about that, especially when I see your prick of a father made it? I'm fucking furious, Connie, but being pissed is not gonna save their lives. It's not gonna keep any of us alive. So get your shit together cuz we got a lot of work to do."

Connie sniffed and wiped her nose on her sleeve. "Damn, you're good at that, man. Who knew the apocalypse would knock something loose inside you?"

"I don't know." I was as surprised as she was. "I don't think that's something anybody could plan for."

"Uh, guys?" Dennis had pulled the curtain aside and was looking out the window toward Dad's van. Four men were circling it, carrying baseball bats and crowbars.

"Shit." I ran downstairs and out of the door.

A big, fat, ugly dude paced in front of the van. "This is a nice ride. I want it. Get out!"

A thin man with a crowbar leaned into the passenger's side door. "Yeah. We gonna need it."

"Hey!" I shouted from the stoop. "Fuck are you doing here?"

The fat one turned to me. "Oh, good. More meat. Don't worry, sweetheart; we'll get to you in a minute. Boys!"

Two beefy men with crowbars stomped toward us. I turned to Connie. She nodded at me. "Left or right?"

"Left," I replied.

Connie leaped down the stairs. She smashed one of the men's noses into the back of his skull. I jumped down after her and roundhouse kicked the other one in the face. He stumbled, and I shattered his kneecap in half with my boot. Then I pulled the crowbar out of his hands and cracked him across the face with it. Broken and bloodied, the man gurgled as he fell to the ground.

"Now," I shouted, "we could take down the two of you, too, or you can take your wannabe Mad Max asses the fuck out of here and realize you're pussies. We're not scared of you."

The fat man backed up. "Come on, Chuck!"

The skinny man ran as fast as he could to catch up with the fat one, and they hobbled away. Mom turned to me. "Why would you do that? We had this under control."

"No, you didn't." I slid into the backseat. "Besides, those are wannabes at best. They just wanted to intimidate you to see if they could."

"Well, Katie," Dad said, "they succeeded."

"I know, which is worrisome. We need weapons and fast."

"Walmart sells weapons and food. We could cover two things for the price of one."

"Oh, good thinking, Harold. Let's head over there."

Leave it to my parents to think about bargain pricing at Walmart in the middle of the apocalypse.

"I fucking hate Walmart," I said.

"Well, I hate the apocalypse, sweetie, but it seems to be our best option."

I slid closed the door, and Dad puttered the van down the street. He was so happy he'd won an argument against me. I couldn't believe how much it felt like normal, even as we dealt with the end times. With Connie, Dennis and me in the back of my dad's minivan, it felt like I was thirteen again, if only for a moment. And then I looked down at my blood-soaked hands.

I don't like the idea of Walmart on a lazy Monday. Going to Walmart during the literal apocalypse freaked me out to no end, but there was no denying it: They had everything we needed to survive. The problem was that everybody and their mother knew it.

We didn't even get to a mile from the entrance before traffic stopped dead. A line of cars, hundreds deep, flooded like a river into the streets around the store. People crashed through the shrubbery, abandoned their cars, and ran like maniacs to the entrance.

"This isn't going to work," I told Dad.

"No shit, Katie," he replied. "I don't see another way, though."

"No need to snap at me. I didn't create traffic."

"I know. We're all a little on edge. Me included. I'm sorry."

Cars blocked every lane. They lined up in front of us, behind us, and to either side. They were stacked five deep in a two-lane road, and we sat parked dead in the center.

"Switch with me," I said to Dad.

"I don't think so, young lady!"

"Just do it, Harold!" Mom shouted.

I climbed over the front seat, and Dad scooted into the back. I clasped the seat belt tight and gave it a tug. "Buckle up."

"Do you know what you're doing, sweetheart?" Mom asked.

I shook my head. "No, but I know this car is bigger than the ones on either side of me, so I have an idea."

"Don't destroy it."

It was a stupid request, given our predicament. I gunned the minivan and slammed it into the Prius in front of us, then shifted to reverse and crashed into the Volvo behind us. Its airbags deployed. Luckily, there were no airbags in our decades-old behemoth.

I rotated the wheel and revved the car forward. It smashed into a hatchback next to us and nudged them out of the way. I reversed one more time and slammed into a Civic. Then, with one more heave forward, I plowed through the cars and jumped the curb. A half dozen pissed-off motorists leered out of their cars, but we were free.

"Call Barry," I shouted to Connie.

"Do you think the cell phone towers work?" she asked.

"There's only one way to find out."

* * *

It didn't take us long to get to my apartment, but by the time we arrived, our minivan barely sputtered along, burping oil as it lurched to a stop.

"I think the car is dead," I said.

Dad stared. "I had this car for almost two decades. You drove it once and destroyed it."

"Yeah, I did. It's like your worst nightmare, huh?"

"Not at all, Katie." Dad smiled and gave me a pat on the shoulder. "I'm proud of you. I could never have done that."

"I know."

I led the group into my second-story apartment. I'd left it just a couple of hours earlier when it was still a bright, fun, sunny day. Now, it was dark, gloomy, and cold. And Apocalypsey. I had a feeling it was going to stay that way for a while.

I tried to open the door, but it wouldn't budge. "Barry!" I shouted. "Let me in."

"How do I know you are you?" he said. "I've been hearing some shit on the news."

"Goddamn it, Barry," Connie shouted. "Just open up."

There were a few seconds of silence, then I heard something move inside. The door finally opened and I pushed my way in to find our couch perched near the door.

"Sorry. I've been hearing some shit," Barry said. "That horde of monsters is running up the coast. They already got to San Francisco and are slaughtering their way up the Five."

"Shit," Dennis said. "Those fuckers are fast."

"And that's not the worst of it," Barry continued. "There's already five militias organized in Portland alone. They declared martial law in the whole state. Everybody's going ape shit."

I nodded. "I know. Do you have the drugs?"

"They're in my room."

Kilos of weed stacked up to the ceiling covered the bed. "Holy shit. How much did you have?"

"I broke down the farm all morning. Do you think it will be enough?"

"I don't know. Did you make the call like Connie told you to?"

He nodded. "Carl should be here any minute. If he's got any guns, he'll bring them."

I stepped forward. "Wait. Barry, did you tell Carl we needed guns?"

"Of course."

"Fuck, Barry!" I shouted. "I just told you to get him here. Do you know what this means?"

"What?"

Dennis smacked his forehead. "It means they know we're unarmed and have a ton of weed."

The door crashed open. Three assholes with guns stood in the doorway. One with a shotgun. Two with pistols. Carl strolled between us, carrying an AK, smiling ear to ear. His sunglasses reflected the shame on Barry's face.

"Oh," Barry said. "That wasn't smart."

"Alright, you mother fuckers," Carl said. "Get the fuck down and stay there. Boys. Take the drugs. Girls. Don't fucking move."

"I can't do that," I said. "You take this weed, and we got nothing to bargain with. We're as good as dead."

"You don't move, and you'll be as good as dead, too."

I stepped forward. "What do you think we have to live for right now? There are monsters in San Francisco. They're gonna keep coming, and they're gonna rip us apart."

I studied his eyes. Beads of sweat formed on his forehead. "You—you gonna die!"

"We're all gonna die, Carl. Every one of us. Even if we make it through today, we're gonna die. This is the new reality. The new normal." I took another step. "Do you understand that?"

Carl blinked. It was only a second, but it was enough for me to lunge forward and knock him in the face with the butt of his gun. His grip loosened, and I spun the weapon out of his hands. The other guns in the room turned to me.

"Hey! Hey! Hey!" I shouted. "I'll make this easy for you. Drop your guns, kick them to me, and fuck off. That's more than fair. Otherwise, at least one of you is gonna die right now. I might die too, but I'm gonna take as many of you fuckers with me as I can."

"What about your family? They get caught in the crossfire?" one of them asked.

I lifted the gun. "I'll be doing them a favor. They won't have to be ripped apart by monsters. Now, drop your guns and get the fuck outta here."

The assholes looked at each other. They dropped their guns and kicked them over to me.

"Connie! Dennis! Barry!"

They picked up the guns and pointed them at the assholes, who quickly shit themselves and ran away. I kicked the door closed. "Holy shit. I can't believe that worked."

"I almost pissed my pants," Barry said.

I laughed and slung the gun over my shoulder. "Go pack up the weed. We should get out of here. They'll be back and in greater numbers."

* * *

The most religious bitch in my apartment complex was also the only one with a massive van. She used it to take parishioners to and from church every Sunday. And Saturday. And every other morning, too. Did you know there was church every fucking morning? I didn't until I moved in here.

I knocked on her door. "Mrs. Blick? Oh, Mrs. Blick?"

Her husband died a few years back, but she always wanted to be called Mrs. Blick, not Norma. "My husband," she told me, "is still here in my heart. And we'll be reunited in Heaven."

I wondered if that was true. I didn't know him, but from the pictures, they both seemed like religious folks. Since that's all it took to enter Heaven, I guess they were in. Good, upstanding people weren't in, but scumbags who went to church were in. That's how the unjust system works up there, I guess. Not much different from the unjust system down here.

"Mrs. Blick!" I shouted, opening the door. What was it with religious people leaving their doors wide open? If I were some sort of criminal, I would only target religious idiots.

Across from me when I opened the door was a massive Jesus statue, crucified on the cross. I almost blew it in half when I saw it, thinking it was some dude about to charge at me, but I caught myself at the last second.

"Mrs. Blick?" Are you in here?"

A burning smell emanated from the kitchen. Fire plumed out of the oven. Connie grabbed a fire extinguisher and doused the flame.

"I think these were cookies," I said, using her oven mitt to place the molten baking pan on the stovetop. "I guess she was baking. Let me know if you see the car keys."

After scanning the countertops and searching through coat pockets, I wandered back into the bedroom, where the Pepto-Bismol pink wallpaper had started to curl at the seams. An ancient curio cabinet housed creepy dolls from around the world. A water glass filled with dentures sat on the nightstand. Connie followed me into the room.

"Find anything?" I couldn't tear my eyes away from the creepy-ass dolls.

Connie studied the room with the same unnerved look on her face. "Besides a sick cry for help? No."

"Check the vanity."

"Why do these religious types have to lead such sad lives?" She peeked in a few drawers.

"I guess they give up fun today for a shot at Heaven later."

"Good bet," Dennis said, leaning against the door. "As it turns out."

Connie pulled the keys from a bowl on the vanity. "Found 'em."

"Good," I replied. "Let's get the fuck out of here then."

Mrs. Blick had plastered "First Church of the Savior" on both sliding doors of her van. The thing was a beast. I hopped into the front seat, and the others jumped into the back, except my dad, who sat next to me.

"You sure you can drive this thing, Katie?"

"Nope." I shook my head and threw the van into gear. "Know any gun stores, Dad?"

"How would I know? I don't hunt or do…gun things."

"Connie. Google."

Connie typed into her phone. "Three miles up the road."

"Then that's where we're going."

"Why?" Dennis said. "We already have guns."

"Yeah," I responded. "But we don't have enough ammo."

* * *

Dave's Guns was situated on the corner of a strip mall. There was also a taco stand, a dry cleaner, and a mini-mart. It was as good a place as any to live out the apocalypse.

I barely stepped out of the car before a bullet ricocheted off the ground next to me. "Stop right fucking there!"

A bearded man in a bandana was aiming at me with a sniper rifle. I put my hands up. "I'm not here to fight you."

"Good," he said. "Cuz if you were in for a fight, then we'd have trouble."

"I need ammo. Are you…Dave?" I pointed to the sign

"Yeah, I'm Dave, and I got plenty of ammo. But I ain't got a lot of use sellin' it to the likes of you."

I stepped forward, but a bullet ricocheted off the ground again.

"I wouldn't do that if I were you," the man said. "I got good aim but a lousy temper."

"How much are those bullets worth to you?"

"More'n you got, 'less your sweet ass is on the market. I would pay top dollar for you, little lady."

I turned to Dennis. "Give me a brick."

Dennis handed me a brick of weed.

"I ain't on the market, but we have weed."

I heard him cock his gun. "Fuck I need drugs for?"

"Think about it. This is the end of times, man. People are gonna need two things: weed and guns. Then food and water, but weed and guns first. We got a pretty sweet thing going here. I keep you in weed. You keep me in bullets."

"Why not just shoot you now and take it all?"

I looked up at him. "Cuz we're not bad people. Just because we didn't get called up doesn't make us bad people. You're trying to defend yourself, and I respect that. I'm trying to do the same. That doesn't make us bad. You shoot me and take my weed, though, then you're a bad person. Then God, or Satan, or whoever the fuck started this, was right. We don't have to be like that."

"You make a lot of assumptions, little girl."

"You haven't shot me yet."

The man finally took his eyes off the sight and smiled at me. "Well, you got me there."

* * *

Dave waddled down from the roof of his store. His rotten teeth smelled of decay, but he knew how to conduct business. He exchanged four bricks of weed for twenty cases of shotgun shells, thirty cases of revolver ammo, and four cases of AK shells.

"This is gonna be the most valuable currency on Earth one day," he told me as we loaded the cases into the truck.

I slammed the back of the van closed. "Thank you, Dave. You are a gentleman."

He nodded. "You need anything else, little lady, you let me know."

We exchanged some weed with Bill, too, the owner of the mini-mart on the other end of the strip mall. He filled us up with cured meat, water, and bread in exchange for another brick.

"I'm not going to smoke it," Bill said. "But it does have a lot of buying power."

I smiled at him. "You don't have to lie to me, Bill. It's the apocalypse. Smoke the shit out of it."

He grinned. "Maybe a little."

I shook their hands and returned to the van. We had everything we needed to survive the first days of the apocalypse. We would have to venture out before long, but hopefully not before we learned how to live in the new world order.

I fit Mrs. Blick's van inside my parents' garage, and we set to work. The weed and guns went into the cellar, the food in the kitchen.

Dennis and Connie ripped up the wooden patio and deck and used the boards to cover all the windows and doors so nobody could get in or out. Barry booby-trapped the garage to give intruders a bullet to the chest. Mom and Dad watched helplessly as we turned their quaint home into a fortress.

Finally, when it was all done, we gathered in the living room. Dad walked in with a six-pack of beer. "I think you guys have earned this."

We each grabbed one.

"If there was ever a day to drink," he sighed, "it's today."

I took a long, slow sip and turned on the television. The emergency broadcast reporter looked haggard and scared.

"The demon horde continues to invade every part of this country. It seems the entire world has been overrun with monsters. May God have mercy on our souls."

The broadcast cut out to a green screen and a constant loud beep. I turned to Connie and the others. "This is gonna suck."

We all nodded. We weren't ready for this. We'd wanted a normal life.

But somehow, some way, we would survive.

LIMBO

Rejected from "What Fresh Hell is This" anthology

PAGE 1 - 3 PANELS

PANEL 1 - Dante and Virgil walk through the bowels of
Hell. In the distance behind them is a sign that reads:
abandon hope, all ye who enter here. Think of this like a
carnival sign with big, flashy light bulbs. In fact, the whole
thing should have a more modern tone than the original,
like it was set in 1920 Coney Island. There should be a
boardwalk under them to complete the illusion.
This is LIMBO, which is the first ring of Hell, which
means there are all sorts of ghosts floating around. They
don't so much look unhappy as they look bored. Limbo,
after all, isn't so much about punishment as it is a sort of
holding cell. It's important to note that most of the people
here are children, toddlers, and babies. They are playing
games, but the games don't work, so it's just kind of…not
fun.

DANTE is a young man in a dapper three-piece suit and
bowler hat. VIRGIL is an old man who looks not dissimilar
to Ralph Waldo Emerson, dressed in a gray cloak that
makes him look like a wizard.
VIRGIL - And here we have limbo, the first stop on our
journey through Hell, home of unbaptized children and
virtuous pagans who did not accept Christ into their lives.
DANTE - I've been to a depressing carnival like this
before. It's not fun.
VIRGIL - The purpose of Limbo is not to have fun nor to
have pain. It is to feel nothing and to be nothing.

PANEL 2 - Virgil turns to Dante.

VIRGIL - Its appearance changes with the times. At one time, it was an unpleasant swamp, and at another, it was derelict castle grounds.

PANEL 3 - Closer on Virgil, who looks down at the ground.

VIRGIL - In my day, it was an empty agora devoid of any to hear my proclamations.

PAGE 2 - 4 PANELS

PANEL 1 - Dante walks through the Coney Island fair that
is Limbo. Babies crawl silently around him, devoid of any
feeling. Children walk through as well. Everybody looks
completely bored, but nobody is crying. This shot should
be quite a bit wider than the rest, possibly across the top of
the page.
They pass a milk jug game, where a little girl is holding a
ball. On top of the game are a bunch of prizes that look old
and dusty. Nobody has ever won them. The biggest is a
teddy bear.

DANTE - Let me see if I have this right. This level of Hell
is filled with people who didn't believe in Jesus, including
people who lived thousands of years before his birth.

VIRGIL - That's right.

PANEL 2 - Dante, behind him, a girl ghost throws a ball at
a stack of milk jugs, like in the old-timey fair games. There
are prizes that hang above her head, including a big stuffed
teddy bear.

We need to see the girl behind and get a sense of her
actions. It's important for the rest of the piece. Feel free to
add more panels to draw out the action on its own.

DANTE - And it's also full of little babies who were too
young to commit any atrocities in their lives, some of them
too young to even have a single thought in their heads.
They're stuck here too?

PANEL 3 - Virgil nods. The ball flies toward the milk jugs
behind him. This needs to be a two-shot to see the ball and
not break the 180-degree rule.

VIRGIL - Correct. You truly are the most gifted scholar of your age.

PANEL 4 - Dante, confused. Behind him, the ball knocks off the jugs and flies through the air.

DANTE - And that doesn't seem unfair to you?
GIRL - Aw, man. This game sucks.

PAGE 3 - 5 PANELS

PANEL 1 - The ball rolls across the pier toward Dante. The girl runs up behind them.

VIRGIL - It's best if you don't think about that part too hard.
DANTE - But isn't that the point of this journey?
GIRL - Hey, mister! A little help?

PANEL 2 - Dante bends down to pick up the ball. The girl walks closer.

DANTE - Here you go.

PANEL 3 - Dante hands the ball to the girl.

GIRL - Thanks, mister. I've been trying to knock down those milk jugs for fifty years, but they just won't budge.

PANEL 4 - Dante looks at the girl.

DANTE - Frustrating, isn't it?
GIRL - So frustrating. If I knock 'em down, I get to win a teddy bear, but nobody's ever knocked 'em down before.

PANEL 5 - Dante walks toward the game as Virgil watches.

DANTE - How old were you when you died, little girl?
GIRL - My name is Becky, and I was 7.

PAGE 4 - 6 PANELS

PANEL 1 - Dante stops in front of the game. The big teddy bear is right in front of him. We need to see it because it's important to the action.

DANTE - And you weren't baptized, Becky?
BECKY - I'm Jewish, sir, so no.

PANEL 2 - Dante holds out his hand toward Becky, gesturing for the baseball.

DANTE - Can I see the ball, Becky?

PANEL 3 - Becky places the ball in his hand. Dante smiles kindly at her.

BECKY - Don't lose it.
DANTE - I promise.

PANEL 4 - Dante winds up to throw the ball at the milk jugs.

DANTE - Did you ever do anything really naughty, Becky?
BECKY - One time, I gave a Wet Willy to my brother, but other than that, I tried to be a good kid.
DANTE - That's what I thought.

PANEL 5 - The ball flies out of his hand.
PANEL 6 - The ball hits the milk jugs perfectly and bounces off. You can show the trajectory line, but the ball should be almost off frame.

PAGE 5 - 5 PANELS

PANEL 1 - Dante looks at the milk jugs. Becky kicks the ground, disappointed, behind him.

BECKY - Aw, man. I'm never gonna win that teddy bear.

PANEL 2 - Dante looks up at the bear. Becky is sullen behind him.

DANTE - That doesn't seem fair, does it, Becky?
BECKY - No. This game doesn't seem fair at all.

PANEL 3 - Dante reaches up toward the teddy bear.

DANTE - I meant your particular situation, but the game doesn't seem fair, either.

PANEL 4 - Dante grabs the teddy bear.

PANEL 5 - Dante hands the teddy bear to her. Her face lights up.

BECKY - Thanks, mister! But aren't we gonna get in trouble for stealin'?
DANTE - I think you've gotten into quite enough trouble already. A little more won't hurt.

PAGE 6 - 6 PANELS

PANEL 1 - Virgil walks up to him.

VIRGIL - You shouldn't have done that. It's not the way we do things here.

PANEL 2 - Dante.

DANTE - You led a good life, didn't you?

PANEL 3 - Virgil.

VIRGIL - I like to think so.

PANEL 4 - Dante watches the little girl play with her teddy bear. For the first time, he sees a smile.

DANTE - And yet, you still ended up here, even after everything good you've done.

PANEL 5 - Dante, watching other kids gather around excitedly.

DANTE - For no other reason than you were born at the wrong time, into the wrong religion. That is not fair.
VIRGIL - Not everything is fair.
DANTE - God should be.

PANEL 6 - Virgil and Dante walk away from the game.

VIRGIL - That is a bit naïve, don't you think?
DANTE - No, I don't.

PAGE 7 - 5 PANELS

PANEL 1 - Virgil and Dante walk across the pier, past the milk jug game.
DANTE - Tell me, is there any way to get out of Hell?

PANEL 2 - Virgil, scoffing.
VIRGIL - Of course not. That would be preposterous.

PANEL 3 - Dante.

DANTE - Even if you are the most virtuous person in Hell, you can never leave, right?
VIRGIL - That is the burden of your actions on Earth.

PANEL 4 - Dante and Virgil.

DANTE - Even after a hundred million years?
VIRGIL - Not ever.

PANEL 5 - Dante looks at Virgil.

DANTE - And you expect me just to accept that this whole place is built on injustice?
VIRGIL - I expect you to observe and report back what you have seen here. No more, and no less.

PAGE 8 - 1 PANEL

PANEL 1 - Dante and Virgil walk into the fog. In front of them is a sign for Level 2. Virgil has placed his hand on Dante's shoulder.

DANTE - I don't like this story at all.
VIRGIL - Then you really won't like what is to come, my friend.

THE LAST BRAVERY OF DULCIE EYNES

Accepted to Eynes Anthology, never drawn

PAGE 1 – 5 PANELS

PANEL 1 – Dulcie Eynes, curly hair, pigtails, bows in hair. The cutest girl you've ever seen in your life. Every parent's dream. I don't know about her parents, but I would prefer her to be mixed race if possible. If Ben and Mary are both white, then white is fine.

She's wearing a schoolgirl outfit, skipping home. The cuter she is, the more heartbreaking this story will be.

It's important there is an alleyway in the distance of some type, which is dark.

DULCIE – Ring around the rosy.

PANEL 2 – Dulcie passes over a crack.

DULCIE – Pocket full of posies.

PANEL 3 – Dulcie passes into an alleyway.

DULCIE – Ashes, ashes.

PANEL 4 – Two big, yellow eyes appear in the darkness.

DULCIE – We all fall down.

PANEL 5 – A smiling mouth appears with the eyes.

MOUTH – Hello, Dulcie.

PAGE 2 – 6 PANELS

PANEL 1 – A massive lizard monster, scaled and scarred, slithers toward Dulcie, who balls her fingers into fists.

MONSTER – Do you know who I am?
DULCIE – Y-y-y-y-y-yes.

PANEL 2 – The monster curls around Dulcie's shoulders.

MONSTER – And yet you aren't afraid. You must be a very brave girl.
DULCIE – Mama and Papa taught me to fight monsters like you.

PANEL 3 – The monster smiles, now face to face with Dulcie.

MONSTER – And yet they left you all alone with no way to defend yourself.
DULCIE – Papa will come. Papa always comes.

PANEL 4 – The monster chuckles.

MONSTER – I'm sure he will.

PANEL 5 – The monster slides toward a dumpster.

MONSTER – Do you know why I am here, Dulcie, my sweet child?
DULCIE – You are here to do evil things, just like all monsters.

PANEL 6 – The monster scoffs.

MONSTER – Evil. You think me evil? That is childish, Dulcie. Do you know what your parents have done to my kind over the years?

PAGE 3 – 5 PANELS

PANEL 1 – The monster towers over Dulcie.

DULCIE – They saved us from you.
MONSTER – Saved? That is one way to put it. I prefer to say they murdered everybody I loved. Have they told you how many of my children they slaughtered in front of my eyes?

PANEL 2 – Dulcie's lips quiver.

MONSTER – Have they told you how many of my kin they brutally eviscerated? Hundreds of my brothers and sisters. Dozens of my children cut down in front of me.

PANEL 3 – A tear comes down Dulcie's cheek.

MONSTER – Do you not think that is evil, little Dulcie?

PANEL 4 – Dulcie is crying for real now.

DULCIE – I don't want to die.

PANEL 5 – The monster looks away.

MONSTER – Neither did my blood. We just wanted to be left alone.

PAGE 4 – 6 PANELS

PANEL 1 – Dulcie looks up at the monster, feigning bravery.

DULCIE – Will it hurt?

PANEL 2 – The monster lowers his eyes.

MONSTER – I'll make it as painless as they did.

PANEL 3 – Dulcie looks back.

DULCIE – He's not coming, is he?
MONSTER – No, my child. That will be his suffering.

PANEL 4 – Dulcie closes her eyes.

DULCIE – Tell Papa I loved him.

PANEL 5 – The monster raises his claw.

MONSTER – No.

PANEL 6 – The alleyway from the first page.

DULCIE – Screaming.

NEW ARMOR

Originally accepted into Manthology, but never finished

PAGE 1 – 6 PANELS

PANEL 1 – A lone warrior, clad in shadows, stands on the battlefield. He should be in complete shadows, holding a sword. It's, like, super important for the joke that you can't see him. Just so you know, it's a he and a big-ass bruiser at that. And he's wearing something analogous to Witchblade's costume. It doesn't have to be Witchblade's costume, but something like that.

CAPTION: On the battlefields of Siggrath.
WARRIOR: Man, this is gonna be awesome! Can't wait to test out this new armor.

PANEL 2 – The Light shines on his face. Again, we're just seeing his face. So shoulders up, this should look like male armor.

The warrior screams. His mouth takes up most of the panel.

WARRIOR: I HAVE THE POWER!

PANEL 3 – Again, in silhouette. He runs through the battlefield with a bunch of other battles going on around him. There's a giant sword in his hand, dragging behind him.

SFX: AHHHHHHH!!!!!!!! (This is a battle scream, not a scared scream. You can change the lettering as you see fit.)

PANEL 4 – Over the shoulder, he sees an orc, or goblin, or some shit. Just make it some cool monster fantasy peeps would dig. Not too big, though, because he's going to take it down with one swing of his sword.

WARRIOR: Finally, some action!

PANEL 5 – The sword is raised over his head. He jumps in the air.

WARRIOR: Taste my steel!

PANEL 6 – Now we see him in all his glory. He is huge, but he's dressed in a very skimpy costume. You know the type they always make women wear in games.

This is the biggest panel on the page. I would like it to go across the whole bottom and take up the bottom third. The rest can be rather small, but I would like this to be striking.

WARRIOR: DIE!

PAGE 2 – 6 PANELS
PANEL – The Warrior stands over his dead body, wiping down his sword. His friend in regular traditional male armor stands next to him. This should be like the daedric armor from Skyrim or other completely badass armor. The more badass it is, the better. He is a PALADIN.

WARRIOR: That was so much fun!
PALADIN: What are you wearing?

PANEL 2 – These should all be beauty poses for the Warrior. Make him look as objectified as Starfire in the New 52.

He looks back at his ass. His back is arched. The Paladin is behind him with a hand on his face.

WARRIOR: Like it? I picked it up in the caves of Fibjegar. Nifty, right?

PANEL 3 – The Paladin takes off his helmet.

PALADIN: No, that's not nifty…

PANEL 4 – The Paladin screaming.

PALADIN: You are wearing girl armor!

PANEL 5 – The Warrior scratches his head.

WARRIOR: Sooooo?

PANEL 6 – The Paladin throws his arms out in front of him.

PALADIN: So? What do you mean, so? It's girl armor. You are a boy!

PAGE 3 – 6 PANELS

PANEL 1 – Warrior stretching. Again, beauty pose.

WARRIOR: So what? It's comfy and stretchy in all the right places.

PANEL 2 – The Warrior picks his butt. I mean, this is basically a thong. Maybe make it a thong. The Paladin is behind him.

WARRIOR: Except for this epic wedgie, of course, but they say you get used to that.
PALADIN: But it's girl armor.

PANEL 3 – The Warrior is slightly perturbed now, but he's more confused than anything.

WARRIOR: Yeah, you said that before.
WARRIOR: Let me ask you…what's the armor rating on that big, hulking thing you got?

PANEL 4 – The Paladin puffs out his chest.

PALADIN: 759. Highest in the Kingdom.

PANEL 5 – The Warrior laughs.

PANEL 6 – The Warrior is serious again.

WARRIOR: Not anymore. Try 1237 bitch.

PAGE 4 – 6 PANELS – (can we make sure these pages have different layouts, too? Dynamic paneling is important to an epic story of wedgies ☺) Feel free to redraw this page in any way you see fit to make it look dynamic and cool.

PANEL 1 – The Paladin is perplexed. His eye is cocked, and his brow furrowed. The Warrior leans down. Do I have to say beauty pose again? Just all the beauty poses. The Paladin leans down to check out the tag.

PALADIN: You're lying.
WARRIOR: Check it out.

PANEL 2 – A close-up on the tag. The tag says: Armor rating 1237. Repels fire. Weak to water. Do not machine wash. Hand wash in the volcanic fires of Mount Doom only. Air dry.

PALADIN (O.P.) – Well, I'll be damned.

PANEL 3 – Paladin. An ogre rushes up behind the Warrior. The Warrior holds his sword.

PALADIN: Let me get this straight. I can get a better armor rating, wear less, and maybe even get rid of this epic back problem from lugging a hundred pounds of armor on by wearing girl armor?

PANEL 4 – The Warrior flings his blade at the ogre.

WARRIOR: It's not girl armor. It's just armor. Not only that…
WARRIOR: You can feel the breath of your enemies so much better.

PANEL 5 – Dead ogre in the front of the panel with a sword sticking out of his face. Behind, the Warrior and Paladin talk. Along the battlefield, there are hundreds of dead bodies. The Paladin has his hand on the Warrior's shoulder.

PALADIN: Where did you get that thing again?
WARRIOR: Don't touch me.
TEXT: The End.

ABOUT THE AUTHOR

Russell Nohelty is a USA Today bestselling author, publisher, and speaker. Russell is the author of dozens of novels and graphic novels including The Godsverse Chronicles, The Obsidian Spindle Saga, and Ichabod Jones: Monster Hunter.

He has a very entertaining newsletter, which you can join at www.russellnohelty.com. He lives in Los Angeles with his wife and dogs.

Get free books for signing up for my newsletter at:

www.russellnohelty.com/mail

Facebook:

www.facebook.com/russellnohelty

Twitter:

http://twitter.com/russellnohelty

Bookbub

https://www.bookbub.com/profile/russell-nohelty